CRYSTAL KING

JOHN M. OLSEN

IMMORTAL WORKS

Immortal Works LLC
P.O. Box 25492 Salt Lake City, Utah 84125 Tel: (385) 202-0116
© **2017 John M. Olsen**
johnmolsen.blogspot.com

Map illustrated by J. Riley Horn
www.rileyhornart.com

ISBN 978-0-9990205-2-4 (paperback)

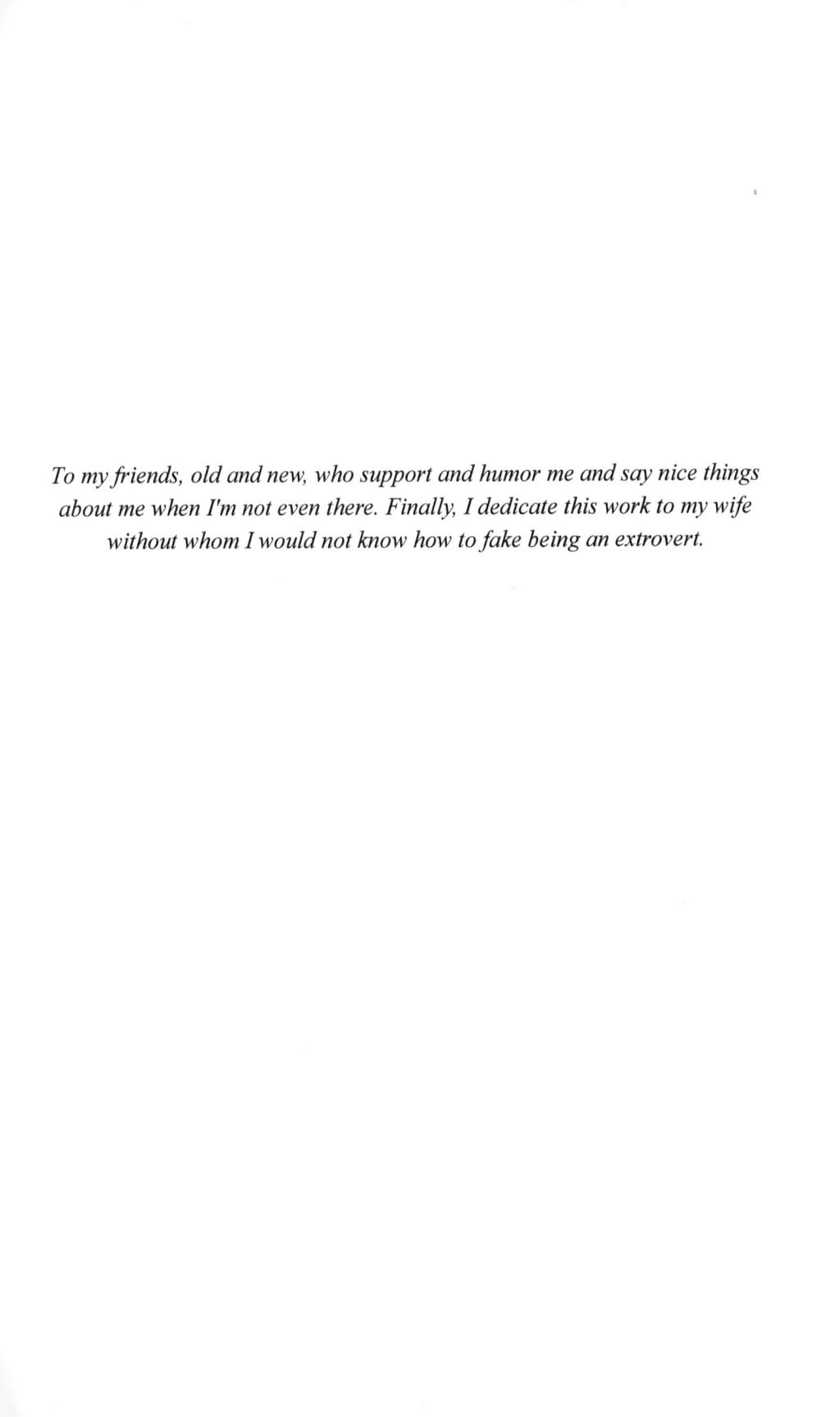

To my friends, old and new, who support and humor me and say nice things about me when I'm not even there. Finally, I dedicate this work to my wife without whom I would not know how to fake being an extrovert.

Map of Riland Kingdom

CHAPTER

ONE

Gavin glanced up from the castle roof as clouds floated by like dreams; they were nice to gaze at, but impossible to reach.

He took a bite from a fresh apple pilfered from the kitchen, and leaned back against the cool stone. Across the roof, boots rapped out an approaching rhythm as Master Draken Mboli rounded the bell tower, looking like a thundercloud ready to spew lightning bolts.

Draken placed his hands on his hips and waited. His imposing form was terrifying at times. His umber skin told of his far-southern origins in the unclaimed wilds and matched his glaring brown eyes.

Gavin smelled smoke and nearly attributed it to Draken's temper rather than the chimneys of the adjacent village. The thought of Draken's temper letting off smoke made Gavin laugh under his breath, but he had sense enough to squelch the noise before Draken heard.

Finally, Draken spoke through clenched teeth. "Is it too much to ask you to show up for weapon drills and crystal training at least once this week? I refuse to further justify your behavior to your father, and I refuse to let you get away with this laziness any longer."

Gavin didn't think of himself as lazy. He just didn't place any value on the things his father, his trainer, or even his brother wanted from him. They already had the barony leadership well in hand, which left him unsure of where he fit. Why should he put any effort in to study and training when he was the throw-away second son of a baron, and the king of Riland would never hear his name?

He shrugged and tossed his apple core over the parapet. As he stood, a voice from below cried out in alarm. He looked over the edge. "Sorry, Goodwife Moody. I didn't see you there."

A more cheerful voice from below called, "Oh, it's you. I'll toss it in the compost for you." At least some of the villagers liked him.

Draken let out a long breath and shook his head. "Follow me. Your father wants to see us before he leaves for the Baron's Conference."

"Right. The conference he's taking Stephan to without me. Without you, too."

Gavin knew it was risky to antagonize Draken, but it was a well-worn routine, and he fell into it out of habit.

Draken turned around. "You are the age of full consent now. It's time you acted like an adult. What you do influences those around you whether you like it or not. Right now, you're making it hard for me to do my job."

He leaned against the wall next to the stairway down into the castle and shook his head. He showed all the signs of a buildup to a colossal lecture. Was Draken willing to make them late just to make a point?

"Your actions impact others whether you want them to or not. What you believe makes no difference until you put effort into it. The sooner you come to terms with that, the better off you will be."

Gavin wanted to explain, but he didn't know how. He tried anyway. "I know actions are important. I choose what I do for my reasons rather than my father's. I'm not like him, and he knows it. You see how he treats me. All expectation and no reward. I'm expected to be a happy little appendage to the family and do what I'm told."

Draken's voice dropped to just above a whisper. "You have the baron's blood in your veins. You bear the family name. Do you think that counts for nothing? Don't you see the rights and responsibilities that gives you? Why should your father go out of his way for you when you've done your best to make a mockery of your name? You bring shame to your mother's grave."

Gavin stood with his mouth open. Of all the insults he'd received from Draken, this was the lowest. Finally, he recovered and pointed a finger. "Leave her out of this."

Draken ignored the gesture and turned to walk down the steps. "Your actions reflect on her. It's time you learned to honor her memory."

"She died when I was born. You have no idea what I would give up to remember her, to have a memory to honor."

Draken scowled. "I never met your mother. Do you see that stopping me?"

Gavin followed down the worn stone steps in silence, his thoughts a jumbled mess.

GAVIN HATED his father's private council room. It brought back too many unpleasant memories, and each visit added a new memory to the list. An almost physical burden settled on his shoulders as he entered.

Baron Gerald Stoutheart sat at his table with his eldest son, Stephan, at his side.

The baron gestured across the table and spoke. "Have a seat, both of you."

Gavin chose the high-backed seat off to the side.

Draken gave a short bow, then flipped his chair around backward and straddled it. He leaned his folded arms on the back of the chair. It was the only way Gavin had ever seen him sit at his father's table.

Draken said, "I'm sorry for the delay, sir. I had to retrieve Gavin."

The baron rubbed his forehead as if to lessen a headache. "Thank you. We leave within the hour, and I must go over a few things first."

He turned to Gavin. "With both myself and Stephan gone, that leaves you as the ranking member of the household here at the castle."

Gavin took a deep breath in anticipation, breathing in the scent of the flickering oil lamps. Could it be that he would finally get some responsibility and do something important?

"I'm granting your request to visit the Tanners and fetch the cattle from the mountain pasture, but I need you under Draken's supervision and training for two days first. He will run the barony while I'm gone. I expect you to learn something from him before you leave." His father's tone indicated the decision was not negotiable.

Gavin knew enough to run the barony for a few short days, but wouldn't be given a chance to do so. He bit his tongue on a reply to keep from losing even the privilege of the trip. He had no desire to be on Draken's short leash until his father returned, so he nodded his acceptance.

The baron turned to face Draken and made a conciliatory gesture. "I'm sorry to leave you behind, but I need a firm hand here while I'm gone. I'll take most of my personal guard and several of my advisers, which leaves a large hole to fill. All the healthy war animals are going along as well, so crystal training must be set aside for now. I intend to dominate the king's hunt this year by taking everyone I can. I'll have more than double the staff of any other baron. I'll be back before you know it, and we'll put things on a solid path forward."

Draken nodded. "Are you sure it's wise to leave so little here for defense? The only war-trained animal left is the injured wolf."

The baron rummaged through a pouch until he found what he was after. He tossed a faceted crystal on a cord to Draken. "See to her recovery. Reports are all quiet with the Graven Kingdom along the north. I'm certain you'll be fine."

Draken said, "Yes, sir. I will keep the castle running for you while everyone's gone." He put the cord over his head and tucked the crystal into the neck of his tunic. His nostrils flared.

Gavin knew disappointment when he saw it. Draken was no fan of administration. Even the thought of military action or a good hunt put a glint into his eye. But Draken always took the baron's side on any argument, even when Gavin knew Draken felt otherwise. Where did that respect come from?

"That will be all. We have things to attend to before we leave."

Gavin was familiar with what he called "the dismissal." His father had no more need of him, so he was to get out of sight and not interfere.

He stood and headed for the door. Before Gavin could stop himself, he said, "We'll get along fine without you."

The baron came to his feet so quickly his chair toppled over behind him. "Gavin!" his father's void boomed as his fists hit the table.

Stephan stood and put a calming hand on their father's shoulder. "I'll talk to him."

Stephan followed Gavin into the hall and fell in beside him.

"You know he means well. He wants you to make something of yourself."

"No, he doesn't. Everything will be yours. You've trained for it, and I'm nothing but an extra piece of unwanted baggage."

"You can't mean that. He's given you every opportunity. You've ignored what he offers."

"What? Should I be like you, a perfect copy of him, but without any responsibility or chance to make a difference? He looks at the village and sees subjects and resources. I see people. He considers me a burden because I'm not like him. He always has."

Stephan caught his brother by the shoulder and forcefully turned him, so they locked eyes. "I've seen the efforts he goes to for you. I know you disagree with his methods, but he has plans for greatness for the Stouthearts, and you're part of that. You share the name. You're family. He hasn't told me the full measure of his plans, but I know they include you. This will be an important conference, and he's working for our future. We have to build the barony to be better than it has ever been. It's not just for me. Do you want to have that childish comment be your last word to him before our trip?"

Gavin ran his fingers through his hair. Everyone had a plan for him and knew what was best, but never valued the time he spent among the villagers learning about them. "Tell him ..."

"Yes?" Stephan waited with a hopeful expression.

"Oh, never mind. You can regale me with tales of greatness when you get back."

It wasn't just Draken or his father. Even his brother tried to get him to conform to proper ideals.

They played their game, and he would play his. There was no reason to stay at the castle running through drills for two days to appease his father. He would use his leadership skills and initiative to leave early for the mountain pasture. Nobody would care or notice except Draken.

GAVIN WATCHED from an arrow slot near the castle gate as the train of wagons left with the crystal-controlled war animals. The larger animals, like his father's one-eared bear, rode in cages, while others followed along on leashes.

The village lay before him. It was half-vacant, the result of the last war that had cost so many lives across the kingdoms of all six Crystal Kings. He was too young to remember the war, but the old folks talked about it from time to time to blame their problems on the other kingdoms.

The afternoon sun warmed him as he watched the wagons crest the hill. They rolled out of sight.

It was too late for anyone to interfere, so he set out to prepare for his trip to the pasture. Soon he had provisions and a bedroll ready.

The last thing on his list was his leather breastplate from the practice arena. He heard the staccato clack of metal on wood from the practice floor as he approached. Draken performed sword drills on the wooden dummies with a ferocity Gavin rarely saw. Now he knew how Draken worked out his frustrations.

He would have to cross the arena to get his armor, but Draken would see him if he tried. He could wait for his trainer to tire and leave, or Gavin could go without the armor.

It wasn't a hard choice.

CHAPTER

TWO

G avin hadn't walked the trail for a year, yet it felt like coming home. Every fall he fetched the cattle herd along with the Tanner family who cared for them. He was allowed this personal trip because the Tanner twins, Saleena and Ned, were his closest friends. They had turned eighteen during the summer, a month after Gavin's birthday.

Out here in his father's private grazing lands, Gavin did as he pleased with no interference and no obligations, but this time was different. He spent his time in thought about what his brother and Draken had said. Maybe they had a point. Maybe he'd been wrong. Had he been too selfish?

He'd try to talk to Stephan and Draken, and maybe even his father, when this trip was over. Their expectations weren't as outrageous as he made them out to be. It was often hard to remember, but he lived an easy life compared to the people from the village.

The cattle trail rose at a slow, even pace through the hills. Evergreens stood on both sides of the trail as Gavin rounded a corner where granite boulders forced a sharp turn. Two strangers stood less than twenty strides away, gawking at his sudden appearance. Nobody had permission to be up there.

The smaller of the two swore, and then said in a northern accent, "That's him. He's early." The speaker lay down on the ground and entered a trance without another word. Gavin saw a crystal the size of two thumbs on a chain around the man's neck and wondered what animal wore the other half of the matched pair.

Based on the size of the crystal, it was a massive, war-trained predator that could catch him with little effort if he ran.

The other man shirked off his pack and grasped an iron-shod fighting staff with both hands. He took up a defensive guard position between Gavin and the man on the ground. The guard wore a worked leather breastplate with a spaulder covering his right shoulder. The man's armor was functional and well used, but the stained and mottled armor didn't fit well. He must have come by it recently. Gavin was outclassed by the bandits, with no armor and only a short blade on his hip.

After a quick glance around the scattered evergreens, to check for signs of their animal, Gavin drew his blade. He scanned for terrain he might use to his advantage and found none.

Gavin made a fake lunge and discovered his opponent's fast reflexes as the staff grazed his shoulder. He had to get past the guard and hurt the man in the trance to disrupt him, but there wasn't much time.

He circled to the right, away from his opponent's weapon. Over the past year, he'd given Master Draken a string of excuses to get out of formal weapons training. Now he regretted it.

As he circled, Gavin asked, "Who are you?" He took in the man's smirk as he stood guard over his companion.

The man said, "Makes no difference who we are, only that we've come for you." This one also had a northern accent.

As the man glanced down to step around a large stone, Gavin charged with a dodge to the right to force the guard to intercept his path with his staff held up in a defensive block. The burly thug didn't have to take chances. All he had to do was keep Gavin busy for a while, and he'd win by default when the animal arrived. Gavin skirted farther to the side and pulled wide enough to avoid a swing at his back.

His meager skills returned in fits and starts. Still, no sound came from the trees. Even though his opponent had better skills, strength, and reach, the man stood his ground over his entranced companion rather than chase Gavin down. That made him predictable, but Gavin would tire fast as he worked to force an opening.

Gavin feigned a thrust and drew back again, inviting yet another swing from his opponent. Something about the swing was off. He knew enough about combat, despite his best efforts to skip training, to recognize the man targeted Gavin's torso rather than his head. The man wasn't trying to kill him. They regained their stances.

Why the man held back didn't matter. What happened next was all that mattered; Gavin had to control the duel, or it could cost him and the Tanners their lives.

A branch snapped in the trees to the north. He circled to the right of his target again, maximizing the distance from his opponent's weapon to make it look like he would try the same attack as before. More branches broke as something large crunched through the undergrowth. The animal was big and fast, as he'd feared. If he didn't break the trance immediately, it would be too late to do anything else.

He heaved in a deep breath scented with sour sweat. He had to commit everything. It was a gamble, but Gavin counted on the thug not going for the kill. He dived in almost as he had before, but at the last moment spun and ducked across to the left under his opponent's swing. The man continued his swing around in a great circle as Gavin had hoped, but he hadn't counted on the man's strength and speed as he brought his staff down.

The staff caught Gavin square on the back as he dove forward with his small blade, aiming for the man on the ground. The force of the impact knocked him on top of the prone man blade first, with the hilt against Gavin's belly. The tip of his short blade caught on the man's leather breast-plate, but it was too thick to pierce easily. His opponent crashed onto him and grabbed Gavin's arms. The hilt punched into Gavin's gut and forced the blade through the prone man's chest and into the ground. The impact drove the air from Gavin's lungs like a powerful sucker punch to the stomach.

He tried to breathe, but failed as the thug rolled Gavin onto his back. The man gawked at his partner pinned through with Gavin's blade and said, "Oh, splinters." He jumped up and fled along the trail. After only ten steps, a large bear emerged from the brush and hit the man at a dead run. The thug tumbled like a rag doll and lay sprawled on the ground, shaking his head. The animal was no longer under control and sensed the death of its master. Rage and confusion drove it now.

Gavin gasped a tiny breath and tried to pull his blade free, but it was stuck fast. The crystal around the dead man's neck caught his eye. He pulled it off and dropped it around his neck. Such powerful crystals were usually only available to nobles. How this pair of thugs had such an expensive thing mystified him.

It could take hours to build a bond to bring such a large wild animal under control through the matching crystal fastened around the bear's neck. Gavin dragged himself into the brush beside the trail to hide. He hoped the bear would be satisfied with the thug while Gavin recovered.

Gavin wanted to get away as fast as he could, but he knew enough to not run away from a predator. Only food runs away from bears. The beast had his prey, but Gavin didn't want to gain its attention. He hunkered down in the brush to wait.

Unwilling to watch the one-sided fight, Gavin turned away as the beast took to its grisly task with claws and teeth amid a series of screams that soon gave way to silence pierced only by the occasional crunching noise. Its rage temporarily blunted after mangling the thug, the bear seemed content to feast.

The crystal warmed against his chest. The control link between Gavin and the bear was a thread of spider silk, too tenuous to grasp. He wouldn't be able to achieve a full trance for hours. He couldn't even discourage it from attacking before then. Eventually, it would be a mental window, ready for him to throw open and reach in to control the body of the bear. For now, he crouched in the bushes with no weapon, a dry mouth, and lungs only able to pull in one shallow gasp at a time.

When the noises stopped, Gavin peeked out across the scene of the attack. The bear and the thug were both gone. A crimson trail was the only sign of where the bear dragged the remains for a future meal. He decided it was safe enough and crept from his hiding place.

Although it sickened him to do so, Gavin levered the blade back and forth to free it from the dead man's sternum. He choked back the urge to vomit as the blade came free with a gurgle of dark blood. He forced himself to inspect the body for anything that might tell him why they had attacked him.

The dead man had dirty blond hair, and his light complexion pegged him as from the Graven Kingdom, which matched the accent Gavin had heard. The man had set a small camping pack beside the trail. It contained a bedroll, a water skin, and some dried fruits and meats, nothing to tell Gavin who the man was or why he was there.

The dead man's armor was leather, but not quite as well used as his companion's. It was small enough to fit Gavin's light frame, although it needed a good washing. Leather armor would be useful if there were more attacks. A world of trouble would land on him from both Master Draken and his father for having left so unprepared, but he hadn't thought the trip would be dangerous. He'd come to visit Tover Tanner and the twins without incident for over ten years, and had traveled alone for the last four.

His hands shook as he unfastened the armor and hauled it downhill to a small stream where he rinsed off most of the blood. The bedroll worked as a towel to dry the armor enough to wear. The wet leather was slimy, cold, and stained red in splotches, but at least it would dry in the right shape as he walked. He adjusted the straps to fit, and then repacked the man's camp kit. He saw the bigger thug's pack on the ground and picked it up as well. He used the fighting staff across his shoulders like a peasant's yoke to hold the gear on both sides. Thankfully, he didn't have far to go with the additional burden.

CHAPTER

THREE

S aleena watched over the pasture through the cattle's eyes, basking in their contentment, as she controlled them through the crystals around her neck. The cut crystals her brother, Ned, had made for her were illegal. She felt a small thrill of excitement at doing something the law would punish, but she also knew how useful the crystals were to train and protect the herd. The baron's herd.

The Accords were simple, as agreed to by the six Crystal Kings. First, kings and barons were the only ones who could authorize the use of crystals. During times of war, kings allowed the army to access crystals, but normally they were limited to noble families. Second, crystals were to be used only one at a time. Third, they were to never be used to control another human. The reasons behind the Accords were debated endlessly, but the rules themselves had remained constant through generations, with deviations stamped out ruthlessly by all six kingdoms.

In their far-off corner of the world, who would notice?

Her father had built his children's curiosity with tales of warfare and conquest achieved with the animals he controlled in the battles of the last war. His tales of the pooka marks on crystals were always her favorite, how in the ancient days it was said the pookas had given the patterns to the Crystal Kings. Some said it was a gift meant to curry favor. Others said it was the result of a treaty to prevent war, while yet others said the patterns were captured in a daring raid into a dark underground lair.

Most didn't believe any of the stories and chalked the crystals up to the cleverness of men in ages past. It was clear from the range of stories; nobody knew for sure where they had come from, or when the first crystals had fallen into the hands of men. Like the folklore of gods, demons, and sea monsters, very few adults believed the fantastical stories of cave-dwelling creatures.

Saleena had never expected it to work when Ned began experimenting with cutting, polishing, and engraving the rough crystals dug from above the pasture, but she was happy to continue their forbidden experiment after the first success.

She directed the cattle to areas where the grass was longer and less trampled to keep the pasture healthy, and scanned the field with thirty sets of eyes. All those eyes had driven her to distraction when she'd first connected to several cows at once. Her training had challenged her in several ways, but she'd worked her way through it, and could now watch the entire pasture as if it were a single image in her mind.

Unexpected motion near the valley's entrance caught the attention of the herd, and Saleena's multi-eyed gaze swung around for a closer look as the cattle's curiosity pushed lightly against her control.

Was a predator on the loose again?

No, it was just Gavin, two days early. She shut off her connection to the cattle and sat up with a dizzy rush, disoriented and shaky from exiting the trance.

Early? This was bad. They'd hidden their use of the crystals for years. Not even her best friend, Gavin, knew they controlled the animals with crystals in the pasture each summer.

She stood as he tromped across the field to meet her. He was sweaty, carried three packs, and wore a damp leather breastplate with nasty reddish-brown stains. Concern for his safety replaced her concerns over getting caught.

"Gavin, what happened? Are you hurt?" Maybe he hadn't noticed the cattle and the crystals around their necks. Twenty master-crystals hung around her neck, but wrapped inside a scarf over her frilly red blouse. She wore leather breeches up in the pasture for practical reasons, but she wore the blouse because it was her favorite.

He breathed hard from his hike and moved with a slight limp. "I'm alright. Two men attacked me." He paused and swallowed hard. "There was a bear, too."

Gavin looked across the field, then at Saleena. "Please tell me you don't have all these animals crystal-trained."

So, he had noticed after all.

"You know the laws, and how the baron feels. You could be sent to the mines or be banished."

She stuck her chin out in a defiant pout and glared at him. She held a hand up to feel the knuckle-sized crystals on their cord around her neck. "You're early. If you'd been on time, you wouldn't have seen anything at all, just like for the last three years."

"You've hidden this from me for three years? I don't like having to lie to my father, even for you." Gavin pushed his sweat-matted hair out of his eyes, a clear sign he was upset. She'd seen him do it often enough. "This will have to wait. I need to talk to your father and Ned. Some armed men were waiting for me an hour down the canyon. It's not safe here."

"Da's back at the house. Ned's hunting for mushrooms and cattails farther down the canyon. Ned's down there!" She turned and ran to the cabin yelling for her father. Gavin dropped his extra packs and followed, arriving just after Da came through the doorway.

Her father was a tall, strong man, and loved to share his soldier stories with them around the hearth at night. He'd told them how he traded soldiering for family life, took a wife, and became the baron's cattleman. He stuck with the cattle even after his wife vanished when Saleena and Ned were five years old. He didn't like to talk about that part but never blamed their mother for anything.

"What's all the ruckus, girl? You know the cattle don't like the noise."

"Da, Gavin was attacked by some men down the canyon. Ned's down there by himself. We need to go get him."

Her father gave her a stern glare. "You speak with respect and call the baron's son 'sir,' missy. I don't care how long you've known him. Now, let's see where Ned is." Da put his fingers to his lips and let out a piercing whistle. No answer came back.

Gavin said, "I don't know if there are more men out there in the woods. The two men I saw are both dead now. I hope they were alone, but I don't know for sure."

Da reached inside the doorway and pulled his longbow down from a hook. He nodded back toward the side of the house. "Runner's napping out back. Take him to search for Ned down the canyon." He gave Saleena a look loaded with meaning. Da intended to use Runner, the family's herding hound, to go along with her and Gavin.

Da looked back to Gavin and hooked the bow behind his leg to string it. "I'll keep an eye on things here to keep the herd safe, good sir." He'd grabbed his bow, but not his quiver of arrows. Sometimes he was forgetful like that. The bow was just for show, for Gavin to see.

Gavin rolled his eyes, and addressed Da like a displeased schoolmaster. "Tover, you have a crystal on the dog, too, don't you? You're going to be the death of me." He threw his hands in the air. "You stay in the cabin while you control Runner to come along with us, then. We'll work out this mess with the crystals later."

Da grinned. "Will do, good sir." He stepped back inside and shut the door. A thick bar clunked into place to lock the door. Da knew enough to stay safe while he controlled the dog. Saleena had heard all about staying safe in his stories. Without protection, you were the weak link in the chain.

Runner trotted around the corner and stopped in front of them, wagged his tail, then headed down the trail, sniffing the ground. Da knew how to use Runner's acute senses to good advantage, and could track just about anything. She'd given up trying to hide anything from Da as soon as Runner wore a crystal.

"Hold up a second. Saleena, there's a spare blade down there with those two packs if you want it. You held your own with the practice sticks when we were little. You might even be better with it than me." Gavin rubbed the middle finger of his right hand. "Remember when you broke my finger with a practice sword?"

Despite the stress of their impromptu search party, she smiled at the memory, and how she'd managed a lucky hit against him. He didn't give himself the credit he deserved. She poked the hole in his stained armor. "But who is it that killed two bandits on his own without a scratch? You'll never convince me you don't know which end of a sword is dangerous. Let's get moving. Ned's out there."

Runner bayed and held his position until she retrieved the blade, and they hurried back to him. The dog pointed down the trail like a hunting dog would, even though he was bred for cattle herding. Da was good at giving signals through the dog.

Movement caught her eye at the tree line. For an instant, Saleena thought it might be Ned returning, but instead, a creature lumbered from among the trees, and she screamed, "Bear!"

It tromped into the clearing near the main trail, a good distance from them, and scanned the area, possibly drawn out by the sound of Runner's barking.

Gavin said, "I have its crystal, but I can't control it yet. Run to the cabin. Go!"

A lot of good it would do him if she ran. Was he going to pull some noble sacrifice and let the bear kill him so she could run away? She had a better idea. She dropped to the ground and entered a trance to control the cattle. Immediately, Saleena saw the whole pasture again in her mind. Runner howled. He'd seen her lie down, and would never leave her unprotected. She might not need their protection if this worked out as she had practiced.

Gavin said, "What's she doing? Oh, great. Now, neither of you can talk to me."

The bear looked at Gavin and Runner as they guarded Saleena. Then it glanced at the cattle. Saleena examined everyone's position. This might work.

The bear turned from the cattle and trotted in Gavin's direction. It raised its head to sniff the air and slowed as it approached, wary of Runner's growl.

She launched the first wave.

The ground rumbled as more and more of her cattle broke into a carefully timed run. Gavin watched the bear and held his useless short blade out.

The cattle converged from behind the bear first, each coming from what looked like a random direction. They ran past in rapid succession. First, she stomped the bear with a hoof, then gored with a horn. Some of the cattle were better at kicking or biting, so she used what they were each best at, encouraging them to attack however they preferred. The herd was an extension of her, a body made of many parts. It was a dance, and she was their choreographer. They each attacked the target at full speed, never bumping into each other, never hesitating as she interwove their movements.

The bear swiped at one of them, but missed as she hit it from behind to keep it off-balance. The cattle looped around and continued their attack in a constant stream. She wondered why her father's stories never included anything like this, but all he'd said was that it was forbidden to control more than one animal in the Accords.

The bear let out a grunt and turned to face her cattle as they ran past, but it was only able to catch one with a claw. She felt a shock of pain on the flank of the bear's victim but nothing felt broken. She continued her careful stampede, with all its energy focused on the bear.

A minute later the bear collapsed with both of its rear legs broken and an untold number of puncture wounds and smaller injuries. Saleena continued the rain of hoofs and horns until the bear ceased moving, then trotted the cattle back to their pasture where she gathered them together into a defensive ring. They breathed hard and needed a rest.

Saleena pulled back from controlling the cattle and wavered to her feet, unstable from the transition. The disorientation and weakness were the same every time. She gave Gavin the look she used when she had won an argument. "That's why we haven't lost a calf to a predator in the past three years. I say it's worth it, even if the king's law says it's wrong." She turned to Runner, who was still controlled by her father. "I'll clean and bandage the cow's flank injury when we get back. It doesn't look too bad. She's still moving around well, even though it hurts. Let's go."

Runner nodded and barked, then loped over to the trail where the bear had appeared.

Saleena pulled the crystal from the bear's neck and looked it over. Da said large crystals cut by a master craftsman were worth years of common labor, yet the much simpler ones crafted by Ned worked well for the cows and Runner.

Ned got the polish right, but they had only a few of the markings that were on the bear's crystal.

She handed it over to Gavin who pulled the one from his neck. He stored them both in a pouch.

Gavin said, "You're going to have to tell me how you made those crystals."

Saleena said, "After we find Ned. He can tell you. It took him a long time to figure out all the shortcuts on the pooka marks."

Ned's trail led down the path and off to the side of the spring near some cattail patches. Runner tracked his scent for the better part of an hour.

Gavin said, "This is close to where I saw the men. They were down there next to the trail."

Runner growled and pointed with his nose. Gavin approached to look at the ground with him and said something under his breath.

Runner whined and glanced back at Saleena as she joined them. "Did you find something?"

Gavin continued his conversation with Runner. "There's a chance he got away. He might have made it into a tree or a cave. Any number of things might have happened." It had taken her a little time to get used to talking to Da through the dog, but Gavin had training and took to it quickly. It only took five minutes for them to come across the blood and drag marks, and a single shoe lying on the game trail. Saleena gasped, and ran along the trail where Ned had been dragged across the ground.

The bear had stored two bodies back against a small cliff, hidden away from easy view. The larger body belonged to Gavin's thug, but the smaller body was Ned's.

Saleena ran to her brother's side. She rolled the thug away from him, spewing a stream of the vilest of insults she knew, then sat next to Ned and screamed in anguish as Runner let out a long howl.

Gavin stood behind her but remained quiet. She and Da mourned their loss, cradling her brother's body. They had taken him from her. Behind her, Gavin set to work gathering stones.

Finally, he sat to rest from his labor. He picked up and studied a spaulder which had come loose near the bodies. How he could concentrate on details like that with Ned dead was beyond her. She held her brother's body close as Gavin made a second pile of stones a distance away for the thug. Why would he build even a small cairn over the bandit who was responsible for her brother's death?

She sat up beside her brother's body and turned to yell at Gavin. "This is your fault. You said they recognized you. Why else would they be here?" Runner stood and watched as grief flooded through her.

Gavin came back and knelt beside her. He held his arms wide, leaving her free to punish him however she saw fit. Why didn't he fight back? She wanted him to do something, not just sit there. She had no idea what he could have done to prevent it, but nobody could ever make up for Ned's death.

She pounded her fists on his leather breastplate, then collapsed onto him and sobbed on his armored shoulder. He gently patted her back. "You're right. I'm sorry. I don't know what I could have done better, but I will not fail you again. That's what a baron's family is supposed to do, isn't it? Protect the people?"

Saleena sobbed as Gavin sat with her. He had been their closest friend for years. This didn't sound like the Gavin she knew. He sounded more mature, more thoughtful. Maybe something had changed. She knew she shouldn't blame him, despite her desire to make it all his fault. Someone's fault.

Finally, she spoke, bitterness flavoring every word. "When you find the one who did this, let me see them. Let me ask them why."

"Of course. You deserve that."

Once the bodies were buried under proper piles of stone, they returned to the camp, much more subdued and somber as the evening approached. As they came near the cabin, Runner lay down in a grassy spot, and Da opened the cabin door and stepped out. He wrapped his arms around Saleena and stood for a long while without saying anything.

When the embrace ended, Gavin said, "What can I do to help? We need to pack and leave as soon as we can in case more men are coming."

Da straightened up, took a deep breath, and glanced around. "Right. Perishables from the cabin need to go into packs. We can tie those extra packs of yours together and string them across the back of one of the cattle. Since we're not exactly hiding anything anymore, good sir, I have some raw uncut crystals to bring with us. If you would be so kind, the packs are stored up in the rafters."

They were right. There was a lot to do. Saleena dried her eyes on her sleeve and stood up straight. "I'll go gather the things you dropped in the field. I can see them from here." She wanted to collapse and sob for her brother, but she didn't believe in sitting idle while others worked. It was best to stay busy doing something—anything. She wiped a tear from her cheek and sniffed as she set to work.

Gavin's breath caught, but he turned away as he scrubbed his face. She wasn't the only one hurting.

Packing only took an hour.

Da had the largest pack by far, loaded down with all the uncut crystal pulled from its hiding place behind a loose stone in the hearth. Saleena had insisted on digging out the secret spot behind the stone after making their first successful crystal. Others wouldn't understand.

Gavin saw the bulging bag and said, "There must be enough for twenty or thirty crystal pairs in there. Where did it all come from?"

"Well, good sir," Da said, "there's a rich crystal deposit up in the hillside near where the creek bubbles up out of the ground. Rough and impure, but clear enough to see through. My Da knew about it, but didn't know the first thing about cutting them. I'm not sure why he never told the baron, but I learned young to not stick out, so I followed his lead. I learned the shape to cut from a fellow soldier during a campaign to the north. We had our assigned beasts and crystals, and took lots of notes and made wax molds of them. Bored young soldiers got no sense, you see, even for things that might get them banished or killed. Don't never let your soldiers get bored, sir."

The thought of watching Gavin lead soldiers was noble and inspiring, but his brother Stephan was the one to do all that.

Da was stubborn about manners and always used 'sir' to address anyone in the Baron's family. He reminded her to do the same. He'd ignored Gavin's requests to be less formal over the years, and sprinkled in more 'sirs' to make his point.

Saleena made good use of the time to treat the wounded animal, and had it cleaned and bandaged before Gavin and Da packed the last of their things from the cabin.

Gavin asked, "Will the cattle move in the dark? I hate to stay here any longer than necessary."

Saleena answered, "Leave it to them, and they won't go anywhere in the dark. They might get hurt, or get sick if we push them too hard, and they need their rest. They don't work the same way a single animal does with the crystals. It's almost like they're one big creature with dozens of bodies. I call it a herd-brain. They're used to working together. I can give them an idea and coordinate it, but it's a lot easier to get them to do something close to what they want anyway. They won't want to move in the dark."

"I've never heard of herd-brains. It seems useful."

She frowned. "All I know is the Accords forbid it for some reason. I don't understand why, since it's helped us to protect and train the herd. Barons don't want to line up cattle and march them around a field to eat the best grass. The other barons would make them a laughingstock. With them, it's got to be a wolf, bear, mountain lion, or some exotic thing with large fangs and such. The bigger, the better. They want war animals. Barons don't have herd-brains, and I bet they don't know how to use them either. Even something like Runner here is beneath most of them, though he's got to be the best herd dog around."

Da looked at the sun, low in the sky as evening approached. "We need to keep a watch tonight and leave first thing in the morning. As you said, good sir, there may be more men out there. I'll take Runner out tonight to keep the first watch."

That night, Saleena lay with her eyes open for a long while, unable to sleep. Had the men killed Ned by controlling the bear, or had the bear found him on its own? The men were probably after Gavin. Had Ned gotten in the way? They could all still be in danger. Were there more men waiting in the woods? Who was behind the attack?

Would Gavin tell his father about their crystals, or would he lie and become an accomplice? The law was clear. They had broken the law while protecting the baron's herd. She had broken two of the three Accords of the Crystal Kings without ever considering the consequences. It had been an adventure at first, but later it had become a matter of pride, caring for the animals to keep them safe.

She thought of controlling the cattle through the night even if they didn't leave until morning, but being in a trance wasn't like being asleep. It was still a lot of work, and not the least bit restful. She suspected nobody but the cows would be rested in the morning.

THEY LEFT EARLY, just as the stars faded in the growing twilight. Gavin watched as Runner, true to his name, directed the herd with precision. Crystal training enhanced his natural instincts. He knew exactly what every whistle command meant, and what to do about it. The dog knew more commands for driving cattle than Gavin did. Come to think of it, the herd knew more commands than he did. Animals remembered everything their master did while controlling them, and they learned quickly through example and patterns.

Unfortunately, Runner's and the cattle's training violated laws of both the kingdom and the barony, and even agreements among the six Crystal Kings. The restrictions made sense from the viewpoint of those in power. Crystals were used to train war animals, and what business did peasants have with war animals?

Emotions ran close to the surface for everyone. Gavin concentrated on the business of getting home to keep himself under control. He and Tover split watches to provide extra security for the trip now that they had to watch for more than ordinary predators. A horse would have been a great help, but his father did him no favors so long as he didn't act like a proper baron's son. Gavin refused to fit the mold of his father's expectations.

Saleena was silent for the first day on the trail, and Gavin kept his distance to allow her to grieve. He found nothing to say or do to ease her pain because he, too, felt a keen loss. He had no idea how to lessen his own emotional turmoil, much less anyone else's.

Even into the next day, their conversations were sparse and stilted, but Gavin drew her into some idle chatter from time to time as they hurried the cattle on their way. Saleena had thrown herself into the work, watching after the cattle. She regularly checked bandages and watched the trail ahead for trouble.

Gavin figured she kept her emotional demons at bay by staying too busy to think of anything but the work. That might work for her, but his demons were always there in the background of his thoughts and feelings.

They were a half day away from the castle when they set camp late in the afternoon on the second day. They couldn't make it by nightfall, so there was no sense in making it a long day on the trail. Saleena approached Gavin before his first patrol around the resting cattle.

He spoke before she could. "I can't just show up with the crystal pair from the bear with no explanation. I'm going to have to make up something about killing the bear myself to keep your secret. Nobody will believe me, but they're less likely to suspect the truth if they're wondering about my motives. If there's a way to get around the law, I will. But secrets don't last forever."

She gave him a shy shrug. "I'm sorry if I hurt you when we found Ned's body. I've had a lot of time to think about it, and I know it wasn't your fault he died. I miss him terribly. Thank you for everything you've done, Gavin. Or as Da would have me say, sir."

Gavin cringed. "Please don't do that. Don't be like your father. I grew up with you. The more we keep things the same, the better it will help me to remember the good times with Ned." He paused to gaze out across the brush and grass beside the trail. Faint smells of sage and cattle drifted on the air. "However, when it comes to the crystals, I need to try to keep the rules because the baron is my father."

Saleena's jaw dropped open. "You're a hypocrite. Since when did you care what your father thought? I know how you dodge responsibilities. I've been there to see it. I've helped you with some of your schemes."

"Saleena, please just listen for a minute. I also need to look out for you and your father as friends. You've acted more like family to me than my real family. It's going to be tough to find the right middle ground. I will do everything I can to keep you safe."

She nodded a slow acknowledgment and continued on a different topic. "I looked through those two packs you salvaged from the thugs. I used their sleeping gear to pad the backs of the cattle. I stored their locked case with the spaulder you salvaged."

"What locked case? Was it inside their packs? I never looked through their things with so much on my mind the past couple of days."

"Just a minute. I'll get it." Saleena stood to fetch the case, but stopped as three horses thundered up over a hill to the south.

Gavin drew his blade and stepped forward. Saleena and Tover had removed the crystals from the cattle the day before. No controlled stampede would rescue him this time. Still, Tover had a bow, and Saleena knew the basics of swordplay.

Master Draken called from horseback as he approached. His dark skin made him easy to pick out. Gavin slid his short blade back into its scabbard and began to breathe again.

Draken's voice carried across the field as the three trotted closer. "Sir, I have to get you back to the castle immediately. Come with me, if you please."

Whatever this was about, it couldn't be good. Master Draken was never this polite. Draken wouldn't discuss anything sensitive within earshot of commoners, so Gavin would learn nothing here. The other two men dismounted, and one of them handed Gavin the reins of his horse with a quick bow. The other tied his horse and strode across the field to speak with Tover. "The two of us will escort you the rest of the way to the castle."

Gavin whispered to Saleena, "Tell your father I'll talk with you both before I share information with anyone else. Hold tight and hope for the best. Keep them all hidden."

Gavin mounted and rode into the early evening beside a scowling Master Draken. Gavin had seen him in a range of moods over the years, but to see Draken in such deep frustration was rare.

CHAPTER

FOUR

Gavin would rather have met anywhere but his father's private council chamber, yet Master Draken insisted they both go straight there as soon as they handed their horses off to the stableman. It was a relief his father wasn't there to meet them.

Draken hadn't spoken the whole trip, allowing nothing more than a vague insistence about waiting until he knew they were safe from prying eyes and ears. It was unusual for him to be quite this paranoid.

The baronial map covered most of the table as Gavin's father had left it, with weights holding the corners down to the thick oak tabletop. Master Draken pulled the iron-banded door closed, then tossed his dirty cloak onto the back of his usual chair, but remained standing. With Master Draken, the longer he remained silent, the more extreme the lecture. This one would be legendary.

Gavin interrupted the silence. "I don't know what you've heard, but–"

"Of course, you don't know. How could you know? Word is only reaching us now as wild rumors spread among the locals."

Gavin bit his tongue, removed his cloak and hung it on a wall peg before easing into a chair at the table, not caring if his trainer still stood. It was a breach of protocol, but he needed to sit on something besides a saddle. He wasn't used to riding, and they had ridden hard to make it by sunset. Only after he sat down did Master Draken flip his seat around to sit across from Gavin with his arms resting on the chair back as he always did.

Gavin gestured at the chair and raised an eyebrow to let Draken know he'd noticed the lack of rebuke for his rudeness. "Do I go first, or do you? My news is important, but now I'm not sure who has priority."

Draken wiped dust from his dark face with his sleeve and glared at

Gavin across the table. "Based on the battle-worn and blood-stained armor you're wearing, I'd say you've earned speaking first, but I have an obligation to fulfill. Unless I'm mistaken, I suspect we have two sides of the same story. We've had no time to confirm the rumors yet, but there are reports of an ambush at the Baronial Council."

"Is my father in danger? Has he been hurt? What about Stephan?" As much as Gavin and his father had fought and argued in this room, he loved his father and wouldn't wish him or his brother Stephan any harm.

"We don't know. According to what we've heard, a large force ambushed them. King Vargas' family, every baron, and a good portion of the baronial heirs may be dead."

Gavin placed a hand on the table. "Dead? What do you mean? They can't be dead. They had the best of the kingdom's war animals on hand, and the best of the guardsmen." He tried to put a stopper on his emotions to better consider and understand the problem, but his heart raced as he realized he might be the only Stoutheart left. All dead.

"The king's annual council isn't known for its military discipline, so there may have been a weakness to exploit. The rumors are already spreading among the people. To deny it would only lend the rumor credibility and speed. Luckily, most of the locals don't understand the consequences if the rumors are true. If the news has reached us, it will spread whether it's true or not. The late harvests may slow the rumors, but every barony will hear before snow flies, and whatever remains of those ruling families will have their hands full keeping the peace. It will be the greatest loss of power in centuries. The kingdom itself might collapse without any other effort, much less if an outside force is at play."

The stories were not final or proven. Gavin took a deep breath and exhaled slowly. "So, we need to verify the news first, and then act. We need to either dispel false rumors or take control of the barony, depending on what we learn." He forced his emotions under control, at least for the moment, and analyzed the situation to decide what to do next.

"Your strategic grasp of the situation is far better than your swordplay, but you have the order wrong. You need to take temporary control as your first step in keeping the barony stable." He paused and squinted at Gavin's dirty armor. "You have a hole in that breastplate right about where your heart should be. I'm sure your news has something to do with why you're not wearing your own armor. I found it in your locker after you left. I'd hate to think you risked your life for the sake of comfort. It's your turn now, sir." Master Draken tilted his head to the side, ready to listen. Draken always paid close attention to the formalities of address, but he'd never let formality get in the way of a stern rebuke.

Gavin's concern for the Tanners and their cattle grew while possible reasons for the attack crystallized in his thoughts. If the same enemy killed everyone at the Baronial Council, Gavin would have been just one more target. Things still didn't add up.

He described the attack by the two men and the bear in the broadest of terms, avoiding details which would incriminate the Tanners. Gavin decided all Draken needed to know was that these men tried to kill him, and they had, directly or not, killed his friend Ned Tanner.

"A bear. You expect me to believe you killed a crystal-trained bear and two men?"

Gavin pulled the bear's crystal and its master from his pouch and dropped the mated pair of stones onto the table to shimmer in the lamp light. "I don't care what you believe at this point. What we do next is more important. We've got to find out if my father and Stephan are still alive. You can keep running things here as you have. I can take a handful of men to check out the rumors." It ate at him that he had parted with his father and brother on such bad terms.

Draken gawked at the sparkling crystals and reached out to touch them. "Those could be from a royal guard! I've never seen better." He wrenched his attention back to Gavin. "I'll accept your account, though it changes little. All we know with your input is the attack was more widespread than we thought."

His visage became grim as he continued. "But as usual, you have a head for strategy, and you're daft as a rock at the same time. How do you do it? There is a large enemy force out there somewhere, and you want to gallivant around with a few armed men. Until we know for certain about your father, you're the Baron Regent. You're not going anywhere. To top it all off, I may grind my teeth down to nubs because I am your senior adviser. Sir."

Gavin's mouth hung open as his train of thought evaporated like a summer mist. "I can't be the Baron Regent. I'm too young, I don't have the training, and I have no desire to fill my father's shoes, or my brother's. Besides, they may be out there still, and we need to find them."

"Do you think any of your stupid excuses matter? Do you think I'm happy about you being our best option? The people will look to the Stout-heart name for security. You're not much, but you're all we have. It's time for you to grow up and step up. You need advice, you need information, and you need a plan. But before that, you need a backbone."

Gavin sat back in his chair, his mouth open. Draken had been sharp with him before but had never been so blunt. Was he right? Did the people need him?

"How long have you wanted to say that to me?" Gavin asked quietly.

"About ten years now. I seem to finally have your attention."

Gavin nodded. "A few years late, I suppose."

Draken continued, "You're great at plans and schemes. I've seen the extents you've reached to get out of training. Now you need to lead."

"Am I really the best option? You could do it."

"Well, sir, that depends on how many people you want to die if the subjects and guards believe I've attempted a coup to gain control. You've got a brain. Use it. We need you as the regent."

Gavin was running out of options. Maybe Draken was right after all. He could stand in for a few days until they figured out what was going on.

"Okay, I'm the Baron Regent for the next little while. How do we find out about the rumors? That has to be our top priority."

Draken said, "Before I fetched you, I assigned some of the castle guards to track the rumor back to its source. With your blessing, I'll follow up to see if we have a person to bring in for a chat. I suspect one of the locals started the rumor. We need a first-hand account."

Gavin no longer felt irrelevant or useless, and he wasn't sure he liked the difference. "Right. Finish your hunt, Master Draken. Tomorrow, I'll go make sure Tover and Saleena made it back without any more trouble."

Draken pinched the bridge of his nose and closed his eyes. "If I might give you more counsel, sir, you have people who can do those sorts of things, and who *should* do that work for you. You do not understand this yet, but your time has become more valuable than you can imagine. Learn to delegate." He stood from his chair and grabbed his dirty cloak. "If I can find our rumormonger, I'll be back tonight. Don't get too comfortable, and don't go anywhere alone. Now, if you will excuse me?" Draken walked over to stand next to the door and waited.

Gavin looked him over. "Do we have to go through all this protocol?"

"Yes, we do, *sir*. If you must, consider it to be out of some vestigial respect for your father."

Gavin lowered his gaze in shame, a rare thing when it came to Draken's barbed comments. "Then you are dismissed."

Gavin gazed off at the alcove used to burn memorial candles. "Missing. Maybe gone. I'll never be able to replace them and do what they would do."

Draken paused with his hand on the door. "Replacement isn't the goal. You must do your best with what you have. Learn who you are meant to be, and then be that man." He gave an informal salute.

Gavin returned the salute. He stood and walked to the door as Draken opened it and left to hunt for his source of information.

A footman just a few years Gavin's senior stood at ease outside the door. After a bit of thought, the name came to Gavin. "Jase, please let me know when the Tanners and the cattle arrive. They should get here mid-day tomorrow. Also, Tover lost his son Ned to bandits. I'd like to light a candle for him. Just have someone bring a box of candles; I may need several by the time we're done."

Perhaps the candle meditation would bring him peace. The Priests of Order always brought plenty of new candles when they visited, so there must be several on hand. The alcove in his father's study had seen generations of candles burned for generations of loss. Now it was his turn to mourn.

"Of course, sir. I'll see to it." Jase pulled a cord near the door to summon a servant and looked Gavin up and down, lingering on the stained hole through his armor with wide eyes. "Do you, ah, need anything else, sir? Bandages maybe?"

Explaining would be too much work. "No, thank you." His heart had a hole, but not the kind left by a weapon. Gavin shut the door and sat back at the table to reflect on his upside-down world. A baron should be someone with skill and power. A lot of good people would look to him as their protector, and they deserved his best, as Draken had said. Would his best be good enough? The puzzle still had too many unknowns.

Gavin was still pondering when Jase delivered the candles a short time later.

GAVIN KNELT on the old mat, worn from use over the years in front of the candle alcove. He struggled to stay awake as the small candle for Ned burned down to a flickering nub, when there was a sharp knock at the door.

"Come," Gavin answered through a wide yawn.

Draken opened the door and strode through, followed by one of the local men who stared about the room as if it would eat him whole and spit out his bones.

Gavin stood up, rubbed his eyes, and stretched. He considered taking his regular chair, but noticed Draken's subtle nod toward the baron's seat. Gavin inspected the new arrival in silence for a few moments, and then sat.

He had seen the man in passing before but had never talked to him. His fox fur cap marked him as a small game hunter. Gavin tried to formulate a reasonable question with his sleep-fogged mind, but Draken spoke first. "We found the source of the rumors, sir. This is Mick. Would you like me to proceed with questioning him now?"

Leave it to Draken to know how to intimidate and terrify the locals. His methods wouldn't work at all if they wanted the man to put thought into his answers. Gavin wanted to learn whatever he could immediately, as much as Draken did, but felt compassion for the man. He nodded to two of the chairs across from him.

Gavin tried a smile, working to ease Mick's fears. "Have a seat, both of you. Master Draken didn't wake you, did he?"

"No, sir. I was out drinking with the boys when I got summoned. Am I to go to the stocks? I never meant to spy on the king's council with his barons. By the shards, I didn't mean it!" Mick sat with his arms to his side as if he expected to be tied down. At least the man stopped flicking glances back and forth like a wild rabbit in a dog kennel.

Draken flipped his chair around, as usual, and sat. "What we want from you is the truth. A careful and correct account of what you saw. I'm not interested in the tales you told to the barmaids and your friends. Keep to the facts, as plain as you can recall, and we can stay friends."

Mick blinked and nodded with enthusiasm as he twisted his hat in his hands. "Well, those woods are one of my reg'lar trapping runs, so I was gathering pelts and meat. I got mouths to feed."

Draken folded his arms and raised an eyebrow.

"So, you see, I wasn't sneaking or interfering or nothin'. I figured if I got too close, the patrols would send me back. Anyhow, the first time I seen a royal patrol, they was already dead. Ripped up. I didn't want nobody to think I done it, so I marked the spot in my head and then made my way to their camp to let the proper authorities know."

Draken interrupted. "Do those authorities include your friends at the alehouse where you've been flapping your gums?"

Mick licked his lips. Gavin was about to intervene to soften the mood when Draken backed off without insisting on an answer.

Draken said, "What colors were the dead men wearing?"

"Why, King's colors, of course. They all wore dark blue. It was his yearly Council after all. But like I said, I hiked to where their camp was, straight away. When I got there, all I saw was bodies and trampled tents. The whole place was a mess, except for one spot at the king's banner."

Gavin held up a hand to interrupt. "All the banners were left up? That's not normal."

"No, sir. The King's was the only banner flying, like a signal. That's why I risked a look. The king and his family was all set out in a neat line right under his banner. The queen, both sons, and his daughter, all dead. I seen their paintings in the big hall here at the castle, so I know it was them. Women and children executed, not torn up by war animals like the other bodies I saw out in the camp. I got scared. I didn't want to be dead myself. I ran back to my camp, got my horse and rode as fast as I dared back here to stay safe. I got here two days back."

Gavin balled his fists at the man's description. He leaned forward with his knuckles on the table to keep his hands from shaking. "Did you see Baron Stoutheart, or did you recognize any others there?" He dreaded what he might hear.

"Sorry, sir. I never got close to any but the king and his family. The people I saw was all dead and the whole camp wrecked. Even some war animals got killed. That ain't a good sign for the men controlling them. Men, beasts, women, and children all killed. None were spared as far as I saw."

Gavin raised knuckles to his temples and looked at the desk. "So, no news specifically on the Baron. He might still be alive." It wasn't very likely, but he refused to say it aloud. He'd never dreamed something this horrible might happen, to violently take away the last of his family all at once. The lack of solid information frustrated him, yet there was the thin hope of his father's miraculous escape.

Draken leaned forward. "You're a hunter. You've seen animals that have been dead for a while. How long had these men been dead?"

"I never thought about it, but I guess they was all fresh dead. They hadn't bloated up or gone to rot yet, and the blood wasn't all soaked into the ground or dried out. It was less than a full day."

Gavin tried to ignore the images conjured up by the description, and instead figured the numbers in his head and considered the time it would take to ride from the site of the Baron's Council. It coincided fairly well with his attack in the upper pasture. The events fit together better now but were still confusing. Why try to capture him rather than kill him? If they wanted to capture an heir, they had all the heirs they needed at the King's Council. With the dozens of bodies Mick had seen, the odds were low anyone survived. Gavin was no closer to fixing his confusion.

His biggest question was still unanswered. Had his father and brother survived? It was impossible to tell based on what they knew, but it didn't look good. He heaved a sigh and ran his fingers through his hair, which was still thick with dust and sweat from the trail. He would happily sacrifice a little time to wash up. Maybe clean skin would help to clear his mind. "Master Draken, do you have anything else to ask?"

"No. Mick, as far as I can tell, you're lucky to be alive after such a near miss with the ambush. You're dismissed, but stop spreading stories. As of this moment, you no longer remember visiting the king's camp. If you talk about it, I will hear. You don't want that. Do you understand me?"

Mick bobbed his head up and down. "Yes, of course. Thank you, Master Draken, and you too, sir." He gripped his hat tight in both hands and beat a hasty retreat.

Gavin waited for the door to close, then said, "The king's whole family is gone, too? What were they even doing out there?"

"The eldest princess was approaching marriageable age. The heirs of all the barons were there to show off and gain her father's attention. That may be why your father took a larger group of guards and advisers. A show of strength. With them all dead or on the run, we have a problem."

Gavin leaned back in his seat. "I don't see how that has a lot of impact here in our barony."

Draken said, "You're thinking on the wrong scale. What happens to our country if most of the barons and their heirs are gone?"

Setting aside his worries for the moment, Gavin thought through this new puzzle and whistled. "Right. Kingdom-wide confusion, waiting for word from dead barons, then scrambling to take over. Just like us."

Draken said, "Gather your advisers for a formal council tomorrow. All the craft masters, everyone of rank. Shall I attend to gathering them for you?"

"Do you tell my father what to do like this?"

"No. I never felt the need to lead him by the nose. He's never been one to shy away from a decision, but you're still new at this. I pray you'll learn some of his skill before this crisis is over. If you'll grant me my leave, I'll take care of those invitations to get everyone here by noon tomorrow. Some of them live out in the countryside."

Draken's tone irritated Gavin, but his request made sense. "Of course, Master Draken. The people need some form of leadership until we have a real answer about who died, so I'd better get used to it. Tomorrow at noon, then."

Gavin followed Draken to the door, and said to Jase, "I'd like to go to my room now."

Jase wrinkled his brow and gave Gavin an odd look. "Master Draken had us move your things to your father's sleeping quarters. He said it was for security, but if you're to be the new Baron Stoutheart, these will be your rooms permanently, sir."

"I'm not the new baron. Not while my father might still be out there." Gavin leaned his forehead against the door frame. "Forget it. It's not your problem to deal with. Thank you for your help."

"Sir, if I might give you one piece of unsolicited advice?"

"Sure. Go ahead. I'd better get used to it."

"As much as I like you to thank me for doing my job, your father trained us to be invisible. Ready at a moment's notice, like a good tool, but out of the way. Begging your pardon, but if you spoke to a guard as you would to a peer in front of another noble, they would see you as weak. In his more generous moods, your father would thank us with a slight nod."

Gavin turned to go back into the private conference room and the chambers beyond. "I'm not my father. I'm only here to fill in while he's gone."

CHAPTER

FIVE

The main council chamber was half-empty as Gavin sat at the head of the long table. His father had taken several guards and advisers with him which left the seats nearest to Gavin vacant, isolating him from the rest of the men who gathered at Draken's request. Mottled, mid-day light made its way through the small windows high up on the wall, while wall lamps tossed yellow light across the stone floor. It smelled of decades of soot, oil, and wax.

Captain Zachary spoke first. "Sir, we need to respond to the situation."

Gavin looked up, realizing the Captain of the Guard had spoken to him. His eyes itched, and his bones ached, not entirely from lack of sleep. "Yes. We have a lot to do." The reports he had read earlier in the morning described the duties of the Captain of the Guard. Even as tired as he was, he mentally built a list of high-level goals. "You're down several men. This situation could turn into anything from a false alarm to war on our doorstep. What is your recommendation for changes to the guard?"

The captain's eyebrows raised with a look of pleasant surprise as Gavin asked him for input instead of telling him what to do. The captain cleared his throat. "If we call the villagers inside the castle walls for security, I can draw on the retired military men to make up the shortage. It will crowd us in tight, but we'll manage. Our walls aren't very tall, but they'll do against a small force. I can expand patrols inside and outside the walls with a dozen more men. If there are more men with the right training, I can use them, too."

Master Draken nodded discreetly at the local Merchant's Guild Master who scowled with concern. Picking up on the cue, Gavin said, "Master

Quincy, you look worried." Gavin didn't know why the merchant was upset, so he leaned forward to listen.

"Moving people in before the farmers finish the harvests will make it harder, if not impossible, to do the work. Farmers will need to go out in shifts rather than staying in the fields."

That sounded right to Gavin on the surface, but there was another level of concern he felt he missed. Gavin ran through all the new information and put mental puzzle pieces together while staring up at the ceiling. He'd always excelled at puzzles and had spent his winters trading riddles and creating complex rules to games played in the dark halls of the castle. He had never considered the management of the barony as a puzzle until now. He needed to identify the resources that best matched the needs as they came up. He drummed his fingers a few times and then looked back at Captain Zachary.

"You said you want to expand external patrols. Can you make those patrols consist of farmers already done with their harvests? They can guard the remaining farmers and lend a hand as well."

The Captain nodded. "Yes, sir. I can do that. I think I know the right families to call on. Some of the early crops are already in." He leaned back in his chair.

Master Quincy folded his arms and leaned forward. "This is all highly irregular. Coming up with the budgets for this will be —"

Draken interrupted him. "It will still be your job to manage the grain harvest and trade. Everyone here needs to adjust, to prepare for what may come." He looked around the room. "Each of you send a status report of your responsibilities in the morning. That will tell us where we stand."

A rumble of agreement surrounded the table, although some joined in later than others.

Why had Draken insisted Gavin run this council meeting when Draken knew better how to do the job? Perhaps Draken had shifted to a different form of training, to show Gavin what was required to stand in for his father. There was no dodging the training this time.

Oddly enough, Gavin didn't want to skip out. He saw better how things worked, and how each choice had an impact on real people within the barony. It was his job, temporary or not, to give the people what they needed to keep them fed, housed, and safe. They weren't just people. They were *his* people.

Gavin moved to the next agenda item. Despite Draken's warning the night before, he said, "We still lack information on my father and brother, and need to learn what happened. We need to send scouts. I know I have duties here, but it's my family and our baron that's missing. How many searchers can we spare?"

Several of the Masters glanced back and forth all around the table. It was Gavin's first clue he'd misspoken.

Master Smith slapped his meaty hand down on the table. "We just heard how short we are on guards. Are you daft, boy? You can't have it both ways. We don't have dozens of people to go traipsing across the countryside."

Draken stared daggers at Master Smith until he sheepishly added, "Sir. My apologies. I got carried away. What I meant to say is that we need every spare body here. As our Baron Regent, you listen to us then make the hard choices. Everyone's heard your father is missing along with your brother. It's got us on edge."

Draken nodded. "If I may, sir? Master Smith has a good point, even with his lack of manners. I believe I'm the best candidate to confirm or debunk the information. No team is necessary. I know every game trail within a day's ride. I've traveled nearly all of them with the baron. I know where he'd go if he's managed to escape the ambush. I've cared for the baron's injured wolf since before the trip, so I'm attuned to her crystal. I'll take her with me. That leaves you free to be seen here, which will ease the growing fear in the village."

He used the same tone as before, issuing instructions while making it sound like he asked for permission. At least it seemed as if he was asking permission to go. It was clear that Gavin wasn't going anywhere.

Gavin nodded. "Very well. This is Stoutheart Barony. As the only Stoutheart here I will make myself seen, and keep everything moving forward. Master Draken, do what you can to find them." The choice made the most sense, even though his heart wasn't in it. He wanted to be out searching, but he would do this for the people. They deserved his best, despite him not feeling very inspirational under the cloud of concern over his family.

GAVIN SAT at his table and looked idly at the burned-out candle stub in the alcove. Draken paced the floor.

Draken said, "That wasn't quite a disaster. Close, but not quite."

"What? I thought it went pretty well."

Draken looked up at the ceiling for a few seconds before he spoke. "Your job is to prepare for the worst while hoping for the best: weapon storage, increasing stores from the fletchers, and ordinary things at the same time, too, like the harvest and pest control at the granary. But that's what this council is for. Part of your job, sir, is to be confident and be seen by the people. They need someone to follow, more now than ever."

"I'll tour and mingle while you're gone to improve morale. I won't just sit around, despite what you think of me."

Draken flipped his chair around and sat. Gavin had never been brave enough before, but now he asked, "Why do you always do that with your chair?"

"People in this country don't know how to make a proper chair. This is as close as I can get to the way they use them in the wild lands. Maybe I'll build a proper chair one of these years and show you."

Gavin made note of their give and take. Gavin offered to be more responsible, and Draken opened up more as he would to a friend. Gavin wanted to ask more, but they had work to do. "You think I let you down in the meeting. What did you learn from it?" If nothing else, Gavin needed to identify his failures and correct them.

Draken said, "Let me fill you in on the things you didn't see, and a little on why you missed it. You need to be more aware of what's going on around you."

Gavin snorted. "You realize I've never spoken with most of those men before, right? Fine. What did I miss?"

Draken held up one finger. "You have Captain Zachary eating out of your hand because you asked for his advice, which your father hasn't done in over a decade. I'll give you points for that one, but it seemed like an accidental win."

He raised a second finger. "On the other hand, Master Quincy is learning to hate you because you're impacting his ability to squeeze extra rent out of the farmers from their personal crops on the baron's land. They all try to grow a little extra and skim it for themselves. If they harvest quickly, he doesn't have time to visit before they've stored their private stashes and delivered the barony's quota."

He raised a third finger. "Master Smith still sees you as the little boy who hammered his finger black and blue at eight years old, but at least he wants to take you under his wing and be helpful."

Gavin thought back to the conversations and body language and saw that he missed all the information Draken had gleaned from the visible hints. He had not paid attention to the right things. Now he knew more what to watch for. He might not catch everything the next time, but it wouldn't be for lack of trying.

Draken said, "Again, your job is to be seen and to be confident as much as your job is to lead. More importantly, you must always be aware. You need to direct people and get out of their way. You're to act as the mind and soul of the barony. You're not the feet, or the hands, or even the eyes and ears. Others feed you the information, and you decide what to do."

Gavin said, "It appears dodging all that combat training is about to pay off if I'm meant to run the barony from here, away from fighting and danger."

Master Draken gave him a withering glare. "Yes, but you must also be seen to care. Do you?"

Gavin glared at Draken for the rebuke which hit too close to home. He cared about the people, perhaps more than anyone in his family because he spent more time among them, but he had never been able to make a difference before. He caught on that thought. He had a fresh chance to do what was best for the people. As Draken implied, the decisions all fed back to him. He could make a difference. He *would* make a difference.

Draken stood and walked to the door. "I expect to be no more than three days on this scouting mission. Don't accidentally burn the castle to the ground while I'm gone, sir."

"You're still bringing that up? The fire wasn't my fault. I never could convince you, or my father, I didn't start it." Gavin understood Draken meant well, but his strict methods and rough exterior rubbed people the wrong way, and Gavin was the most frequent target of his insults and insinuations. But Gavin expected nothing better after he'd ignored Draken, disobeyed him, and returned insults freely for years. He had been so caught up with not being the heir that he hadn't been much of anything.

But, things were different now. Gavin had to build a working relationship with Draken and with a whole council. Even if Draken found his father, and Gavin reverted to the ignored second son, things would never be the same. It might not be permanent, but he had no choice but to step up. He owed an obligation nobody else at the castle was qualified to fill. Not an obligation to his father, but to the people who had supported and befriended him as he had grown up.

Gavin embraced the job at hand and said, "If you find my father and bring him back, the two of you can take turns telling me what I did wrong. I'm sure it will be a long list." Yes, things were going to change.

WITHOUT FOOD, the barony was nothing. Gavin felt a need to check on the granaries and food supplies, after visiting the main wall and the trade carts, with Jase following along behind as a personal guard and assistant. It hadn't occurred to Gavin that his father always had an armed shadow, and the constant escort made him uneasy. It had seemed second nature for his father to always have a guard ready at hand, sometimes to do nothing more than stand and frown while wearing a sword. For him, it seemed a terribly inefficient use of time.

Jase picked up his pace to walk beside Gavin. "I received word the Tanners arrived while you were in council."

Gavin nodded. "Thank you. I want to visit them later."

Two servants in the courtyard stood aside to make way as he walked past, which came as a surprise. Before, he had gone wherever he wanted without anyone paying particular attention, and he was the one who dodged those who walked with purpose. He wasn't sure whether he should say something to them or not. Did one thank people for getting out of the way? He was sure Jase would frown on it.

Word of his arrival preceded him along the entire path to the granary. Despite wearing his usual breeches, shirt, and vest, everyone noticed him. He nodded and waved to acquaintances who were oddly distant, yet respectful. As a middle-ground decision, he smiled when people acknowledged him.

The granary stood behind the main barony castle, but within the outer wall for protection. Gavin bypassed the stand-alone silos for storing corn and wheat and entered the wing of storage rooms filled with bags of flour and barrels of pickles and other sundries. Salted meats hung from the rafters, and barrels of ale were stacked and stored against the coming fall and winter. The air smelled of meal and vinegar.

Jase led Gavin to a small door. "The rat catcher lives here. He can tell you about the granary." Jase knocked, and the door opened immediately.

A scrawny boy of sixteen stood at attention inside. "Baron Stoutheart. Thank you for visiting, sir! I'm Willem. What may I do for you?" It was a well-starched speech, as if he'd given it before. Maybe it was how the boy addressed the old baron.

Gavin had only seen him out and about once or twice. The boy either kept to himself or was too busy to join with friends.

"Tell me about the granary, Willem. What do you do here?" If Gavin stuck to open-ended questions on his tour, he could leave all the hard thinking up to the people he met.

"As the rat catcher, I guard against pests, not just rats. Things like mice, bats, and bugs. I protect the stored food within the castle walls." He stood straight and looked Gavin in the eye, obviously proud of his position.

Gavin glanced around the poorly lit room. Willem occupied a tiny sleeping area barely large enough for one person, with a cot and makeshift table next to a small fireplace. "You do this alone? You catch all the vermin?"

"Yes, but I get help from Doom Bringer, Death Claw, and Skull Crusher. That's Doom Bringer up there." He pointed to the top of a stack of crates where Gavin spotted a black shadow with green eyes. The cat stood and stretched, and then hopped down from one box to the next until he head-butted Willem's leg and walked past to plop down onto a pile of rags beside the small cot.

"Well, from the looks of you, you're certainly not raiding the pantry." Gavin considered Willem's wiry frame and smiled at his own joke before realizing it was rude to point out Willem's poor state.

"Oh, no. Of course not. I'd never dream of it. I eat what I can get from hunting or trading, sir."

Gavin looked around and saw no hunting equipment. "What is it you hunt?"

"I already told you. Sometimes they'll bring down a pigeon, too."

Did he consider squab a special treat? This wouldn't do. Gavin made a mental note to have the cooks set aside some fresh bread and cheese for Willem. "Thank you. Keep up the good work. I'm sure your effort helps a great deal. It's been a while since I thought of all the hard work that goes into running all the daily details of the castle. I'll get back with you soon."

Gavin would give compliments and build friendships wherever he found them. He needed allies and information sources, even among the lowest of the common laborers. He was responsible for everyone, after all.

Jase scowled as they walked, so Gavin said, "What's bothering you? Is it Willem's condition, or my response?"

"I know that look in your eye. He's been there a few years now. If Master Draken comes back with your father, it won't go well for you if you change how things are run."

"You're right. Thank you for your concern, but I owe the people my best, not what my father would do. If my father doesn't like the things I change, he'll tell me when he gets back. Loudly and several times."

Gavin thought a great deal about the idea of allies as he traversed the main hall on his way to the cattle pens. He had misread or failed to notice many of the signals at the council meeting, and he risked losing their trust and cooperation if he didn't learn from the experience. He wouldn't fail like that again with the council or with the people at large.

Even if his father came back tomorrow, Gavin was better equipped to set goals and meet them rather than slide by with minimal effort as he had done for years. He was determined to do something to make a difference, to make life better for the people. For *his* people. Lurking in the shadow of his brother had never gotten him anywhere, and now he was in charge and on full public display, for good or for ill.

———————

GAVIN CAME to a stop near a corner off the main hall as he pondered his new influence. Lack of sleep had made him easily distracted, but the voices of servants in the main hall brought him back to his current errand.

"Pshaw. He don't look strong to me, but he's got a heart of gold. I don't know how he whipped the council into shape when he's still in mourning. I hear he burned candles all night long."

A second voice replied, "No, I'm telling you. The new Baron Stoutheart ain't one to be messed with. I heard he killed a bear and two men with nothing but a short blade. He's stronger than he looks. Did you hear he's hiding a stab wound? There's a hole right through the armor he wore as he arrived, but he's walking about like nothing's wrong."

Gavin motioned to Jase to move back quietly and then spoke in a loud voice as they approached the hall for the second time. "Jase, when we get to the pens, I would like to talk to the Tanners in private for a few moments."

They rounded the corner as Jase replied, "Of course, sir."

Two of the household servants were on their knees with heads down, scrubbing furiously at the floor. They didn't glance up as Gavin and Jase passed them.

Once out of earshot, Gavin asked, "You didn't say anything to anyone last night about the candles or armor, did you?"

He'd never believed his father's paranoia about the flow of information being the key to power, but now he began to understand. These wild stories about him could impact his ability to make choices and enforce orders if people got the wrong idea. Stories always got more outrageous as they passed from mouth to ear.

Jase raised an eyebrow. "Of course not, sir. Well over a dozen people saw you arrive, and several servants helped to fetch the candles for you or saw someone else involved. I didn't say who they were for. Someone made assumptions."

Gavin's mistakes from his meeting motivated him to listen and watch for signals. He listened to Jase's tone and watched his body language for clues. Jase was obviously appalled at the idea he would spread any gossip learned through his post.

Gavin tapped a finger on his chin. "I think it's time you start saying more, but selectively. These rumors are sheer idiocy and have to stop. I'm not the baron yet. I didn't get run through with a blade, and the bear–"

"If I may be bold, sir, you can't catch up to a rumor once it's started. These sound harmless to me."

Gavin grimaced. "Maybe I'll start some true stories to make up for all the false ones, then. Gavin never got stabbed. Gavin can't fly or eat rocks for breakfast. How about this: I never wanted those two men to die."

As they passed the hall's exit, the guard there snapped to stiff attention and said, "Sir." Gavin hadn't seen such a formal response, even to his father, in years.

Jase broke his stern guard visage with a quick grin. "It seems the guard staff will be receptive to your direction. Captain Zachary has spoken to the men about you."

When they got to the cattle pens, the beasts had been let out to pasture for the day. Runner would earn his keep, chasing the cattle from pen to field and back every day. Gavin finally found the Tanners at the edge of the outside pasture.

Jase kept a watchful eye on the area, barely out of earshot as Tover waved and came over to talk. "Baron Stoutheart. To what do we owe the pleasure?"

"Really? Unless I miss my guess, you probably changed my soiled pants more than once when I was a toddler. When my mother died, you and your family filled in quite often. Must you still be so formal all the time?"

"No, good sir, but my parents taught me manners. I do my best to keep them."

Gavin lowered his gaze as red crept up his cheeks. Tover was right. "Could you at least not call me Baron Stoutheart? My father may still be out there and on his way back."

"As you wish, good sir." Tover nodded to emphasize his compliance.

"I burned a candle last night for Ned. Shall I send candles for you and Saleena? You seem pretty busy with the cattle."

"No, sir. We'll be fine. Saleena lit candles for Ned and your family as soon as we got back, but she's still awful quiet and wants to be alone a lot. I'll get by herding the cattle without her for the moment. I'm younger than your father was, after all. Um, I mean, younger than he is." There was an awkward pause.

Tover put a brave face on things, but Gavin knew the man suffered because of his son's death and would feel the loss forever. Despite the rocky relationship Gavin had with his father, grief struck without warning. He'd held it at bay since the day before. He wasn't ready for his family to be gone. Gavin and Tover both gazed across the grassy field where Saleena worked rather than acknowledge the tears on their cheeks. A few moments later, Gavin sniffed and blamed the cold weather for his running nose, and Tover picked at his sleeve and looked anywhere but at Gavin.

Finally, Tover spoke. "So, about the crystals. What do we do next, good sir?"

Despite the grief roiling under the surface, Gavin nodded and moved on. "I haven't talked to anyone about your crystals. Master Draken is on his way this afternoon to find out what happened, leaving me as acting baron. I need to hold things together here until he gets back, either with my father or with a confirmation of his death. I have an idea to increase our safety, but it could get me into a whole new kind of trouble."

Tover folded his arms across his chest. "Troubles are coming, either way."

"You have no idea. I'm going to do everything I can to make sure you and the rest of the people are safe. Father will be most displeased."

CHAPTER

SIX

Baron Gerald Stoutheart glared at the guard stationed at his north-most watchtower. "No word at all? That's unacceptable."

The watchtower was the most remote within the borders of the barony, and it had taken careful maneuvering to get this particular guard to be stationed there during the invasion.

The old stone border watchtowers had served long and well to aid travelers and give warning of invasion in times of war. This time, no warning was sent.

"The scouts are a day late, and the Graven King is behind me with his entire band of war animals. Hungry war animals, I might add. He won't be happy if those feed cattle are missing. They're vital to our success. Do you have any idea how much it slows an army if they have to forage? And my son! It should be no great challenge to fetch one rebellious child."

The baron stomped back and forth outside the tower with an occasional glance to the south for the wayward scouts, then to the north for signs of the approaching army.

"Did they tell you anything as they left? You gave the note to them, didn't you?"

"Yes, sir. I gave them the note. The big guy locked it in a travel case. I told him it was critical like you said."

Baron Stoutheart shook his head. "The instructions weren't difficult. Get rid of the cattle herders, capture my son, show him the note, and bring the cattle. How could this be so difficult? They had King Ithan's war animal with them, didn't they?"

The guard nodded. "A large bear, bigger than old one-ear. They said they would put a scare into him first to make him compliant, but they said it was an easy job."

Lack of any word about his younger son prompted memories of the ambush at the council of barons. It had taken delicate planning to achieve everything up to this point, and Gerald had given the power-hungry King Ithan all the information and help he needed to succeed against King Vargas and his gathered barons. The sleep drugs had been horribly expensive but had done their job. King Ithan had been in a position of power and had lost only a handful of men.

The choice to betray his own King Vargas was easy once Gerald recognized King Ithan didn't suffer from the sloth and foolishness of Gerald's peers within the kingdom. King Ithan's quest for power matched Gerald's hunger to control and organize what was a sloppy, careless arrangement. The barons were dilettantes, weak and soft after too many years of prosperity and excess. The baronies needed a firm hand to govern them, and they hadn't seen real leadership from his king. Gerald's betrayal would cut the fat from the kingdom and put it on a much better course. The country would have new barons and a new king over them soon.

The new king would not be King Ithan, of course. He was a means to an end. The invasion wiped out Gerald's competition, just as he had planned. Now he only needed to arrange the death of King Ithan after they reached the capital, and he would control both kingdoms and be hailed as a hero for saving the people. For now, he needed to wait. He had to get all the game pieces into the right positions on the board before King Ithan figured out Gerald's game.

The guard asked, "Where's Stephan? Wasn't he supposed to come with you, too?"

"Stephan isn't coming," Gerald said, a flash of annoyance spilling into his voice.

The guard hesitated a moment, then said, "Why not?"

Gerald looked up at the scattered clouds as events replayed in his mind. "Years of training are wasted because he jumped to my defense needlessly. I warned him. I ordered him, but he ignored me and charged the war animals of King Ithan to defend King Vargas and his useless pack of sycophant barons. King Ithan's animals cut him down before I could intervene. King Ithan is useful to me, but he's certainly not worth the life of my son."

The guard gasped. "Dead? But then Gavin is your heir."

Gerald nodded and clenched his jaw. "Indeed. And if that untrained and unwilling whelp is our best hope, then may I live a very long life." He hoped to have the long life his wife was denied when Gavin's birth killed her. When life was unfair, he took control to make his own luck.

He waved his arm to the south as he scanned the horizon. "Climb the tower and check again for the scouts and cattle. The army will arrive soon."

THE WOLF, with Draken watching through her eyes, pulled back tight against the tall tower's back wall on the side away from Baron Stoutheart. The guard couldn't see her from the stone parapets without leaning over to look straight down, but Draken still took a great risk to get this close. He'd heard the baron's talk of betraying the entire kingdom for the sake of power. Every other baron in the kingdom and many of their heirs gone!

It was true. The kingdom was leaderless. Now the enemy could march through the center of the crippled land to the capital with only minimal resistance. Draken knew enough of politics to see the kingdom could collapse, and would likely merge with the Graven Kingdom despite Baron Stoutheart's efforts. The country of Riland would no longer exist.

Draken agreed with Gerald Stoutheart on many things. King Vargas and many of the barons had become complacent and soft, enjoying their drink and the comfort of their padded chairs more with each passing year. It led to Draken's ejection from the capital years ago, for being too vocal about problems he saw. They didn't take the law seriously, and they abused power. Draken understood how their indolence had made betrayal easy.

Baron Stoutheart was one of the few who respected structure and order, so Draken had taken service with him. He understood why the baron betrayed the king and the people, but understanding did not mean he agreed with Baron Stoutheart's actions. Draken had sworn an oath to the kingdom, and Baron Stoutheart had once shown a matching dedication. His admiration for the baron had been unassailable before, but his respect flew like ash in the wind, replaced with a bitter anger.

Draken considered killing both the baron and the guard, but there was no way he could pull off such a feat with only himself and an injured wolf against two well-armed and armored men. Leaving the old baron in place wasn't all bad since reliance on the baron would make King Ithan more predictable. A predictable enemy was easier to beat.

The baron wasn't the type to roll over and serve someone unless there was no other option. He must have plans and contingencies. After betraying and killing the king and other barons, it didn't matter. Draken would never forgive the baron for such a dishonor. It was a shame to have served him.

He twitched his wolf's ears and listened as the guard tromped around on the rooftop. He waited until the man moved to the south rim, opposite from where the wolf crouched. Once he was sure of the man's position, the wolf sprinted for the tree line. Draken continued his observations from a distance. It was too bad he wouldn't be able to listen in on any more conversations here, but he felt content. He'd met the objectives of his scouting mission to find out what he needed to know about the baron. Anything else was a bonus.

The wolf crouched down next to his body as he lay in a trance, hidden within the shadows of the trees. His horse waited farther back into the woods. It was dangerous to leave both his body and the horse unguarded, but the risk had paid off.

The wolf's instincts played into Draken's seething anger. Her hackles rose as Draken thought of the betrayal, and a low growl escaped from her throat. Rather than let the instincts run wild, he controlled and directed the anger.

He would wait and learn more about the Graven King's army. The people of the barony couldn't fight an army, but anything he learned would prove useful as he planned his next move. He saw dust to the north. It wouldn't be a long wait.

BARON GERALD STOUTHEART squinted along the trail to the northeast, noting the increasing dust, and called to his guard. "Any sign from the south?"

The guard poked his head over the parapet. "Nothing, sir."

"Well, that's it then." Gerald strode out a few steps from the tower and waited for his new king to arrive. The vanguard of the army appeared in the distance. His promise of meat for the army's war animals had failed. At least the watchtower supplies would feed the men of the army for a time. His saving grace was his knowledge of the land and its inhabitants. He would have to strike a proper balance between humility and shrewd resource to maintain his position. His modified plan was firm in his mind by the time King Ithan Talandor, ruler of the Graven Kingdom, approached and planted his feet apart to glare at the baron.

Gerald knelt with one knee pressed against the dry fall grasses, head bowed. "Welcome to my barony, Your Majesty."

"Yes. Your supposedly well-provisioned guard outpost. I believe you promised cattle to speed our trip? I accepted your offer to join us in this venture because of what you promised. You keep us in provisions, and we leave the people and the crops in place. What would Stoutheart Barony be worth stripped to the bone for our war effort? I assume you want your barony to avoid destruction."

"Your Majesty, if you would join us on the lookout? My man is watching for the provisions, but there has been a delay."

Gerald led him into the tower with the king guarded fore and aft by his men as they climbed the three flights of stairs to the outlook on the roof.

The baron met all the protocols of courtesy and made introductions. "This is His Majesty the King. Your Majesty, this is my loyal servant Martan Mallory, who has secured this site and maintained our supplies." Gerald understood one could be formal and proper and still throw someone to the wolves.

"I see." King Ithan stepped back, snapped his fingers and gestured to his guards who grabbed the tower guard and heaved him, screaming, over the crenellations.

The king turned back to Baron Stoutheart. "Strip him down and haul him out into the field for my war animals. I've saved you one cow from your missing herd. This is your land, and I respect that, but I expect you to point out where we may hunt successfully. I'm afraid your settlements will have to contribute the difference. We can't afford to wait or slow down, or the news of our coming will spread too far ahead of us."

Gerald nodded, relieved to be alive.

As he stripped Martan's broken body, he decided he must adjust his plan to take the throne of Riland. Originally, his son Stephan would have wed King Ithan's only child, a daughter, after Ithan's death. That plan would have bound the families together to give him the leverage to conquer his temporary ally on two fronts. Plans shifted and adjusted as needed.

If the king continued to kill the baron's loyal people, he would have to take precautions. The king must die before he took the capital and gained the throne, rather than after. The people were suckers for a savior, and the baron would set himself up to fill the role and take the throne for himself earlier than planned.

Gerald pursed his lips and grunted in disappointment at one more unanticipated corpse on the path to the throne. He dragged Martan's body to the waiting war animals.

CHAPTER

SEVEN

The reports in front of Gavin were both tedious and critical to the daily functions of the barony. He reviewed the new report on guards assigned to patrol both inside and outside the castle. There wasn't enough manpower to repel even a large group of bandits for any length of time. The fletchers had been assigned to build a stockpile of arrows, but without the baron's war animals, his defenders would lose against any large-scale organized attack. It was a foregone conclusion an attack of any size would destroy the village outside the walls.

Gavin regretted the loss of the war animals at the Baron's Conference, and felt defenseless. At least the wolf was available for Master Draken, but only because she had wandered into a patch of dragon-head vines, and her paws weren't healed by the time the baron left. The thorns of the vine were barbed and mildly poisonous, leaving behind an infection that lingered for weeks if untreated.

Gavin heard a rap at the door. "Come." He'd learned Jase and the other guards wouldn't open the door to enter until invited, unlike Draken.

Jase held the door open as Tover entered. "You sent for me, good sir?"

"Yes. I've figured out my plans and I have a question for you. First, our conversation doesn't go beyond the two of us. I'm sure you'll see why. We only have one man within a day's ride of the castle who has ever *officially* cut crystal. He has only apprentice experience, but he's the only one I know. We've always had our best work brought in from the capital. Did Ned cut all the crystals, or did you help?"

"No, good sir. Ned did the crystal work, rest his soul. I tried a few times, but they never turned out. Mostly I broke them when I tried to split the master and servant halves apart."

"Well, then. My job for you is to take ten of the best uncut rocks from your stash to Roben Sharp with one of Ned's crystals with the simplified pooka marks. See if he can copy it. Tell him it's from the baron's supplies. You know the tinker, don't you?"

"I do, sir. But why are you taking this risk? There will be trouble if your father comes back, and not just for you."

Gavin knew very well the trouble he was stirring up, but he didn't want to burden Tover with thoughts of the weakness of the barony, or their poor ability to gather information. He decided the personal wrath of his father was worth it if it would protect them from invaders.

"If you take these from baronial supplies, you can't be blamed for following my orders. This will all fall on me. If we need to defend the people, I'm going to use every resource I have. A few more cut crystal pairs might tilt things in our favor even if they're not perfect. My next step will make my troubles so far seem like spitting in a thunderstorm. I never was good at listening to my father."

It was a huge risk for him personally, but Gavin had to fortify the castle and village against attack to protect the people. His people. He would deal with the consequences later.

Gavin walked Tover to the door and paused with his hand on the handle. "One other thing. There's a young man named Willem who keeps the pests down at the granary with his Cats of the Apocalypse. I've asked the cook to set aside something for him. Can you and Saleena make sure he gets taken care of? He needs a solid meal."

"We'll see to him, sir. And thank you." Tover bowed, both hands to his heart in a gesture of respect that had gone out of style at least a generation back.

As Tover left, Gavin turned to the guard. "Please send for Captain Zachary. I'll need him to open the castle vault for me."

"Yes, sir. I'll have him here shortly."

Jase was good to his word, and a few minutes later Gavin stood at the vault door with the captain, who held a large iron key ring in hand. If there were any unused crystals in the castle, this was the place to look. He also needed to pay Master Sharp for his services to cut the crystal, and the treasury books indicated there were plenty of coins if the tinker didn't want to barter food or materials for his services.

"Sir, I can open it, but it's a bit premature. We have all the commodities we need for trade. The Baron was always protective of this vault, and never let me inside with him. Most of the time he came alone, despite my recommendations to keep a guard with him."

Gavin considered abandoning his plan as he examined the vault door. After a few moments, he decided the defense of the castle was an all-or-nothing event. He couldn't approach it with half a heart. "Open it anyway. I hope you're good at keeping secrets because you'll be my witness in the vault."

"If your father comes back, I'll burn a candle for you."

"He doesn't expect a lot from me, and that's always given me extra flexibility. But keep a candle ready just in case."

Captain Zachary unlocked the door and swung it open on well-oiled hinges. They stepped inside, and Gavin lit the wall lanterns from the small candlestick he had brought along. He held up the candlestick and peered around the room, taking a quick survey of the crates, boxes, and cabinets.

"If I were my father, where would I store crystals?" He dismissed the larger containers and gave a critical eye to a set of shallow cabinets mounted to the wall at eye level. "Maybe here?"

The captain gave a noncommittal shrug. "That seems as likely as any."

The first two were empty, but the third contained a series of hooks with three crystal pairs hanging on cords. Gavin hadn't expected to find much, but the three pairs were minor training crystals to be used with smaller, less dangerous animals. Back in the corner of the case, a single beautiful mid-sized crystal sat by itself where it must have fallen. His father had taken the rest with him, along with the animals. Gavin took the single crystal and put it around his neck. If an animal wore the other half, he would attune to it soon. He might have a chance to figure out what the other half belonged to if it was near the castle. He pocketed the three matched pairs.

The small number of crystals gave him little to contribute to defending the castle immediately. They needed better defenses, and a few war animals would have made a huge difference in their ability to repel attackers. Then again, they had no trained animals, either, aside from the cattle.

He was tempted to requisition the entire herd under the control of Saleena but held that back in case of an emergency. He wasn't keen on his father's rules and methods, but he risked rebellion if he introduced too much change at once. The people of the barony had to see a good reason for each of his changes.

"While we're here, we might as well take a quick inventory. The accounting books in my father's study show we should have over five thousand gold coins and ten thousand in silver." The coins of the kingdom held an image of a crystal pair front and back, and were used primarily to trade with the capital, and sometimes with other baronies when they couldn't barter.

The crates were not locked. Gavin lifted a lid to peer inside, finding old cloth bundled up in rolls. The scent of cedar wafted out. He pulled one bundle out and unrolled the cloth. It was an intricately embroidered gown.

Captain Zachary took a sharp breath. "I had no idea the baron kept those after your mother passed on."

His mother's? The sense of loss from the recent deaths threatened to come to the surface. Gavin reverently rolled the dress back up. "You saw my mother wear this?" He ran his fingers along the collar's delicate thread flowers.

"Yes. It was one of her favorites. She wore it to all the winter feasts. Your father wanted to have a new one made for her, but she refused. The people expected to see her wear it every winter, and she was happy to oblige them."

"Thank you. My father never spoke ..." Gavin backtracked. "... never speaks of her. He never told me what she was like, what she spent her time on, or the things she enjoyed. I think he blames me for her death." He laid the bundle back inside and set the lid in place. He made sure it was tight enough to continue to protect the old cloth as it had for over eighteen years. This connected him to the mother he never knew. She was more real in his mind now, someone he could hold onto and care about rather than a vague concept. He wanted to go through the entire crate and ask Captain Zachary about everything, but there was no time.

Gavin sighed and wove his way past the crates to a set of small chests lining a table against the far wall. The captain followed along behind him with crisp steps, his hands clasped behind his back. He was clearly uncomfortable in the forbidden vault but was attentive to his assigned duty. He was a good man.

The first chest was empty, as was the second. Gavin's concern grew as he opened empty chests, one after the other. One held a handful of mixed gold and silver coins. Finally, he reached for the last one and opened it. With a sigh of relief, he saw it was full of gold coins. He tugged the chest to the front of the table, surprised at the weight, and pulled out a coin. He saw a portrait on it instead of an image of a crystal. He pulled another out, and it was the same. He rifled through and found every coin was the same, with an image of a bearded man.

"Do you know where this would have come from, Captain?"

The captain stepped forward to take the proffered coin and held it up to the light. "This is a Northern coin. It's from the Graven Kingdom." He flipped it over in his hand a few times, studying it.

"Why would my father have almost none of the coin the books claim, yet have this? I would understand a few coins mixed in from other places because of trade, but this chest is all Graven as if he's traded with them exclusively."

"Perhaps he arranged a trade agreement, or took the rest of the coins to the conference for a planned purchase." Captain Zachary put a positive spin on the situation, but Gavin knew those were not plausible answers. His father had spent a fortune on something which wasn't recorded in the books.

Gavin put aside the least savory of the ideas which ran through his head. "Right. We'll go with the trade idea, and assume he took all our coin to the Baron's Conference. As I said, you're my witness should the need arise. This changes things."

CHAPTER

EIGHT

Saleena listened, along with the rest of the locals, as Gavin's proclamation was read in the courtyard. Gavin would either be the subject of heroic story and song among the people, or they would string him up by his thumbs on the outer wall. It depended on whether his father ever came back.

The herald's words rang out in a clear tone that carried across the courtyard. "And whereas Stoutheart Barony must provide for the defense of its subjects in these challenging times, all past use of crystals by proscribed persons is pardoned. Each subject with crystal experience, whether in wartime or peace, is asked to come forth and make themselves available for our defense. Crystals shall be allocated where they will be of the most use to protect the people."

Saleena held a pouch with three crystal pairs, given to her by Gavin. He had told her they were for Willem, and for whoever else she thought might be trained to use them, based on their affinity with animals and their experience. He expected her to train Willem and any others who came forward since his father's crystal trainer had gone to the doomed conference.

One of Willem's cats was a good choice, he had said. She agreed to the task of training Willem, even though she'd much rather spend her time with Gavin than in the granary with Willem who was two years her junior. She missed the winters of the past with Gavin, spending hours on mischief and exploring the castle's many hallways, talking about everything and nothing as they wandered. She understood the threat to the barony but didn't like being away from Gavin. She wanted to lean on him when the loss of Ned hit her unexpectedly.

She stamped her way to the granary with a loaf of fresh bread and a hunk of cheese from the kitchen under her arm, taking her bad mood out on the ground with each step.

She saw no good outcome for Gavin. If the old baron came back, Gavin would surely be exiled, or even killed as a rebel. If the baron never returned, Gavin was the new baron, and would never consider a herd-girl as anything more than a friend, or possibly a dalliance, which was worse. There had been rumors about his brother Stephan and the young women he spent time with who would never become the Baroness. She wasn't going to be like those women, used then tossed aside. Gavin would never do such a thing anyway. He had always shown the best of intentions, which sometimes annoyed her when she wanted to garner his attention with a new skirt or hair tie.

Saleena found Willem in his tiny living area with his hands to the small fireplace. As she entered, he turned with an alarmed look. "What is it? I didn't do anything."

"Easy, Willem. Gavin, the baron, whatever he is now, asked me to bring you some things." She tossed the loaf of bread to him.

He caught it, pulled a knife from his boot, and cut it neatly in half with the wickedly sharp knife, then tossed half the loaf back to her. "Thank you. Sorry, but I wasn't expecting anyone. I get a little jumpy."

She sat her half of the loaf on his rumpled bed along with the wrapped block of cheese and pulled out the small pouch of crystals. Each was a much higher quality and more detailed than the ones she used with the cattle and could be divided up among three different people. Then again, she could put them to immediate use if she gave them all to Willem for the Cats of the Apocalypse, as Gavin had called them. She could retrieve two of them later for others to use. She'd been asked to train Willem, and she would do it for Gavin, to show him how her three summers of constant crystal practice were of value.

"Did you hear the proclamation in the square? Gavin said anyone who has used crystals without permission wouldn't be punished. He intends to defend us and wants everyone's help."

"Yeah, I heard some of it. I was over at the window listening. It's got nothing to do with me, though. I've wondered what it was like to use a crystal, but I've never even touched one before."

"Hold out your hand." She placed the crystals in his hand where they shimmered and sparkled in the light of the flames on the tiny hearth. "There. Now you've touched some crystals. These are more expensive than you can imagine, but they're also designed for smaller animals. They're more for practice than for full-size war animals in actual combat. Put the ones with the longer loops around your neck and wear them close to your skin. The short cords are for the cats. I don't know why, but Gavin thinks you should be trained to use crystals even though nobody's ever used cats as war animals. All you do is keep the rats down, right?"

He called the cats and gently put the crystals around their necks, just snug enough to not come off by accident. The black cat was closest, so he attached his crystal collar first, followed by the blue-eyed tabby, and then the calico. "That's my job. I keep the grain free of pests. Are you sure he trusts me with these?" He rubbed the calico's ears.

"He can always change his mind if it doesn't work well, but yes. He trusts you. He may not realize it, but he's quite good with people aside from his father and a couple of others."

Willem appeared skeptical. "Maybe you're right, but it still doesn't seem likely. You've used crystals before? Why would the old baron allow that?"

She shrugged. "The baron didn't know about it. But the pardon has gone out, and I don't need to keep it a secret now. I used a whole set of home-made crystals to control the baron's cattle herd."

"I feel a little warm spot on my chest. So, what do I do now?"

"Now, we wait. I'll be back this evening. While you're waiting, lie back and rest. For me, it's like feeling around inside your own head for a set of small windows to look through. I'll tell you what to do with them when I come back. By the way, do you know what Gavin calls your cats?"

"He didn't call them anything when he was here. I told him they were Doom Bringer, Death Claw, and Skull Crusher." He pointed at each in turn. "Skull Crusher is a girl. I know it's silly, but I wanted them to sound scary to the rats." The animals rubbed back and forth against his legs and purred.

Saleena giggled. "No wonder he calls them the Cats of the Apocalypse. He did the same thing you did, gave them a name to inspire fear. You have to admit, it's shorter than calling each by name."

She sniffed the air. The aroma of roasting meat overrode the smell of vinegar from the nearby barrels. "Are you cooking something?"

"Uh, it's nothing. I'll see you tonight then. Thank you for your help." Willem made to usher her toward the door.

She dodged around him to get a peek at the small hearth. There, over the fire, was a miniature spit where a small animal roasted. She put her hand to her mouth as she recognized the size and shape of a rat.

"Oh, I'm sorry, Willem. I have to go." She rushed to the door as her gorge rose, hoping to gain fresh air before her lunch decorated his floor. "I'll be back later."

THAT EVENING, Saleena sniffed the air as she approached Willem's little alcove, but detected no smell of cooking meat. She sighed in relief, making enough noise he was sure to notice before she knocked and entered. She had no idea of the training process used by the baron's old crystal trainer or the military crystal users, other than a few war stories she'd heard from her father. She'd learned it all by trial, error, and feel.

Willem lay back on his bed, his eyes closed with his fingers laced together behind his head.

"Hey, Willem."

He didn't respond. He must have entered the control trance on his own. She eased his arms down to his side to keep them from going numb from the loss of circulation. She knew it could happen because she'd done it.

She gingerly stepped back and turned to search for the cats. They were right behind her. They were quiet little creatures. No wonder they made good hunters.

"You figured it out pretty quickly. Wake up, and we can talk about it. I still don't know why Gavin would invest in controlling cats, but you can ask him yourself. I'm here to give you some pointers since I've done this with a herd of cattle."

The cats all meowed at her.

"You can't talk to me through them with their voices. You have to wake up first."

They trotted past her to the inert form of Willem and patted at his face and hands with their paws.

"Oh! I never told you what to feel for to end your trance. I didn't expect you to be this far along. It's like leaning back, pulling your head in through the window."

The cats turned to stare at her.

"Let me think." How was it she had learned to connect to her herd and then disconnect from it? She'd started with one crystal and worked her way up from there. Maybe it was different with three at once to start. The crystals were better, and the link was stronger, too. Her first time with more than one crystal hadn't gone well, either.

She prodded him. "It's not working. What else have you tried?"

The black cat licked Willem's finger which showed a small bite mark.

"See if you can pull yourself back. You have to do it with your thoughts instead of your muscles. You've got no control at all over your muscles now."

The cats' ears twitched a couple of times, but they meowed again in unison before settling down on the cot next to Willem's unconscious form.

Saleena put a hand on his shoulder. "I'm sorry. I should have warned you, but I forgot how hard it was to pull back from more than one link the first few times. I expected you to take longer to get used to the crystals. It took me a lot longer, but my brother Ned cut our crystals."

Mentioning her brother sent a pang of loss through her. She looked away to prevent the cats from seeing the tear she wiped away.

She sniffed and turned back, trying to dismiss her weakness. Besides, she was curious at the differences between cattle and cats. "We have to learn how to do this, before Gavin gains some common sense and realizes he's entrusted a fortune in crystals into the hands of a couple of peasants. What's different here? The cattle are a herd. They do things together naturally. Are the cats the same?"

Doom Bringer shook his head.

"But I've heard how cats hunt together. But not like a herd? Can you get them to each do different things at the same time? I always need to make sure whatever the cattle do can be done together."

The cats each took up a different task. Doom Bringer climbed the boxes, Death Claw paced back and forth, and Skull Crusher came over and sat at her feet.

"That's pretty good! I've never been able to take complete control of more than one or two cows. The way it usually works is you control one animal's actions using one crystal. It's too hard to split my concentration between many bodies. I ride the surface of their minds as a whole. Somehow, they each pick out their part of what I want the herd to do. Can you give hints or ideas to the cats then, a bit like I do?"

Skull Crusher nodded and meowed.

She sat for a moment in thought, and then said, "Well, we'd better give this a try. You might not be able to come back on your own."

Her first time using two crystals at once had scared her. Da and Ned both said one at a time was all they should do, but she'd tricked them into staying in the field while she was locked in the cabin for safety. She used the cattle to show them what she'd done, then watched through the cattle's eyes as her father simultaneously cursed, and prayed, and removed one of the crystals from the cattle in a desperate attempt to break her free. She awoke with Da and Ned pounding on the cabin door, and her head feeling like a crushed melon.

"This is going to hurt like a brick to the head, but I think I can break the connection by taking the crystals off the cats one at a time. I'll do it as slowly as I can. I'm not sure if going slow will make it better or worse."

She glanced back and forth between Willem and the cats and chose a crystal to remove.

CHAPTER

NINE

G avin sorted through piles of paper on his table as Draken pounded on the door and came in. It was funny how Gavin thought of the room as his now. He looked up at the open door, fully expecting his father to stride in and stamp mud from his boots as he always had, but the hall remained empty save for Draken and the evening guard. Gavin rested his forehead in his hands and stared at the wood grain of the table.

"You're alone and you're early. I'm not an idiot, but I want to hear what you found anyway."

Draken stood a little straighter at attention than he had before the trip. "The Graven Kingdom's army is on its way, led by its king. We're right in their path. I give us a few days at most before they get here. They're living off the land, pillaging and hunting as they advance."

"Master Draken, I understand the information on an invading army is critical, but why do you make me ask the hard question? What about the baron?"

Draken stood even more stiffly, which Gavin wouldn't have thought possible, and then he said, "Your father is ... gone. Though it pains me to say it, you must be the baron in fact now, and not standing in his stead. The barony is yours, and the people are your responsibility. It will be my job to continue your training and to advise you. I know you don't like my advice or my methods. Should you feel this is a problem, you may release me as your trainer and adviser, and find someone more suitable."

Gavin considered Draken's change in demeanor and bit back the first several replies that came to mind. The man was an odd combination of insulting and humble. He was manipulative, yet compliant. Above all, his dedication to the barony was beyond question. Gavin was still getting used to this side of Draken where he reluctantly played the part of a servant and adviser.

Finally, Gavin spoke. "You don't get off that easy. We don't see eye to eye, but I trust you, and I need you. The people also need you. I must have someone they respect at my side. Trust is critical."

Draken seemed about to say something else, but he slumped slightly and nodded. He glanced at the stacked papers spread across the surface of the old oak table. "You've made yourself familiar with the capabilities of the guard, and of our possible defenses?"

Gavin gave a wry smile. "We're good for defending against a small force, but these walls were never meant to repel an army. We don't have a chance against the army you saw, even if we put everyone on the walls to repel attackers, do we?"

Draken stepped up to the table and pulled the map out from under the other papers. "No, we don't. The army is north of us, marching south." He jabbed at the map as if he could squish the army with his finger. "We have to leave. We can go south through Greenvale, through Richland Barony, and then on to the capital. If we take more than a day to pack, we're at risk. If we have breakdowns on the road, we're at risk. If they get close enough to spot us with forward scouts, we're at risk."

"But if we leave the castle, it will drop into the hands of the enemy." Gavin scowled.

Draken leaned forward and placed his hands on the table. "When I say we are at risk, I mean we are at risk of all being killed."

It was a stark trade-off with no winning position, other than short-term survival. With no experience running Stoutheart Barony, Gavin was forced to abandon it. "How do we evacuate? What's the procedure?"

Draken shrugged. "I don't know. It hasn't been done in over a century. In case you couldn't tell, I'm not *that* old. I've only served your father for ten years."

"At least the treasury will be easy to pack. Did you know it was nearly empty? My father had most of the crystals with him, and the only gold to speak of was a chest of Graven coins." Gavin watched for Draken's response to determine whether he knew anything about the situation with the empty treasury and the foreign coins. Draken's training on watching for reactions had made an impression on Gavin.

Draken didn't disappoint. His eyes narrowed, and his lips drew into a line. "Empty? This time of year, we should have a significant surplus." He smacked his fist down on the map. "The crystals are another issue. I know he took most of them with him. What crystals do we have?"

"There's the pair you used for your scouting mission with the wolf. I found three small training sets unused in the vault, and one master crystal I'm now wearing. I can tell the other half is worn by something, but it's a long way from here, somewhere to the south. I, ah, also pardoned anyone who may have made illicit crystal pairs, and set the tinker to work on a stash of cheap crystal. There are crystals among the people we can draw upon."

Draken's voice edged up in volume, and he placed both fists on the table, knuckles down. "You don't have the right to pardon people when they've broken the king's law or the Accords! You may have the shortest baronial tenure in history." He stopped, glanced up at the ceiling, and then continued in a calmer tone. "Then again, the king and the barons are dead. You may not end up before a royal court at all. How many crystals are we talking about among the people?"

Gavin cringed at what Draken might assume from the answer but told him anyway. "Thirty or more. All of them are rough cut, but they're good enough for a full control trance."

"You mean to tell me we've got thirty or more crystal-trained people in the castle and village? I wouldn't think we have more than five ex-military men with formal crystal training."

"No, I've learned you can use them more than one at a time. There's no reason for that rule in the Accords to forbid it." Gavin thought back to having seen Saleena control the entire cattle herd as one unit, and of having given the three small crystals to her with instructions to train Willem and others. He'd never heard of using cats with crystals. He was eager to see what the Cats of the Apocalypse were capable of.

"The reason is that it's one of the easiest ways I know to kill a man. You should know how dangerous it is to use more than one crystal at a time. It's always been possible, but it's a bad idea. Oh, yes. You skipped too much of your training to know these things." His biting tone was like a dagger in the back. "If you double up on crystals, you can get locked in, and nothing will break you back out of your trance. I once saw a man die when we took two crystals off his neck because he couldn't back out. That's why the Crystal Kings wrote the Accords to forbid using multiples. Something about leaving part of your mind out wandering away from home."

Gavin thought again about the three crystals and his instructions. Saleena had used her cheap-cut crystals all at once for three years without a problem, but he had given her three high-quality crystals. They might be different. He stood up and headed for the door. "The three crystal sets. I sent them with Saleena and told her to train Willem. She might have given him all three for his cats."

As they ran through the halls, Draken berated Gavin. "You drop almost everything from the vault onto a peasant boy, and you assume everything will work out well? Even if you haven't killed him, do you expect him to magically turn his pets into a special assault team of war animals? They're cats! I leave for less than two days, and you singlehandedly risk the financial stability and safety of the barony, maybe kill one of your subjects, violate several of the king's standing laws, and one of the Accords. And all *before* you heard my report about your father!"

They burst into Willem's living quarters, and everything turned into a blur of action. The Cats of the Apocalypse yowled and flashed into action landing against Draken's chest from the front and his knees from the back. Draken fell to the ground with a yelp at their coordinated pounce. The cats bounded from Draken's prone figure into position between Draken and Gavin. Their hackles were up, and the cats growled and hissed as they wove back and forth among themselves with tails fluffed out and backs arched.

Saleena's voice overrode the noise. "Back out now, Willem. Everyone hold where you are," she said, desperation in her voice.

A few moments later, the cats scattered and Willem let out a cough. He sat up and saw his new visitors, then shot to his wobbly feet. He nearly knocked the cot over as he staggered forward, shaky from exiting his trance. "Sir! I'm sorry. I didn't mean to take you to the floor, but you startled me. Are you hurt?" Without waiting for an answer, he turned to Saleena. "My head still hurts when I come out of the trance, but it was better this time."

Gavin helped Draken up to sit on the end of the cot, all the while trying to hold back laughter without much success. "Willem seems to be a fast learner."

From the cot, Draken shook his head in dismay. "Maybe I should consign myself now to hang from the gallows at the capital when they learn we've thrown the Accords to the winds. It would be the simple way out."

CHAPTER

TEN

Gavin leaned against a wall tapestry while waiting for his advisers to arrive in the main council chamber. It took great effort to stay in one place and not pace away his nervous energy. Draken had gathered the full barony council again. Two members were new since they had met last, added to replace those who were dead. They had little idea of how such meetings were run, much like Gavin.

As the last man entered, Draken thumped on the table. "Everyone, take a seat, please. Baron Gavin Stoutheart will address us." Some of the men glanced back and forth at each other, but none spoke any objection. They shuffled around into their assigned seats.

Draken nodded at Gavin. "Sir, the floor is yours."

Gavin moved to the head of the table, pulled out his notes and placed them before him. He reminded himself he was in command, and nobody could see his hands shake. Even if he wasn't confident, he had to sound and look as if he was. "We have reliable reports that the Graven Kingdom ambushed the king's Baronial Council. Their king is leading this assault personally, and we know of no survivors." He stopped to look around the room for their reactions and saw the downcast nods of acceptance. None of them showed the least surprise. This was merely a formal confirmation of the rumors that had spread over the past few days. Draken's suggested wording of the announcement softened the blow by implying rather than declaring his father's outright demise. Draken's news left no margin to hope for his father to return, and they had work to do.

"I'm sure you feel, much as I do, that my father would have known what to do and how to do it. I can't do things as he would. I don't know how. I don't know what my father would have done, and I would probably disagree with him." Some awkward chuckles arose around the table. Most of these men had years of service with his father and were well aware of Gavin's reputation.

"I must rely on you for information and ideas to keep the people safe. This is your chance to make a bigger difference than you have in years." He couldn't tell if their looks were of appreciation at their greater influence, or if they were considering how to peddle the situation into a grab for more power. He hoped most would take him at his word and do what they could to help.

Strategically, Gavin knew he must keep a careful balance in what he offered them. Give too much and the strongest would work to use Gavin as their personal puppet. Give too little and they might rebel or silently sabotage his efforts. For all he knew, he would get both extremes anyway, and all he could do was minimize the damage as he maximized the progress.

"There is only one item on our agenda, and you will understand why nothing else makes a difference at this point. Captain Zachary, please describe what size of a military force we can repel here at the castle." It was a gamble to rely on the other council members to back up the case he was about to make, but including them might rally them all to a common cause.

The Captain of the Guard stepped forward and cleared his throat. "We've already increased our patrols both outside and inside the castle walls. We can withstand an attack of fifty men, possibly a hundred if we have additional time to prepare and train. We could meet and defeat such a force in open battle if we had to."

Draken interrupted. "How many large war animals can you hold against? Bears, wolves, bison, mountain lions?"

The captain rubbed his fingers through his short beard in thought. "We've never faced war animals at this castle in my lifetime, but I've seen it done in other locations back in the last war. Maybe twenty or thirty depending on their size and training. If Ithan Talandor is at the head of his army, they'll be well-trained. Twenty animals from his force are enough to challenge us. With that many, they could force a weak spot and breach the gates."

Draken said, "They have over fifty trained war animals and over five hundred men on foot. I saw their entire force. If we stay, they will run through us with minimal losses."

Gavin looked around to see who showed panic, and who appeared to be thinking the situation through before he said, "We only have one real strategy; we must evacuate to the south through Richland Barony and on to the capital. Anything we leave behind will be theirs. I need your ideas. Each of you has a specialty you understand, so I rely on you to each do your part. I need to know what resources you have, what you need, and how much we can take with us after one day of preparation. We also need a plan to warn outlying villages so they can join us or flee on their own. The most remote may survive unscathed if the enemy doesn't know about them."

The ideas came rapidly from some, slowly from others, while still others sat and watched the exchange. Gavin's leadership skills came into question at one point, with Captain Zachary speaking up in his defense. "He's shown the ability to organize and run the barony in the short time he's served. He's worked to increase our defenses here and planned for better defense as we travel. I, for one, don't expect him to know the details of wall patrols and rotating schedules because that's my job. You should each grant him the same courtesy."

The quiet men warmed up, and soon they argued details back and forth until Draken stepped in. "Gentlemen. I hope you each know what you need now, and have a good idea of where to get it. Anything you can't agree upon among yourselves, send to the baron's desk but make it quick. We pack tomorrow and leave the morning after. No exceptions. The outliers will have to catch up as they can. We need as much space as possible between us and that army."

Gavin decided to risk one last offer to unify them further. He was sticking his neck out, but he hoped it would pay off with better coopera- tion. "You have heard I will not penalize anyone who has owned or used crystals in violation of the law. We need to know what sort of animal forces we have to defend ourselves with, even if it's simple pets, war trained or not. I have a limited number of crystals to be assigned out to those who can use them."

Master Quincy, the merchant guild master, said under his breath, "As if we have anything able to make a difference after the war animals the old baron lost."

Gavin's face flushed as he tried to keep his anger in check and failed. "Do you have expertise using crystals you want to share with us, Quincy?"

"I . . . No, sir. Only with their purchase."

Gavin was sure Quincy implied something but didn't know exactly what he'd missed.

After discussing a few more general questions, Gavin dismissed the council.

Anger crept into Gavin's tone. "Remain here for a moment, if you please, Master Quincy. I have a few more questions for you."

Quincy's brows furrowed and his jaw clenched. Gavin hadn't meant to make it sound like a reprimand, but it was clear that Quincy took it that way.

He had possibly made the man's disagreeable attitude permanent, but Gavin needed to keep dissent in check at all costs.

GAVIN CRINGED at each beginner's mistake he made as he worked with his council and interacted with the people. The day of meetings and planning stretched into a night filled with hard truths. Farmers would lose crops still in their fields. Merchants had carts stored too far away to fetch for the evacuation.

Draken forced him to get some rest, so he collapsed on his bed fully dressed, having left instructions for Jase to wake him at first light.

Gavin lurched from his bed when his outer door banged open and Draken strode in. "What is it? Are we under attack?" He rubbed his red eyes as he stood.

"Hardly." Draken grinned. "You will want to see this for yourself, sir. It's a good omen."

For Draken to see something as a good omen meant it must be spectacular. Gavin grabbed his cloak.

The courtyard held a dozen more wagons than it had the night before. "Where did these come from?"

"The neighboring villages, sir. The first arrived just after you retired. Our riders reached them, and the people responded. These men, your men, hitched their wagons and rode through the night to reach us and lend a hand."

"They came." A lump rose in Gavin's throat, and he smiled. The evacuation might work, despite their challenges.

Draken clapped him on the back. "Indeed. The people know that even with your father gone, a Stoutheart leads the barony."

As the morning wore on, more wagons arrived from miles around to help haul supplies. The barony's wagons were loaded down with food from the granaries and other long-term storage. People milled about everywhere and got into each other's path as he made his way past the cattle pens.

In contrast to the chaos, Tover had a wagon of supplies neatly packed, and the cattle all gathered for a quick exit while Saleena tended again to the animal injured by the bear. The injury would leave a scar, but it was healing well. Gavin hoped the animal wouldn't slow the Tanners. He would be the one to order them to slaughter the animal if it became necessary. They were now his personal herd.

Gavin stepped up to the fence. "Tover, you're set to go already?"

Tover bowed and touched his heart. "Of course, good sir. It's not hard to organize a trip for the cattle herd. I've done it dozens of times. Some folks aren't good at it, though. Not enough practice. I had to convince three different families to leave their furniture."

His words got Gavin thinking. "Say, Tover. Saleena can manage the cattle without you, can't she? You're packed and ready to go, after all."

"She's right good at it, good sir. But you knew that."

Gavin smiled. "Get the crystal you've used for Runner and wear it where everyone can see it. I'm giving you a promotion to Travel Master. These people need someone to organize things, or they'll take a week and get trampled by an army before they get out of the gate. I'll announce it, so they know to listen when you talk."

"Well, good sir, there's a difference between convincing cattle to move and convincing people. The cattle are trained. People think they're masters of their own fate and don't like directions."

"I have faith in you, Tover. I've seen how you care about the cattle. The people will see you care about them, too. But I'd recommend against having Runner chase and nip at people's heels."

Tover laughed and replied, "I'll do it for you, good sir, and I'll keep Runner as my last resort."

FIVE PEOPLE HAD COME FORWARD with the skill to use a crystal, but nobody would admit having a crystal of their own. Perhaps it was a fluke that the Tanners had figured out how to make them. Gavin shook his head. He would work with what he had. As requested, Tover had delivered one of their cattle crystals to the tinker along with several raw stones, so Gavin stopped to visit the tinker as part of his rounds.

"Is the raw crystal any good?" Gavin asked.

"Normally, I'd say no. It won't handle all the fine detailed engraving work, but this crystal pair from Tover doesn't have all that. The intricate patterns are gone, and the core shape doesn't match what I've done in the past. I've replicated the cut already. The pooka marks will be a few hours work instead of weeks. I'd never thought to try such a shortcut. The cost to discover this through trial and error with proper crystal boggles the mind. Nobody would waste the resources."

To Gavin, it made sense. Crude wax molds could only hold so much detail, and that was how Tover obtained the pattern Ned used to mark the crystals. It was dumb luck that it had worked. "Go ahead and try to match the simple marks on your first stone. If you can make them a lot faster, it will be a huge win for us. We can use them as fast as you can make them."

In only a few hours, the tinker sent word he had his first crystal pair ready to test. Gavin picked it up from the tinker before he began another round of tours of the castle compound.

A gate guard, Otis, had a half-wolf named Ruffian he had controlled before with a crystal for training. It was an easy choice to put the guard on the list, and Gavin handed the new crystal pair to the man.

Otis dropped the master crystal around his neck and put the slave crystal onto Ruffian. "They look pretty rough."

Gavin shrugged. "I know the crystals don't look like much, but give it a try."

"As you wish, sir." He held his hand cupped over the crystal as it rested against his chest. "It's warming. It's a little different than I remember, but feels about right. I'll run Ruffian through some paces and report back to you later."

"Remember, with these crystals you're not just serving as a guard. You are one of our front-line defenders. We will count on you. All of us." Gavin waved his arm to indicate all the people in the courtyard and beyond.

"Yes, sir!" The guard straightened his spine and saluted. It was clear the man meant to look serious, but a grin crept into his expression.

Gavin kept a careful accounting of those who could use the crystals he was having made. Most would go to family dogs, which would work to their advantage. Animals that didn't need to be tied up or caged were the most useful, and they would make a good addition to night patrols on the road. One crystal was assigned to train an ill-mannered ox to draw a wagon. Saleena could move the crystal if they found a better war animal, one not needed as a beast of burden.

Travel was one of the biggest challenges of mobile crystal use, and why they still had a slight chance running in front of the approaching army. The carnivores preferred as war animals required a great deal of food, and had to hunt along the way or be provided large stores of meat from ice wagons.

In addition, those who controlled animals had to either make up their travel time by moving in steps alternating with their animal, or they had to be packed into wagons to travel near the animals as they controlled them. There was no easy way to get an army through enemy territory with any real speed unless you could ride the animal while in a trance, and only the Riland Cavalry were crazy enough to try that trick. The larger wild animals didn't always take well to training to be docile and follow along on a leash while not being controlled. They were, after all, bred and trained for violence. The most dangerous were often held in cages on wagons, but they were still limited to the pace of their slowest forces.

It was a dangerous assumption, but Gavin counted on the incoming army being slow as his people learned their way through organizing an evacuation and moving with maximum speed on their own.

He was near the main gate when he overheard a conversation between two men hauling sacks up onto a wagon. "I hear he threatened to have a bear eat the whole council. That's why they work together now. They's all scared of him."

The second man chimed in. "He's let Tover take charge of moving everyone. Don't know if I should be relieved or insulted. Maybe both. I ain't a cow, but Tover knows his travel."

The first man said, "The new baron's got dozens of crystals out of the vault. We'll have an army of war animals in no time to protect us."

It seemed every time he came around a corner, he heard something new the people claimed he had said or done.

Gavin walked between the two men without a word, followed by Jase who accompanied him on his walk to check on preparations for the evacuation. What could he say? If he corrected every wild rumor, he'd get nothing else done.

All he wanted was to get people out of the way of the advancing northern army. Once he got the people to a defensible spot, they would be safe.

He needed a simple task to distract him from the challenges he was up against. Perhaps it would let him ignore all the rumors and gossip from people who believed he was a hero out to save everyone from everything, or a tyrant who would feed them to beasts. With simplicity in mind, he checked on the granary wagons, and to see what progress Willem had made with the crystals.

The wagons held sacks of grain and barrels of ale, yet the granary wasn't empty yet. Gavin grabbed one of the men hauling supplies. "What's the slowdown with loading the grain?"

The man gave him a quick bow. "We can't get more wagons and teams, sir. The grain is never moved all at once like this."

Gavin considered the amount of grain left, and the population within easy reach of the castle. "I have an idea. Jase, please send for Master Draken."

Jase nodded and flagged down a runner as Gavin walked to Willem's small room. After a quick knock, he opened the door to find Saleena sitting next to the bed where Willem lay, obviously in a trance. A stab of jealousy ran through him when he saw them together, even though they trained with the crystals at his request. Willem was a bit young for courting at sixteen years, having not hit his full growth yet, but it wasn't much of a balm to Gavin's unexpected wish to cancel the boy's training. He turned to Saleena and said, "Are you able to get both the training and the cattle taken care of? Your father is spending a lot of his time herding people now."

Saleena picked up Willem's hand and gave it a small slap, at which his eyes fluttered open. She said, "The cattle are ready, so I came here. We're working on getting him back out of the connection to the cats without as much effort. He's about got it. Willem's a natural. He was. . . Is everything all right, Gavin?"

Gavin rubbed his hands through his hair. "Everything's fine. I came to check on the grain transfer." He reached over to help Willem up. Jealous or not, his feelings weren't Willem's fault.

Saleena asked, "What have you learned from your cats? The learning goes both ways. You can train them to do things even when you're not controlling them, and they can teach you how to make the best use of them."

Willem's face brightened with a wide smile. "I already knew they worked together when they hunted, but it's a whole different thing to experience it with them. It surprised me to see how much they notice but don't go after. There are a lot of rats and mice they weren't bothering outside of the storage areas."

Gavin glanced around for the cats but didn't see them.

Willem said, "They're eating some of their catch for the day." He shuffled his feet and continued, "Sir, thank you for the bread. It's the first full loaf I've seen in a long time."

The statement piqued Gavin's curiosity. "Why is it you haven't taken your meals with the other servants?"

"It's by your father's orders, sir. I got here two years back after a disease took all but me on the farm. Once I knew I wasn't going to die with them, I made my way here and set up a deal with the Baron. I'd use my cats to keep pests down, and he would let me have this room. He said as long as I cost him nothing, I could stay on as the rat catcher. The four of us have kept ourselves fed ever since, with a few morsels tossed in from the other servants now and again."

Willem walked to where a stone had been removed from the wall and snapped his fingers. All three cats emerged from the hole to rub against his legs and purr. "Sir, you'll need someone to keep prairie mice out of the food as we travel. I can do that for you if you like."

"I've invested a lot in you, Willem. I've got you training with Saleena. You can do the rat catching as part of your training if you like, but the crystals are more important. You'll also be eating with the other servants going forward."

Gavin wondered what convinced him to trust Willem. He was sure his father would call it a foolish decision and misplaced loyalty. Perhaps the contrast with his father's methods drove him to trust Willem out of sheer stubbornness, but there was much more to it. He needed people who cared about animals and who understood them if he was to make the best use of the crystals he had. Discovering how Willem could use the higher quality crystals as a set, with proper training, was a boon.

Willem said, "If you say so, sir."

Gavin said, "Don't worry. You're paying your way."

Draken called out from the hallway. "Sir, are you in here?"

Gavin gave Willem a solid pat on the shoulder, somewhat harder than necessary, and spoke up as he walked through the door into the hall. "Right here. I had something I wanted to hear your opinion on. Willem and Saleena, you might as well listen in, since this isn't any great secret. We've filled up all the sacks and barrels from the granary and have a lot of grain and beans left in silos and bins too big to move. My idea is to distribute the load and have families each carry part of the leftover food. Can we make the idea work?"

Draken clasped his hands and rubbed his thumbs together as his dark eyes studied the ceiling. "Yes, we might be able to distribute most of the food. We'll need to give the people a reason to load themselves down, or they'll take no more than a token amount to move quickly."

Willem raised a timid hand up waist-high, but it was enough for Gavin to notice. "Yes?"

"Any food left behind will spoil from rats or bugs within a few weeks if nobody's here to care for it. It will go bad faster if water gets to it. If the families are anything like Ma was, they'll hate the idea of wasting the food, especially if you give it to them to keep for themselves." Willem glanced back at his bed. "Ma taught me to never waste anything. Said she'd learned it from the Priests of Order, and it was a sign of respect to both God and nature."

Gavin followed Willem's glance and for the first time noticed the dozens of tiny pelts stitched together to form his blankets. "I'd say you've done your ma proud. Your idea might work to help convince people to carry the load. The people will be cooking and caring for themselves as we travel, since we can't do that centrally very well. Since it would rot or go to the enemy otherwise, I think we should give the grain to whoever can carry it. Master Draken?"

"I'll admit you have a point this time. This is the only way I see to save and use the food. We can spread the word, if it pleases you, sir."

Gavin appreciated Draken's efforts to be civil given the change in their relationship from student-teacher to ruler-adviser, yet he still pointed out Gavin's shortfalls. Their changing relationship worked most of the time, but Gavin knew it grated on Draken and was difficult for him.

It was clear Draken was more comfortable making decisions than following orders from Gavin. Gavin needed Draken's skills and experience, but didn't always know how best to go about making use of him. Gavin's skills lay in high-level strategic moves like choosing to distribute the food, and not in details of how to get it done.

Gavin scuffed his feet on the dusty floor as he and Draken left the granary and walked the hall. "You know, it does please me for you to spread the word, but that's not the point here. I've noticed over the past few days how little I would know to do, and how badly things would go without you. Your eye for detail is critical here. I would make a horrible mess of things in a hurry, or be nothing but a useless figurehead without all the help I've received. What I'm trying to do is say thank you, Master Draken."

Draken let out a single bark of laughter. "Don't thank me, sir. We haven't done anything hard yet."

A short time later, Master Quincy approached Gavin in his chambers.

"What's this I hear about giving away the grain? Resources are power, and giving it to the peasants won't do anything for you, or for me."

Gavin gave him a level look. "I'm not doing it for you or me. We have no more room, and anything we leave will go to the enemy. I would be happy to hear any alternate plans you may have. If you have nothing to propose, then I recommend you load up as much as you can carry, no cost and tax-free. We'll need to ruin any grain we leave behind."

Master Quincy seemed surprised, as if his greatest complaints had become an opportunity. "Right. I see your point. I hadn't been filled in on the whole situation."

The silos were empty within an hour, with Master Quincy taking whatever wasn't loaded up by individuals and families before he got to it. Where he found the wagon space was a mystery. Goods were as much of a power base as information, and Master Quincy knew his goods.

GAVIN WATCHED as the wagons and families formed up on the road, joined by the outliers who had spent a few hours to harvest what they could. Smoke drifted on the air. It held a different tang than the smoke of a fireplace, easily identified as burned crops. Tears washed clean paths down the sooty faces of the men and women who abandoned their farms, doing what they must in order to keep their crops out of enemy hands.

Their burden rested on his shoulders like a sodden cloak. Gavin felt the weight of his decision and hoped he was right to follow the plan they had devised. No other choice made sense, despite his misgivings.

They would pick up stragglers as they marched to the south, but he had never managed such a group. He relied on Tover's skills to get people to where they needed to be on the road, while the other council members took care of all the non-travel details of the evacuation such as supplies, security, and sanitation. It was too much for Gavin to keep track of on his own.

Tover made messengers of some young children ranging from ten to fourteen years old from the farming families. They shuttled messages and instructions to wagons and families. It was often a competition between the boys and girls to see who could get a job done the fastest. The parallels to how Tover used his dog Runner were there for anyone to see, but for the children, it was a great game and kept them busy and out of trouble.

Wagons were full. Carts were full. Even packs on the backs of many villagers were full. There was little space for people beyond the very young, the old, and the crippled to ride. If they needed to travel while more than a couple people were in a trance controlling animals, things would slow down and become more difficult. They would have to limit their crystal training to the evenings.

Gavin had somehow transitioned from dodging training at every opportunity to scheduling training for others. But, in all the confusion, he still avoided his personal training. The difference now was that he didn't have the time, and Draken had also been too busy to force the issue. It didn't take martial skill to move people to safety, and the people were Gavin's top priority.

He waved to Willem, who waved back as he followed along beside one of the grain wagons with the cats trailing around and behind him under his watchful eye.

All the horses were equipped to haul supplies rather than people. As long as they had anyone walking, the walkers would determine everyone's speed. There was no point in anyone riding unless they couldn't walk. There would be a lot of sore feet and blisters after the first day.

It surprised Gavin to see Draken with the she-wolf across his shoulders. Gavin had forgotten the wolf was still building up her stamina as she healed from the injury that had kept her from the king's disastrous council. Draken set her down to walk, and even run, for short stretches, but she still needed to rest her paws. Gavin mentally added Draken to his list of people who could be trusted to care what happened to their crystal-trained animals.

Their path took them due south on the best-maintained road in the barony. While not cobbled like the castle paths, it was built for heavy use by wagons. Plains filled with dry brown grass and occasional low bushes spread before them and to the west, while sparse trees dropped their fall leaves onto the rolling hills to the east in a slow dance to winter. The smell of dust and animals dominated the caravan of wagons.

The day progressed well until mid-afternoon when Draken let the she-wolf down to walk beside him as he patrolled the line. Gavin was a few wagons back behind the granary supplies when he saw the wolf perk up at the sight of the cats and crouch down in hunting mode. He was too far away to do more than shout a warning. "Willem! The wolf!"

Willem crumpled at the side of the road, dropping instantly into a trance. The cats formed a defensive line to support each other and took turns yowling and lunging with claws and teeth to keep the wolf distracted and unsure of her targets. The cats could have fled to safety among the wagons, but Willem's training had all been about hunting, not running.

Gavin ran to them, searching for Draken in the crowd, finally spotting him two wagons farther up. Draken turned as the wolf let out a growl, her legs bunching up for a lunge.

Draken leaped out of the wagon's path and dropped to the ground in a roll as he assumed control of the wolf. She leaped at the center cat with her maw of sharp teeth open, but skidded to a stop just inches from Doom Bringer. The cat, under Willem's control, swatted the wolf on the nose with claws out, drawing deep scratches across sensitive skin. The wolf backed off from its fighting stance with a yelp. The cats hissed as they retreated together to watch the threat from a safe distance.

As soon as Gavin reached them, he looked from the cats to the wolf and said, "I'm sorry. I didn't think to warn you about each other. Is this something you can fix?"

The wolf cocked her head, and the cats sat. It was possible to completely override what an animal would do instinctively, but training and control worked much better when the animal wanted what you wanted. The wolf took slow, careful steps and settled down to sit right in front of the cats with her chin on her front paws as she licked her sore nose.

After a few moments, the cats wandered back several paces, then broke and ran. Willem stirred, and then stood to massage his shoulder where he had landed on a rock. He glared at Draken who was still sprawled on the ground.

Gavin took hold of the wolf's collar, and Draken also sat up, displaying a scratch across his forehead from his rough landing. Tover had taken up a guard position over Draken as he collapsed. He had jumped in to help, not knowing the reason behind the sudden drop into a trance. Tover helped Draken stand.

Gavin said, "Do we need to keep you and Willem farther apart on the trail, Draken?"

Tover laughed. "So, that's what happened. Oh, you'll be able to get them to be friendly to each other, good sir, but it'll take a while. The cattle didn't much care for Runner, but that was easy to fix. The tough one was to train them to stand up to a mountain lion together rather than scatter. It took us a few tries to get them to trust each other. The big cats learned the cattle weren't worth the effort while the cattle learned to trust what Saleena did with them. You'll get there." He trotted off to catch up to his messengers who had not stopped walking.

Draken raised an eyebrow at Gavin. "Something tells me you haven't shared everything you should have. What was Tover talking about?"

Gavin gazed at the ground and tried to start three different explanations, all of which failed to materialize. Finally, he said, "We have crystals for the entire cattle herd, plus a handful of new ones for farm dogs and such. Saleena's managing the herd along with the crystal training." He glanced around to make sure they were out of earshot of the wagon train and continued, "It was Saleena who killed the bear with the cattle. She trampled it to death with moves so precise you would stare in awe. I know I did."

"So, we have both Saleena and Willem running multiple animals with crystals. By all rights, they both should be dead. You're not always going to be lucky when you act with reckless abandon. Someone's going to die, and it will be an even harder lesson when it's your fault, sir."

"I'm sorry I didn't tell you. At first, I was afraid the baron would punish Tover and Saleena, and then I got too busy and forgot. You deserve to know the truth."

Draken gazed at the distant trees to the east as if he would say something more, but he only nodded and headed over to the wolf to inspect her feet after the impromptu cat hunt.

When Gavin thought about the animal connected to his crystal, he had an odd sensation of a mental passage, but it was weak, a vague hint lurking in the background of his thoughts. The single crystal still gave him a rough sense of direction, off to the southeast in the woods, but he had only a general idea how far away it might be. He had to find whatever it was to be able to control it. This new information wouldn't go over well with Draken, but Gavin saw no choice but to bring it up, and then seek out whatever it was.

CHAPTER

ELEVEN

avin cringed as Master Draken raised his voice. "You want to go where? Are you crazy, sir?" Ah, there was the Draken he remembered.

He continued, "We just reviewed this, how the people need you with them. There are benefits to gaining more war animals, but the people need leadership and motivation. Despite your young age, you are the symbol of leadership they look to, for good or ill. We can't afford to have you out of sight for long, and can't risk you for an unknown gain."

They sat around a crackling campfire, its pine logs leaking pitch that doubled as incense to fill the air with its sharp scent. The weather was cool, and the warmth of the fire took the edge off the chill. The wan light illuminated them as they sat on mats and blankets placed on the dry grass.

Gavin raised a hand. "Hear me out. I'm attuned to this crystal, now, and I can tell something is out there and close, but I'll have to get much closer to control it. It may take too long for someone else to attune to it. We only have this one shot to collect whatever it is, and we need war animals. You can take care of things while I'm gone."

When Draken didn't immediately reply, Gavin pulled out his best argument. "Even if someone else could attune to the crystal in time, it's now my job to choose who is allowed to use them. I should go to reinforce my authority as baron."

"Now I know you're daft. You have a point about the possible war animal and your rights, but leaving me here to inspire the people in this motley caravan? Would you describe me as inspirational, sir? Do the people like me? Do they talk about how thoughtful and considerate I am? I use fear to inspire people, as you well know. Besides, you can't possibly go alone."

"Then come with me."

"I can tell you've thought about the trade-offs, but it's a huge risk."

Gavin said, "If the people know we're out finding a way to protect them, I think it will go well. It will give them something to hope for."

It was odd to see Draken at a loss for words. Finally, he spoke. "I can't believe I'm considering this foolishness. You don't understand enough of the situation in the camp, or what we might run into chasing this war animal."

"You'll have me one-on-one to beat the information through my thick skull all the way there and back. I could order you as your baron, but I want your help and support, not your forced obedience."

Draken pinched the bridge of his nose. "I'm sure to regret this, but the wolf and I will come with you. She has healed faster as she's been able to get more exercise. If we take two horses, we can meet the caravan when they reach Greenvale. You may get to learn the joys of traveling while in a trance if we find a useful war animal."

"It can't be that bad, can it?" Gavin wasn't sure what part of his argument persuaded Draken, but it was a relief the discussion was now about how to proceed rather than whether he should go hunt down the crystal connection. He expected resistance from Draken on everything, but it made sense looking back on it. Draken objected only when Gavin said or did something foolish, or when he failed to plan as well as he should have. He did best when he worked out as many of the details as he could, and presented them without excess emotion or hype.

Draken said, "We don't have any cavalry saddles to strap you in sitting up. You get tied with your head down on one side, and feet on the other. It's not much fun even when the horse stands still. Remember the army I saw behind us? The only reason they're still behind us is the time they spend hunting. Even then, they must be gaining on us."

Gavin said, "Gaining? Then we need to move farther each day. We need to speed up, start earlier, or camp later."

"You're traveling with peasants, merchants, and children. You can't push too hard, or you'll leave a trail of those who can't keep up. Anyone who falls behind dies."

"It sounds like we have even more reason to take this side trip. If we can't speed up, we need a way to slow the enemy down."

"The only reason we're talking about this trip is there is more at stake than a single animal. It could be a lone animal wandering around, but it could also lead to a stable of trained animals. We may be able to make use of them to increase our lead or for protection. Either way, we may need them on our side more than we need you to show your face along the caravan every day."

Draken took a deep breath as if he had more to say, but let it back out and shook his head. "Difficult times."

Gavin nodded and gazed at the flickering campfire. The smoke mingled with the smell of grazing animals across the field as the light breeze shifted. "Tover can stand in to deal with anything that comes up. He's done a great job moving people along and organizing the march. He's a great Travel Master, aside from a little trouble getting people going each morning. The other master craftsmen and council members help as well in their own areas."

"Help, yes. But if you think everyone is content, then you don't know people well enough, sir. You're dangerously close to putting the rest of your advisers under Tover's authority, and that will fail. They will harbor resentment that will stew for weeks and hit you with it when you least expect it. I've seen men die for less."

Gavin stirred the fire with a stick as he pondered what to do with the council. "We need a way to keep them busier and to take more responsibility." The puzzle rolled around in his head for a while until an idea struck him. "Can we keep them busy with each other? How about we assign them as a whole to handle everything not related to the migration, so it looks like just the small migration piece is cut out of the workload instead of making them part of the migration? They can use the council to deal with issues brought to them by the people when I'm not there."

"That should help, whether we go or not. They stay out of the way of Tover who does most of the important work, and they keep the people out of his way with the daily annoyances that come up. Even so, I have reservations about leaving the council in charge, even for a couple of days."

Gavin felt Draken's opinion sway. He hadn't refused outright to consider the trip, so Gavin continued the verbal duel with a final push. "I trust them to keep order on the day-to-day things. They've done this for years, and working while traveling doesn't change the tasks all that much."

Draken scowled. "The longer we talk, the more reasons you come up with to go on this trip. I can see this won't end well for me. I suppose we should inform the council members about their slight change in assignments. We can leave at first light."

SALEENA DROPPED into a trance to check on the cattle herd as they grazed. They were tired from the day's travels, but otherwise content. Once she pulled back to herself, she staked the herd out where she had directed them, the older cattle in a protective ring around the yearlings, and left them for the night.

She glanced longingly at the small campfire where Gavin sat, deep in conversation with Draken, but it was pointless to pine over him. He was the baron now, and she had to be responsible just like he was. Still, it hurt to have no time to sit and talk with him as she had in the past. She had work to do, all of it more important than her daydreaming.

She set off to visit her trainees, who had taken to calling her Crystal Mistress. It scared her to have others look to her as the expert, but her confidence with using crystals carried through into her training. Just like when they'd first made the crystals, she saw an opportunity to help and jumped in with full dedication. The old trainer was gone, and nobody else had her experience.

She still reported to Gavin, so things weren't all bad. They were still friends; they were just too busy to spend their time in idle chatter. Most of her evenings were spent with Willem and the other crystal trainees teaching them everything she knew.

The uncut crystals came back from the tinker looking and working even better than the ones Ned had cut for her. An experienced cutter made a difference. The training was easy for the people suited to it, and the tinker planned to deliver a new crystal pair to them every two or three days.

The Crystal Cabal, as they called themselves, gathered each evening to talk and to learn. They were led by Saleena, but they shared everything they learned. Some were eager to try multiple crystals, but she refused to let the new trainees try it.

So far, they had only found one thing in common in learning to use multiple crystals. You always got stuck at first, and when she and Willem had become stuck, the crystals came off the animals first instead of from the person. Was it significant? She didn't know for sure. The one failure described from Draken had gone the other way, taking off the master crystal first. Was it worth risking another life to verify? Had they considered everything? As they got more and more crystals, the question would keep coming up.

When she was alone with her Da, she asked about the first time she'd used more than one crystal. "How did you remove the crystal from the cattle when I got locked in?"

"Why, I held the crystal tight in my hand and cut the cord. Not much to it, fast and simple. I thought I'd lost you. You wouldn't wake up."

He looked around. "Truth be told, your team is right. I think we need people who can run more than one animal in case you or Willem can't be there for us. We need to learn more about how to train multiple crystals. Your class is just learning the basics, so they're no good. The guards will likely report you, so they're out."

It seemed that everyone had been mulling over how to use the crystals in groups. If she didn't make a choice to do it, someone else would try on their own and maybe get it wrong. Someone might die. She counted off the people she saw as likely candidates and grimaced.

"I think we need to try it despite the risk, but you've said nobody can do it."

"Not a word gets back to Baron Stoutheart until we're sure, you hear? He's got enough to worry about. I'll start with the weakest two crystal pairs, just to try it. I'm sure you're right about how to get unstuck. Once could be an accident. Twice means you're on to something. Three examples make a trend, so I think I'm safe. I'll stop by later. Once we prove you right, we can train more people if we need to."

"You can't do it! What if it doesn't work?"

"Saleena, you can't have it both ways. You can't decide to take a risk, and then tell me I can't be the one when we both know I'm best for the job." His gentle voice cut like a knife through her selfish desire to protect him.

She didn't want to risk her father's life, but she and Willem had compared everything they could think of and she knew they had to try. If it wasn't worth risking her Da, it wasn't worth the risk. She gave a reluctant nod. They would remove the crystal from the animal first when he tried it.

A few minutes later, Saleena stood in the center of the circle of students talking about her experiences and comparing theirs. "With one animal, you can control the fine details more easily, like moving ears, looking at things, and fighting one-on-one. You have access to all of their senses, so use them. It's not like that with a group. It's different to feel the herd all at once, or to smell differences across an entire field all at once. There's a lot of information to skim along or sort through."

Willem nodded. "It's like that with the cats, but they're a small, coordinated hunting team instead of a herd. I think with the cattle and the cats, you end up thinking as a group instead of as a single thing. Using three pairs of eyes at the same time still confuses me sometimes, or makes me feel sick or dizzy. It should be a lot easier for each of you with one animal to control." He tilted his head to the side and listened. "The cats found something. I'll be right back."

Willem found a comfortable position and eased into a trance. A minute later, feline yowls rose out in the field, followed by the cats parading back up to the group with their prize. Death Claw led the pack carrying a small gopher.

A minute later, Willem sat back up. "I've made a few peace offerings to the wolf. The cats are getting along a lot better with her. Sharing food is important to animals."

Saleena smiled at his thoughtfulness. "One last thing for the night. Never underestimate any animal's abilities, particularly when they're directed by a human mind. Be prepared to face the most cunning, vicious things you can imagine. Even more important, we need to be prepared to attack in ways nobody will expect. Be the cunning mind behind the animal. We won't have huge beasts with giant claws or bone-crushing teeth. We have to be clever and sneaky. Think of things we can do on a small scale."

She set up new trainees with their large family dogs, which sped up the training. Some were quick studies, while others weren't cut out for it and were glad to go back to normal family duties.

Everyone wandered away after the training session, leaving Saleena and Willem sitting off to the side of the road beside Willem's camp gear.

Willem gazed out across the fields in thought for a while, then said, "You know, we might be able to use a rat or a gopher, or maybe a jackrabbit or badger if we can catch one. I'll try to bring something back alive when we have a spare crystal or two."

Willem glanced quickly around, then scratched in the dirt before he continued, "Thank you for coming back to talk to me and help even after you ran off back at the castle. Most people don't think of rats as food. I'm sorry I upset you."

Saleena wondered how to answer without offending him. She hadn't realized how much his feelings mattered to her until now. "I didn't know you were treated so horribly by the baron."

He shrugged. "Ain't nothing horrible about it. I was the one who offered the terms. It wasn't like the old baron forced me into it. Ma taught me you do what you can with the gifts God lets you keep. I keep myself fed, and have clothes and a place to stay. I was lucky and wasn't ever indentured. I can grow up free. Even better, I've eaten a lot nicer food the last few days."

Regular food had done wonders for his color. He was healthier, too. The best part was his near-continuous smile. She glanced away so he wouldn't notice how she'd been watching him, noticing his change for the better.

How had he kept such a positive attitude, even before the recent changes? She knew he'd lost his whole family, and yet here he was grateful for everything he had. Saleena still had a gaping, raw hole in her heart from her brother's death. Her only hope was to lose herself by staying too busy to dwell on her loss. She felt shame at her reaction to Willem's previous diet but didn't know how to tell him. Rather than try to explain, she stood, squeezed Willem's shoulder and said, "Thank you. You have a good heart, Willem. You're humble and kind and grateful. I've seen men with much more who never appreciate what they have. Things are going to get harder for all of us, so don't stop reminding me to be grateful." She lingered with her hand on his shoulder for one more squeeze before leaving to find her father for his first experiment with two crystal pairs.

CHAPTER

TWELVE

Gavin peered through the dense woods as they rode the game paths with the wolf keeping pace nearby. The scent of decaying leaves and damp earth on the chill evening air made him long for a hearth with a nice bird roasting over the fire. The biggest distraction from the forest was the window within his mind. It had become stronger through the day. The connection clarified into something he could use to enter a trance, although the link had an unfamiliar tang to it.

Before Gavin said anything, Draken held up his hand to signal a stop. He put his finger to his lips then dismounted and found a handy tree to sit against. He held up two fingers to show how many minutes he expected to be gone and slipped into a trance. The wolf, who had been standing obediently beside the horses, shook her head, and ran off among the trees, silent as a four-footed ghost.

Two minutes passed, and Gavin was about to shake Draken awake but decided to risk going into a trance himself to see what had brought them out here. It would leave them both unguarded, but he justified to himself that he could pop in, and then back out if he wasn't needed.

He slipped into a trance and found himself on the ground with the wolf's teeth pressed against his neck. A quick glance around showed men with bows aimed at the wolf. One of them said, "Don't fire yet. If he wanted the boss dead, he'd be dead already."

Gavin felt the position of familiar limbs, and clothing covered his body. The body of another man. Control of another human had been banned as an abomination centuries ago as part of the Accords, and now Gavin was in violation of the Accord through no fault of his own. The penalty for turning humans into puppets was death. Was this how outlaws were made?

Gavin whispered to the wolf. "I've got him now, Draken. He's wearing the crystal."

The wolf backed off two steps, and sat, indicating it would not attack. Gavin had seen this exercise before in training and knew when Draken ended his control of the wolf. He prayed the men hadn't noticed.

Releasing control at this point would be a disaster. The man he controlled already knew everything.

Gavin stood up, careful to keep his hands out in the open. He glanced around and saw several men, all with their eyes on him, on the man Gavin controlled. He wore a dagger at his hip, and a horn bow lay across his back. Neither weapon was useful against so many. He had to buy a little time for Draken to arrive because he couldn't back out without being noticed. They were committed, for good or ill.

He walked over to the wolf and knelt, giving it a subtle hand signal to stay as he looked at the crystal, delaying as long as he could.

The same man spoke again, and asked, "What's the word, boss?"

Well, that tore it. Gavin didn't know whether the man expected a code word or a command, but whatever he said would give him away. A few more seconds and he would have to choose between fighting or quitting the trance. Perhaps there was a third option. He stood and turned to face the man. "I'm not your boss."

They took it all in stride as if this was normal. "Well, you ain't Baron Stoutheart, neither. That's for sure. Now you let him go, or the wolf gets filled with arrows. Your friend won't die with the wolf, but it won't feel none too good for him."

Good. They assumed the wolf was still under Draken's control.

Gavin figured he had nothing to lose by introducing himself. "I'm Baron Gavin Stoutheart. It appears you worked for my dead father."

There was a murmur among the men, as if unsure of their next step.

From back in the trees came Draken's voice. "The last I knew, Adrian Albin was set to be hung for his crimes, yet here he is, whole and healthy. I mean, other than the fresh bites from the wolf. Sir, go ahead and let him go, and bring the horses up. These men won't kill us. At least not if they have any brains left."

How was an insult like that supposed to help? It wasn't the greatest endorsement Gavin had ever heard, but he complied and pulled back from controlling the man, apparently named Adrian Albin. He trusted Draken implicitly, even if he didn't always care for the man or his methods.

Back in his own skin, Gavin stood, then led the horses around a small hill into a glade. The strange men had set up a camp with shelters made of canvas and boughs spread over frameworks of wood. Beneath the framework were tents scattered around a central fire pit. An animal roasted on a spit above the hot coals. The site resembled a temporary hunting camp more than anything else.

The man he had controlled faced Draken. "Mboli Draken. The last *I* heard, you were disgraced in the king's court and told to never return."

Draken said, "You killed a noble over politics. One of the king's trusted men. You don't come back from that, Adrian."

"You set him up to issue a dueling challenge, Draken. You knew as well as I did he was abusing his position, just like most of them do. Then you forced me to kill him when you couldn't. Arguing that he deserved to die got you banished."

Draken said, "If I had died then, it would have been with honor. It was your choice to act. Thus, we both fell from grace."

"At least you were on good terms with Baron Stoutheart. You became his trusted lackey. He turned me into his personal spy puppet, kept out of sight. I haven't had a bed with a real roof over it for years."

Gavin tensed, still not knowing whether they would flee or fight.

The two men approached and embraced like old friends, slapping each other on the back. Draken said, "It's been a decade. I had no idea you were alive. Have you been out here this whole time working for Baron Stoutheart?"

"Well, working for him isn't exactly accurate." Adrian tapped a finger against a steel collar with a crystal embedded on the inside surface. "This was one of the conditions of my release from the king's personal dungeon. It turns out I had certain skills the good baron wanted to use, and he bought me from the king before the trial. Without that, I would have hung. King Vargas worked deals under the table when it suited him, despite his public statements about crystal slavery. The thing won't come off without the skills and tools of a blacksmith, but I haven't tried to remove it." He glanced up to the sparse tree canopy for a moment. "It's a long story I can't tell right now."

Draken glanced from Adrian to Gavin and back, and then said, "I suppose the news hasn't made it here yet."

Adrian gave him a disparaging look. "Really? You wound me. We've known of the incoming army for several days. It's good to meet you, Baron Gavin Stoutheart. I hope it is, anyway, as my life is, quite literally, in your hands."

Gavin stepped forward to clasp hands with Adrian and asked, "If you knew about the invasion, why are you still here?"

"Ah, a quick wit. Your father asked us to camp in the woods near the main road until we received instructions, with a particular warning to not move until necessary. I've found it important to listen and follow instructions to the last detail when I depend on someone's good will for my life. There is always the chance he survived the attack. Now, to save you the trouble, I'll give you the more accurate introduction. I am Adrian Albin, chief spy for your father, and all-around scoundrel, at your service. My men here are the best at what they do."

Gavin looked across the ragtag gang. "And what is it they do?"

"Would you like to be an honest man or a knowledgeable one? I'm happy to handle your dirty work however you would like, sir. Your father preferred to know everything. You strike me as more the honest type."

The man was exceptionally compliant. Cordial, even. Something was wrong. Normal people didn't open up with cheerful acceptance when people show up unexpectedly as they had. Gavin felt him through the link, a short push away from where he could take complete control again. The man had nothing to lose and might go either way to become a dedicated follower, or to free himself from his new master and vanish.

Gavin recognized with a start how easily Adrian and his men could overpower him, Draken, and the wolf if they wanted to. In fact, they had already shown they could and had chosen to spare them. Gavin mentally ticked off his options and threw out all but one as likely to end in death, probably his. He pulled the crystal from around his neck, swung it around his head once and dashed it against a boulder. Shards flew through the air in all directions.

He took in the gaping mouths all around with a quick glance. "So, how about we have a serious conversation now that we're on level ground?" It was a huge gamble to throw away his best leverage, but the crystal was his worst handicap at the same time.

Adrian fell back onto the ground and laughed, pounding the dry grass with a fist until tears leaked out the corners of his eyes. Finally, he took a deep breath and said, "I hope you're this shrewd about everything else you do. You're going to need a lot more help than we can give you."

Gavin stared, concerned at the extreme reaction, and he shook his head. Had the crystal driven Adrian mad, or was this something the baron had done to him? Maybe he was like this to start with. "I'm not looking for an army to fight the invasion. I'm working to get everyone out of the way. I need to get them to safety."

Adrian said, "You're not like your father. What happened to all your training? Aren't you supposed to act like a Gerald Junior?"

Draken tilted his head and sighed. "You see before you an expert at avoiding anything his father wanted him to do."

Gavin glared. "Are you and your men a resource that can help save people, or not?"

Adrian said, "Ah, there's the Stoutheart fire. We can help you, but I'm not sure you're ready to own and direct a spy network."

Gavin shrugged with noncommittal agreement. "Since you seem to be on my payroll already, we can start simple for my sake. Tell me what you know about this invasion, and how we can stay ahead of it."

Time was short, but Adrian and his men filled in whatever details they could on the invasion and its progress into Riland from the north.

Gavin felt his brain was about to overflow following their discussions. The details of his father's orders left him wondering at his father's plans. His father knew the schedules for trade routes, as well as harvest times for various crops on both sides of the border. Had he planned to give the information to King Vargas at the Baron's Council? Had he expected this invasion?

Their discussions ended with Adrian laying out what he could offer. "We keep no written records, but everyone here has skills to draw on, and a memory trained to notice and store details."

Gavin said, "What skills? Hunting and trapping?"

"No, nothing so mundane. We know poison, camouflage, language and dialects, as well as creating mechanical contraptions and traps."

Gavin tossed a twig into the fire. "How about my father's goals? If you're such clever spies, what was he up to? Why all the preparation?"

Adrian said, "I have suspicions about his plans, but they are unconfirmed. He was always careful not to tip his hand, but he was looking for weak spots in the kingdom. Our best option is to concentrate on King Ithan and his resources as he follows you. My scouts will continue to track his progress from a distance.

"He won't have enough wagons to put every man controlling a war animal into a trance and haul the men around, but military men are used to a tough regimen. They do a lot of leapfrogging. At last count, he had nearly fifty big war animals: wolves, mountain lions, several types of bear, all of which must stop to hunt. He even has some moose, but they're grazers. You've got a slim chance to stay in front of them if he's denied local supplies. Otherwise, they'll run right over you."

Draken interrupted. "I've seen their makeup. He has about five hundred men as well as the animals. They've taken provisions from at least one of the border watchtowers. It won't be the men slowing them down."

Adrian smiled and raised his eyebrows. "The armies in the last war were larger, but then most of them died. It seems we have both full disclosure and agreement. I think we'll get along splendidly. You missed one little detail, Draken. Around a quarter of those animals were captured from our side when King Vargas died. I don't know how he did it, but he must have taken them by surprise to take that many. It's like they didn't even fight back. Given the number of crystals they had at the gathering of barons, King Ithan must have sent a large supply of crystal pairs home for safe keeping rather than trust his men with them in the coming battle. He's cocky, and he thinks we're falling into chaos."

Gavin said, "From what I've heard, he's right. There may be no organized resistance between him and the capital."

Adrian held up a finger to correct Gavin. "He may have had no resistance *yet*. We can help you give him something to worry about."

Gavin recognized Adrian's motivation to hurt the advancing army, and

Adrian's men were the only ones in a position to do anything. He couldn't do much with his odd collection of farmers, ex-soldiers, castle guards, and merchants. At least they had a chance of outrunning the invaders if Adrian found a way to leave some difficulties in the army's path.

As they prepared to sleep for the night, Gavin asked Adrian, "Why have you offered to help? Nothing holds you or your men to me."

"You're right. We've never sworn to you. According to the slavery laws, I haven't sworn to anything, despite all the swearing I've done while wearing this collar. But this is home. We've seen how King Ithan operates. He's heavy-handed, and he'll destroy a lot of families. We're here for the people, for the barony, and for Riland. You are the best option I've seen, thus far, for making a difference. I also have some personal matters to resolve, and I'm happy to travel with you to handle them."

Draken said, "That's not enough. I know you, or at least used to, but I don't know your men. Devotion to king and country is great, but I need more than that from you, and so does your new baron. Your crew doesn't look like selfless types who serve out of the goodness of their hearts."

Adrian's eyes twinkled as he smiled and turned to Gavin to plead his case. "Draken doesn't accept the humanitarian angle. He always could see though my arguments. Most of the men also have family members in the dungeons of the capital to ensure their good behavior. They'd like to fix that. You're filling a hole in the power structure as a baron, so you're becoming influential. Friends in high places can help friends in low places, particularly if my men end up as heroes in your employ."

Draken's digging turned up an answer that seemed disturbing but genuine to Gavin. He could work with that. He retrieved the crystal pair he'd taken from the bear and handed it to Adrian. "Here, use this. Nobody in our wagon train can make as good a use of it as your team can if you're going to be out scouting and causing trouble."

Adrian nearly dropped the crystals as he set them down and scooted over to the other end of the log. "If it's all the same, I'll have one of my men take it. I've had enough of crystals." His hands shook as he sat and stared at the crystals. It was no wonder using crystals on people had been outlawed.

"Pick someone. I'll leave it up to you."

Adrian nodded. "Alright, then. I figure we may be able to help here and there to slow down the Graven Kingdom's army by making it harder for them to get supplies from the locals, and by chasing away big game. I have some other ideas kicking around in my head as well. The least we can do is buy you more time to get non-combatants out of the way."

Before turning in, Draken pulled Gavin out of earshot of the others. "I hope you know what you're doing, trusting him. I used to trust him with my life, and I think he'll help us. I agreed with your choice when you broke the master crystal, but giving him one of our few remaining crystal pairs is risky. It's one you could use yourself once we find something to wear the other half."

Gavin stretched out and crawled between the layers of his bedroll. "I've learned a lot about how to tell when I can trust someone to do the right thing. I've always known who would help me escape your training and who would turn me in. I've trusted you, even when I haven't liked what you've made me do. You've helped me by pointing out how to watch my adviser's reactions, and I've practiced. I already know you. I may not always understand what motivates you deep inside, but through it all, your duty and dedication show the honorable man I've always known. If you trust Adrian, I trust him, too."

Draken held a hand up to interrupt then dropped his hand. "I have to speak with Adrian before I sleep. I'll talk to you in the morning."

The next morning, Adrian sent half of his men out in various directions, while the rest shouldered packs of camp supplies in preparation to join the refugees. They would have to speed-march to make up lost ground as the men had no horses. It would be a long and difficult day.

Gavin asked Adrian, "Where are the other men off to?"

Adrian ticked things off on his fingers. "They'll visit outlying settlements and warn them to leave. They'll keep an eye on the advance of the army to warn us what they're up to. Some of them ran ahead last night to lay some groundwork before your group gets to Greenvale. Based on what you told me, the refugees will arrive there today, and it will be better if that is not a complete surprise. I have to keep the boys busy or they'll get into trouble, and if they're going to cause trouble, I want it to be in our favor." The way Adrian grinned, Gavin wasn't sure how serious he was.

CHAPTER

THIRTEEN

Gavin saw a welcoming party approach as he neared Greenvale with his new recruits. They didn't look very welcoming in the evening sunshine.

The homes and shops at the edge of town showed sturdy post-and-beam construction framing their plastered walls. The only buildings showing signs of age stood empty, silent testimony to the losses of the war years before.

His caravan sprawled outside the town where the people still trickled in to set up camp, arriving in a stream over the past hour or more. He wanted to join the camp for some much-needed rest, but the group approaching looked like it wouldn't wait.

Adrian pointed with his thumb. "The one who's about to explode is Baldwin Baker. He's been in charge of the town and surrounding land as the reeve under your father's direction for years."

Gavin rode forward to intercept the group and dismounted.

He needed to calm or distract the approaching man and his entourage for the sake of his caravan, and for the people who lived here. Gavin wanted to ask how Adrian managed to keep all those details in his head, but the reeve marched forward and demanded, "What's the meaning of this? Are you in charge of the rabble ruining our fields?"

Gavin stretched his hand out and took the man's hand, which he offered out of reflex. "Yes, I am. Thank you for your hospitality in letting us camp at the edge of town."

Draken interrupted and gestured in Gavin's direction. "Reeve Baker, might I present the new Baron Stoutheart, who has become responsible for this area following recent tragedy. I'm sure you were well acquainted with his father."

The reeve's eyes narrowed as he scanned Gavin up and down. "Tragedy couldn't happen to a more deserving man, but it won't matter to us unless the old baron's tax collectors died with him."

An awkward silence settled in. What had his father done to these people to deserve such scorn? Gavin would have to check with Master Quincy about how heavy-handed the taxation had been. But things had changed in more ways than one.

"Well, Reeve Baker, you won't have to worry about taxation anytime soon, despite your thriving community."

Reeve Baker stammered, "What do you mean about the taxation?" He was clearly expecting something different.

Without giving the reeve a chance to continue, Gavin pressed on. "Some of my men arrived earlier to warn you we were coming. Did they contact you?"

"Yes. We met this morning. They were talking nonsense. The residents don't want to leave."

Gavin talked over him. "That means you've lost critical time to evacuate. I will summarize for you, in case you missed something important earlier. The Graven Kingdom is invading, and our king and the entire Baronial Council are dead along with most of their heirs and advisers. The invading army is behind us by a few days. We can assist you in your evacuation, and we welcome all those who will join us. We'll travel until we can secure the safety of those who can't fight. We hope to join with enough fighting forces to defend against the invasion."

Gavin glanced to the side. "Did I miss anything critical, Master Draken?"

Draken drawled out, "Normally, this sort of meeting would take an hour of conversation over a meal and drinks, but no. You covered it, sir."

Gavin smiled. "You see, we are in somewhat of a rush, what with the approaching army. Can I rely on you to get the word out immediately to your people that this is a serious matter?"

Without giving the man a chance to answer, he continued, "We leave in the morning. Any who choose to stay are defying my evacuation order, and risk being caught by Graven war animals. Now, if you don't mind, I need to see to the evacuees. I trust you will inform your people of the deadline. Thank you for your help."

Gavin and Draken gave the reeve the most cursory of bows and hurried on, leaving the man staring after them with his mouth open. Adrian had vanished while Gavin wasn't looking.

Draken spoke once they were out of earshot. "If only you were as good with a blade as you are with a tongue lashing. I was unaware of your ability to talk like a cattle stampede. Most impressive."

"We have to do what we can to convince them. People will die if they're still here when the army arrives. I hate to push him so hard, but these are my people. I don't want their deaths on my head, so I'll do everything I can to encourage them short of armed threats."

Draken said, "Just remember armed threats are still an option. He's already defied an indirect order. If he continues, you can make him the token example for defying your direct order. More people will come with us if you have him lashed."

Gavin shook his head. "No. We just need to make sure everyone knows the situation. I don't have the time, or the desire, to judge and punish people. The punishment will come in the form of the army."

"Just remember I gave you the option. More people will obey if they see their reeve in the stocks for defying you."

It took only a few minutes to find Tover, who waved his arms and yelled at the two angry men standing before him. "You should have asked me for help! Going to blows over something so simple as where to tie animals does none of us any good." He looked up from the wagon and grimaced, rubbing his temples. "Welcome back, good sir."

Gavin pointed at the wagons. "What's the problem?"

Tover came closer to Gavin to talk with some degree of privacy. "Well you see, I'm good at keeping a migration going, but we have problems with people all wanting their way. It gives me headaches trying to keep track of it all."

Gavin folded his arms and looked the two men up and down. "Is there anything else you need to resolve, or are you done taking Master Tover's time?"

They looked at their boots and shook their heads, then saw they'd been dismissed by their baron and left at a quick pace.

Tover was pale and looked a bit shaky. Was the stress of the new job too much for him? "Are you ill, Tover?"

"No, good sir. I'm a bit road weary, but I'm feeling much better now with a little help from Saleena. I just wish I knew what to do to speed up the people. Nerves are wearing thin as old boot soles. They're starting to squabble, and I spend more time putting out fires and tracking things down than making progress. I swear, good sir, my cattle are never this much trouble."

Draken nodded. "Regular trade caravans emphasize safety. We need speed, and the merchants don't have the right skills. The priorities are different. We have to handle people and their goods differently."

Tover sighed. "It's a relief to know you understand the problem then, sir. It's going to slow us down more and more over time as we add people almost every day. We will lose our head start if it gets much worse."

Gavin said, "Do you know how to take care of organizational problems, Master Draken?"

Draken gave a grim laugh. "I know how to see the problem, not how to fix it, sir. I recommend you ask your full council and see who can help. It sounds a lot like a military supply chain problem to me."

"We need to meet with the full council anyway." Gavin turned to face the town. "Is there a good place to meet here? I'd like to have a roof over our heads to make the meeting more formal."

Adrian said, "I know where you can meet."

Gavin jumped. "Don't scare me like that. How long have you been there?"

Adrian gave him a quizzical look as if he'd been there the whole time when Gavin knew he had not. It was no wonder his father had put Adrian in charge of spying on people. With the way he blended in and appeared or vanished at will, he could learn things nobody else could.

Adrian said, "Invading Reeve Baker's office would probably be bad politics after such lively introductions. It would barely be big enough, and they won't have food. There's an inn with a private dining room you can use for your meeting in town. It's called the Dragon's Plate. Now, there's a good place for food. I'm sure you'll like it. They may be in the middle of packing, but I suspect there will still be hot food."

Gavin nodded. "That sounds perfect. I'm sure the council won't mind a hot meal not cooked over a campfire. I will arrange the room and review a few things while I wait for everyone to arrive. Draken, can you make sure the various masters and Reeve Baker know to meet there tonight? He should at least respond to a direct order that only requires him to appear and confer with us." At Draken's withering glare he added, "I'll take Jase along with me."

Draken nodded without losing the glare. "Very well, sir. I need to get the wolf settled and pay a few visits first. I will meet you there tonight."

ON THE WAY through the camp, Gavin bumped into Saleena and Willem in the middle of a conversation. A glance around showed the Cats of the Apocalypse keeping pace in the nearby shadows. Willem held a dead rabbit by the ears.

Saleena waved and smiled. "Gavin. I mean, sir. It's good to see you back. People missed you while you were gone. Did you find anything?"

Gavin wanted nothing more than to give her the long version of the story and waste the time away. He missed the time they spent together, but the short version would have to do. He owed her that as a friend. Then again, she was also the barony's crystal trainer. His eyes lingered on the scarf covering her necklace of crystals for the cattle herd.

It dawned on him their relationship hadn't faded, but had changed. Saleena had taken on more and more responsibility. She led the crystal training with confidence and skill, to the point he no longer worried about it. She was one of his advisers, and he trusted her in that position.

Perhaps there was a little time to spare. She might need to know more details for her to do her best. "We found a camp of men loyal to my father, and some of them have come back with us. Others were assigned to scout and report back. Some of them got here before you, but the people haven't taken the warnings of danger seriously."

"What about the crystal? No war animal?"

"One of the men had a slave collar. I destroyed the master crystal since his collar won't come off without good blacksmith tools. At least I'm doing my best to keep *that* Accord, even though the king didn't seem to care about the slavery violation."

"Destroyed a crystal? A full-size crystal?"

With a nonchalant shrug, Gavin said, "It was a tricky situation, and saving lives seemed more important than a crystal at the time."

Saleena rolled her eyes. "It's your barony, but I'd suggest you save whatever crystals you can. We need them."

They didn't see eye to eye on everything, and he doubted they ever would. Friends didn't have to always agree. Gavin changed the subject and pointed at the rabbit. "Who's the prize for?"

Willem's eyes had been on Saleena until he turned to look Gavin in the eye. "It's for the wolf. The cats are making friends with her."

Gavin's train of thought paused. Willem was sweet on Saleena. The two of them spent their evenings together with training, and he had seen them walking together during the day as the caravan moved. His protective instincts made him want to discourage Willem, but that was a fool's errand. First, he knew the barony and its needs might dictate who Gavin married. Second, they would both hate his meddling. It all made sense but didn't do much to ease his sense of loss at the change. Friendship was the key. He would concentrate on his friendships with them both and avoid thinking of the negatives.

Runner barked for Gavin's attention and jumped into the middle of the trio, disrupting the conversation. Gavin rubbed the dog's ears, and then turned back to Saleena, his emotions calmed by the dog's enthusiastic greeting. He knew he should be happy for their growing friendship, right alongside their growing abilities and skill with the crystals. It was unfair of him to ask her for any emotional attachment when he knew he could never be there as more than her baron. "Is training going well?"

"It is. Wonderfully, really. Master Sharp has delivered another crystal pair with the simple pooka marks. I'm searching for someone with a good pet to use, but we may capture something wild and try to tame it. Willem's getting good. He's got focus and knows what he's after with how he trains the cats, and they're learning from him as well."

Gavin said, "Great. It's a relief that you're handling this training as the new Crystal Mistress."

Saleena looked at him askance. "You know, you never told me that was my title. I heard people using it, and tried to correct them until I finally heard that the job and title belong together."

Gavin's cheeks reddened. He stammered, and then said, "I'm so sorry. I didn't think about that. I'll announce things properly for anyone that's still wondering. I keep making foolish little mistakes."

Saleena said, "I don't see you making any mistakes more than once. You're doing great." She always worked to find the positive side of anything he did, but her body language didn't match, and her tone carried the disappointment in his oversight. He would work to regain her full measure of respect. He would do what it took to deserve it.

"I'll do my best. I hope my best improves as I go. Do you have enough volunteers for training?"

She nodded. "We're making progress. Some people have to be turned away because they don't understand what it takes to control the crystals or can't get a feel for it. Some can't handle the sensations of being a furry four-footed animal, but we've got enough people, for now, to match the new crystals as they're finished. My team keeps asking about using more than one crystal. I know what you're going to say, but I know what we did that made it work. I'm sure of it, more now than ever."

"No, I'm not going to risk a life on a test we don't need. It will be better for us to have more people trained. Anyone who wants to should get some exposure to see who is best at it. Also, I need you to join the council meeting tonight. If anything related to the crystals or training comes up, I'd like to have you there to answer as the newly announced Crystal Mistress." He grinned.

She gave a sad smile. "I'll be there. Thank you."

It was a good start to fixing the things he had broken in their changing relationship, but he knew he'd disappointed her.

GAVIN FOUND the Dragon's Plate without much effort, Jase following a pace behind and to the side. The building had a sign hanging out front, decorated with a dragon and an armored man facing off over a plate of food. The place was nearly deserted, but the great room's hearth had a fire going. He flagged down the first person he saw with an apron. "Excuse me. I've heard this is a good place to host a meeting and get some food."

The woman eyed Gavin and his guard. "We don't have a lot left unpacked, but we'll take care of you."

Most of the chairs sat upside down on the tables, and the shelves behind the bar were nearly empty.

She called back to the kitchen. "Chase, get two plates, fifteen minutes apart." She turned to the two men with a confident smile. "Would you like to eat in the private dining room, then? Follow me, sir."

"I'm sorry, but I wanted to have a meal with the meeting later if possible."

"Ah, but you're going to be doing a lot of the talking later. If you eat now, you get a hot meal to eat at your leisure without interruption."

As they dodged a table and passed through the large double doors to the dining room, she said, "The second plate is for your man once you've finished your meal. Can't have him guarding on an empty stomach, but it's improper to feed you both at once. Do you have a head-count for your meeting this evening, sir?"

Gavin wondered if Adrian hadn't primed the pump by warning the woman they were on their way. It fit in with what little he knew about the man. "I'm not sure yet. I'll be meeting with eight from the camp, plus some locals."

"I'll guess the locals are to be the reeve and his two assistants. I'll add three to your party. Four just in case."

Gavin began to ask another question when he heard a faint bell chime. The woman excused herself with a curtsy, and then returned a few moments later with a plate of steaming food and a mug, which she placed deftly on the table along with a silver knife and fork. Gavin recovered from the confusing blur of action and asked, "Were you expecting me?" He sat at the plate of fragrant vegetables and sauced meat, accompanied by a slab of bread and cheese.

"Ah, there's a trick to it. You see, I planned for someone to come from the camp and visit, just in case, sir. As for knowing who you are, anyone in town with half a brain will know by now, I suppose. You came in with a guard. There's only a handful who would have a guard wherever they go. I spent time in military camps in my younger years. I know how military and guards work. It's clear you're not the baron's appointment scheduler, so that makes you Baron Stoutheart."

A side dish held a bounty of nuts and vegetables with different harvest times, all cooked to perfection rather than having been left to steam all day. Gavin had spent his share of time hiding in the castle kitchen and knew the effort it took to fix meals when you fed dozens at a time. "How did you get peas this late in the season? And those pine nuts in the sauce smell wonderful."

She puffed up a little and her smile grew. "I hadn't heard you were so attentive to details, sir. The truth of it is you only need to know where to get what you want at the right time. You see, the Fernel's farm is on the north side of a ridge and up higher in the hills. It's cooler there, which makes their harvest later. Same thing for the early harvests on the sunward sides in the lower valleys. I know every farm within a day's walk, and when their crops will be ready. The baker got a delivery of flour two days ago from the miller, so I knew he would have his ovens fired up all morning baking, despite the news we have to leave. I give the children their shopping orders first thing each morning, and off we go, simple as that."

Gavin noted her methods in case he could use them later. "It's an impressive system. I'd better get to this meal before Jase's food arrives. I'd hate for him to have to wait while his food got cold." He dug into the meal, savoring the mix of aromas and flavors. He wasn't sure if it was the change from camp food, or if this was, in truth, much better than he had eaten recently. No, there was no question. This was an extraordinary meal.

As he ate, she talked about the locals, with only the barest of prompting questions. He stored away details on the various families, businesses, and leaders for later. The woman was a veritable fountain of information. It was no wonder Adrian liked the place. The information would help since Gavin had only this last meeting to get the town leaders and remaining residents on his side.

It was a while before he noticed how she asked as many questions as she answered. She was a master at conversation, and she learned a great deal about the caravan even as she filled him in on the town, making a fair exchange of information.

Between bites, Gavin held up a hand to interrupt her stream of talk. "I'm sorry, but I'm afraid we skipped formal introductions. You know who I am, but I was rude not to ask you to introduce yourself. Let me make up for my poor manners. I am the new Baron, Gavin Stoutheart."

"I'm Lindy Keeper, the owner of the Dragon's Plate since the departing of my dear husband five years gone."

He cocked his head. "The owner? Wouldn't the property go to your oldest son at your husband's death?" The laws were clear about inheritance, but local exceptions always popped up.

"We've run the place as a family since the war, when the last owner never came back. My son's still in training and learning to run an inn. I guess it's going vacant again now with the evacuation. Nobody local presses the ownership issue with me if they want to stop by for drinks and not have them watered, if you know what I mean." She gave him a sly grin. A bell chimed in the main room, and she laughed and walked back out, clearly the ruler of the roost.

THE COUNCIL MET in the Dragon's Plate as the sun dipped below the western horizon. Gavin had to keep the meeting short, while still giving the reeve and his men an incentive to support the evacuation. The more warning people had, the better they could prepare.

Reeve Baker was skeptical of Draken's description of the enemy army, even with the enhanced information from Adrian's advance crew. He also questioned what he had heard about Gavin. "The stories about you seem highly unlikely. They say you personally killed bandits who were accompanied by a war animal, and are a master at gathering intelligence. I hear rumors you are training people to use an army of crystal-controlled war animals. I see no evidence of any of these things."

Gavin shook his head. "Your skepticism is warranted, but I'm not here to convince you I'm a worthy leader. I'm here to save your town from destruction. Your only real chance is to prepare tonight and leave with us in the morning."

Reeve Baker smirked. "It's clear you're far too young to remember the last war. I was part of it. I saw how it worked. An army doesn't work the way you describe when they're out to take land. They'll consolidate as they go to expand their borders."

Gavin stood his ground. "And if they're not out to take land? You've heard the reports on what they're doing. They're on the way, and you are in their path. The facts speak for themselves. It is *your* lives in the balance, and you are gambling on information years out of date."

The reeve's primary assistant spoke up hesitantly. "We can help to spread the news, but as the reeve said, there are those who don't want to evacuate. We won't get everyone. Caben Rockwile wouldn't leave his land if they burned his farm to the ground around him. There are a few other stubborn folks out on the surrounding farms."

The reeve glared at his assistant, clearly incensed at what he saw as a betrayal.

Draken directed his attention to the assistant. "I've seen this army. Everyone who stays will die, or wish they had. We must do what we can to convince people, but we leave tomorrow as Baron Stoutheart said, or we will lose too much of our lead. Time is tight enough as it is."

Reeve Baker's face grew red. "You'll address me when it comes to my town! You're all loons if you think we'll be overrun this far south."

Draken stood, slowly turned to Gavin and asked in a low, calm voice full of ice, "May I?"

Gavin nodded, not sure what Draken had in mind. All he knew was that Draken showed all the signs of erupting like a volcano beneath his calm exterior.

Draken turned to Reeve Baker and slammed a fist onto the table, causing plates to rattle. "Your town? This isn't *your* town. You rule at the good will of the baron. This baron seated before you now. If you can't get it through your head that you face destruction, we'll talk to whoever will save the baron's people. We have no time to waste on debate with you."

The reeve stood. "Barons come and go, but my family has lived here for generations. We're not going anywhere."

Lindy swept in with a tray of drinks and wove her way around the table, interrupting the tension. She handed one to Reeve Baker. "So much conversation must leave you all parched." The drinks were timely and cooled tempers as the meeting continued.

To Gavin it felt odd to have Draken stand up to support him. More than that, Draken had defended him and gone on the offensive. The experience of sharing the same view was new, but they had to work as a team to save as many people as they could. Still, there were differences. He considered the threats of further punishment Draken offered and rejected them. He would not be that kind of a ruler.

Messengers entered and exited through the next hour, and glasses were regularly topped off. At Lindy's earlier hint about watered drinks, Gavin had made a special request for her to keep everyone's heads clear, but suspected she gave Reeve Baker something stronger than normal instead. Lindy was there to hear their discussions but seemed to be completely ignored by the reeve and his men. Gavin made a mental note of how Lindy and Saleena held whispered conversations at the far end of the table. Saleena's practical nature made sure information reached those who needed it.

One sticking point in the discussions was that the evacuation was not moving quickly enough. They were slow to start each day and too disorganized when they camped at night. People regularly lost anything they hadn't packed and taken care of themselves. Common camp resources got mingled with personal items or misplaced and took too long to find.

The reeve glared in stony silence all through their discussions.

With no improvements proposed, Gavin moved on to cover other topics, and asked, "Saleena, how is the crystal training program going?"

Saleena stood. "The new crystals are helping, but the crafting takes a great deal of time. The tinker can only work on them in the evenings. We have a couple of veterans with experience using a crystal and a list of people to train, but only two known war-trained animals."

Reeve Baker slapped his hands down on the table. "You have a cattle herder as Travel Master of your evacuation. You have peasant children using crystals under a young, inexperienced Crystal Mistress. Yes, a woman as your crystal trainer!" He jabbed a finger at Saleena. "You're flouting both law and convention. You may have some people convinced, but I'll have none of it." He stood so fast his chair tipped over, and he stormed out of the room which was left in a dead silence.

Draken moved to stand, but Gavin put a hand on his arm to keep him in place.

The reeve's assistant cleared his throat and stood, careful to scoot his chair back slowly. "I'll see to it that everyone learns of the danger. Those we convince to leave will have everything prepared by midmorning. My apologies for the reeve's disrespect."

Gavin asked, "Will Reeve Baker cause you problems?" He wanted to avoid Draken's more drastic measures with the reeve, but would do what he had to.

"I don't know what sort of baron you will be, but I know Reeve Baker. I don't plan on seeing him again. I'm coming with you in the morning along with everyone I can convince."

Choices became easy when the alternatives led to death or captivity. It was a great motivator to live in fear of destruction. If only Reeve Baker had felt that fear, rather than placing so much value on his misconceived notions.

The meeting broke up, and Gavin walked back to the camp with the others. People were going to die, and it was up to him to save as many as he could. He was unlikely to get any sleep tonight between the preparations still to be made, and everyone's need for command decisions on a host of things. He was glad the reeve's assistant would handle at least part of the supervision as the people of the town packed.

His goal was to keep everyone safe, but the group he was responsible for grew daily. Was Draken right about punishing Reeve Baker? Would it save more people to make an example of him?

He said to Draken, "As baron, I can threaten them, and make people come with us. I could lock up the reeve to prevent him from poisoning the attitude of the locals. There are so many things I could do if we had time, but we don't. Was I wrong? Did I need to do more than offer and encourage?"

"You did well. I disagree with some of your choices, but they are yours to make. Me? I'd clap him in irons and parade him through town. You don't work that way. You earn the hearts of the people, and they choose to follow you. Those who stay will see the consequences quickly enough. You made your choice, and the results are yours to own. You have nothing to be ashamed of."

Such praise from Draken was a shock. Their relationship still had rough edges, but they shared a new level of mutual trust despite their differences.

"You think more people will die because I didn't arrest the reeve." Gavin was haunted by the thoughts of all those who would stay. People he had not convinced.

Draken nodded. "But this is who you are, offering a hand up instead of a slap down. You may be right that your way is best. Either way, it's important we leave in the morning, or we will throw away the lives of the refugees right along with those who don't want to be saved. War is harsh and cruel, and much of it is out of our hands. Whether good or bad, consequences have a way of finding us once we've made our choices."

"I hate to think there's nothing more I can do. I have to give them every chance I can."

Draken said, "You already have."

As Gavin navigated through the last few tents and wagons near his private camp, he found Adrian walking beside him. He'd begun to get used to his spy master's appearances and disappearances. Gavin glanced over his shoulder at the town. "I assume you heard we won't get them all. What can we do about those who stay behind? Did you say something about preparing a greeting for the army? Give me something positive. I need some good news."

"Sir, I'll have to check on supplies, but I think I can cost them a day or two here and create a chance for the holdouts to leave. The army has pillaged everything you left behind at the castle by now. Too bad I wasn't there when you left or I'd have cost them as much as a week with all that fine architecture to work with. Ah, well. No use trying to rewrite the past."

"Draken says I don't have time to do any more for the people who stay behind. Do what you can for them."

Adrian smiled. "Right, then. For tonight, I'll need three empty wagons, shovels, canvas, rope, some fish hooks, and a couple salted hams." He rubbed his hands together with glee. "This will be fun. A couple of my men will spread out to visit side villages just like the men I sent from the camp, so be ready to take in even more stragglers as you come across them. They'll be told to camp alongside the main road and migrate to the capital on their own at their best speed."

It sounded like a disaster in the making.

ONLY THREE-QUARTERS of Greenvale joined the evacuation caravan, but those who came were well-organized. Gavin walked the road to see how soon they could leave. Before long, he came across Tover berating a wagon team who couldn't find their assigned oxen. "You lost them? They have bells on and were tied out to graze! How do you lose two large beasts wearing bells?"

The wagon driver scuffed his feet and looked around as if hoping to spot some way of escaping the reprimand. "I looked where your errand boys took them. They weren't there."

Tover gave Gavin a shrug. "Sorry, good sir. We're a little behind schedule this morning, but we'll be on our way as soon as we track down a couple of loose . . . ends."

There had to be a better way. Gavin hurried to the far side of the camp to visit the locals, who were ready and eager to move. He approached a man as he tied a tarp over a cart while his wife tracked their four small children. "Good morning! Fine looking children you've got there. How is it you can be ready with young ones to distract you? In fact, everyone from Greenvale is chomping at the bit to be on our way." He looked at the children and wished, for a moment, he'd had a family like theirs with two parents, and siblings near his age.

The man's wife smiled and pointed up the road at Lindy Keeper who had a small line of people waiting for her attention. "Those who need it have help." Gavin watched from a distance as Lindy listened to a man who was clearly upset. After a great deal of pointing and waving from the man, Lindy waved another man over and spoke a few words to him and pointed back at the upset man. The two men spoke for a few moments, then nodded and headed off together, allowing Lindy to give her undivided attention to the next person in the queue.

"What's she doing?"

The woman with the children said, "She knows everyone in town because they all either trade with her or spend time at the Dragon's Plate. She talks to everyone endlessly. Whenever one person needs something, she knows who to go to or where they can find what they need."

The husband cinched the last knot on his tarp and glanced at the worn leather breastplate Gavin wore. It was easier to wear than to find a place on a cart to store it.

"You're Baron Stoutheart, aren't you? I mean, sir. I recognize you from the stories." The man gave a short nod of respect.

Again, with the stories. If he had a way to make the gossips and story-tellers stop, Gavin would do it in a heartbeat. "Yes, I am. And don't believe everything you hear in those stories." He noticed Lindy had only a few people waiting for her now. "I'm sorry, I need to go. Thank you for your help." Gavin trotted up the road with a wave back to the man and his family.

As Gavin was almost out of earshot, he heard the man say to his wife, "See, he talked to us like a regular person does. I think we're right to follow him, despite what Caben and the reeve said about staying."

Gavin hoped the man was right about following him. It would tear his heart out to see those children come to harm.

He hurried along and caught Lindy's attention by waving. She waved back and walked to meet him halfway after signaling her petitioners to give her a few moments. "What can I do for you this morning, sir?"

"I hear you're the one who knows where everything is and where it needs to be. We have a couple of missing oxen."

She turned to scan the crowd. "Chase! I have a quick errand for you."

Gavin recognized her son from the inn. He'd manned the kitchen while Lindy served food and drinks at the meeting.

"Go check with the Potts family. They've been up and back down the whole line this morning chasing their wayward son. If they've seen a couple of loose oxen, find the beasts and send them over to the Travel Master." She glanced back at Gavin. "Wasn't his name Tover?"

Gavin nodded, mystified. "How did you know Tover was searching for the oxen?"

She smiled. "If it has to do with getting people going this morning, he'll know who lost them, and where the oxen go." Chase ran off on his search.

"There's one more thing if you have a moment."

"Of course, sir."

"My sources tell me you're the reason the Greenvale folks are on task and ready to go."

She waved her hand as if to dismiss the idea. "They don't need me to help them get ready. I only tell people how to get things from where they are to where they need to be."

Like the sun rising over the trees to the east, Gavin had a moment of clarity where several pieces of information made sense when viewed together.

"You're a widow, right? Was your husband a military man during the last war?"

She placed her hands on her heart in remembrance. "Aye. He made it through the war, unlike a lot of others. I lost him later to a fever."

"I'm going to guess he was a supply chain master, and you followed along behind the front lines as part of the supply chain."

She gave him a cautious nod. "Well, now. It seems you're the one pulling information out of thin air today, sir. You've got the truth of it."

Gavin suppressed a grin, having guessed in one try. He suspected her husband's success during the old war was due to Lindy's natural skills. "Tover's good at keeping people moving, but we have a hard time starting up in the morning like you heard last night. Please take a look at things and meet with him this evening to see what can be improved. I'll tell him to expect you."

"I'd be glad to help in any way I can."

Chase returned, out of breath, and reported. "The Potts family didn't see any stray animals. Sorry."

By the time Gavin got back to Tover, two of Saleena's cattle were yoked up as makeshift replacements.

"What happened?"

Tover waved him closer. "They were killed. We found their bells where the boys staked them out. Runner tracked them over that close hill and found them with their throats cut, good sir. The enemy got an advance scout past us, or someone in town hates us. Thank goodness it wasn't a war animal that attacked. One war animal can cause a lot of damage in a hurry. We have to abandon them. You can't trust meat killed by the enemy."

"Thanks for keeping it quiet. I'll tell Captain Zachary we need more night patrols, and we'll put the animals closer together at night with a watchman. We can't afford to lose the animals we use to haul our supplies."

Gavin failed where he didn't even know he was being tested. He would improve, to guard his people more closely and protect them from future attacks. He was still reacting rather than acting. He knew the dangers of that from even his simple level of combat training. He had to control the situation and act rather than let the challenges dictate his actions.

There was only one logical course of action. "We need to use our patrols to catch whoever did this if they keep following us. They caught us unaware once. I'd be a fool to let them get away with it twice. We can call on Runner and Ruffian for some tracking." Even though he felt the responsibility and ownership of the problem, Gavin knew he wouldn't be the one hunting this cattle killer.

One of Tover's young messenger girls ran up to say the tail of the line was ready to go. The competence of the people around Gavin far outstripped his meager skills in many areas, and he was grateful for those who shared his goal to keep the people moving and safe.

A moment later, a boy showed up to report the head of the line was ready as well. The boy glanced at the girl and made a mean face at her as the girl smiled and twirled her skirts. He'd lost the race. Gavin knew both the smug success of the girl and the pretend animosity of the boy. They reminded him of Saleena and himself where games were always a contest.

Gavin dropped back to the tail of the caravan and glanced back at the town as the evacuees made their way along the dusty road. A few of those who refused to leave had come to watch or to say goodbye to friends or family. A group of them joined the reeve who scowled at him. They turned and walked back into town grumbling among themselves.

From the top of one of the buildings, he caught sight of Adrian giving him a high sign. With luck, the man would convince the remaining towns-people to leave before they were overrun. Gavin had done what he could and left the rest of the work in the best hands available. He prayed it was enough.

CHAPTER

FOURTEEN

Gerald Stoutheart rarely defied King Ithan, but this time, he had no choice but to argue against the plan to overrun and loot Greenvale. Gerald stood at the camp table, fists resting on the worn wood.

"If you destroy the town, you'll have to rebuild it later."

Trees stood in the distance far to the east. The road rose where it approached Greenvale with farms on either side in a large ring around the town, which itself sat on a slight rise. The fields were mostly cleared, with just a few late holdouts of fall vegetables and grains yet to be collected. The crops would be destroyed along with the town. Such waste was unavoidable to some degree, but Gerald preferred to preserve what he could.

King Ithan shook his head. "I can live with that. It's on your head anyway. Your failures have slowed us to a crawl. We didn't even get to your castle before everyone fled with most of the food."

"Your highness, I hardly think –"

"You're here to answer my questions, not to think. I did the thinking weeks ago. We're behind schedule, and this town has what we need to speed our advance. We take them out and try to catch up with the rumors of the invasion before someone organizes enough people to cause us real trouble."

Gerald backed off, wanting to avoid the full wrath of the king. "I did mention Draken was resourceful, especially when under stress. He must have taken control in the name of my son and evacuated."

"I don't care about your little walled home and its peasants. The past is past. The only thing it's good for is to teach us to not be surprised by this Draken, or whoever has taken control of your people. Whoever is in charge is a shrewd organizer, and he's in front of us. All the more reason to flatten the town, take what we can use, and move on to catch up to our target. My spy, Edwyn, has fed me plenty of information on the towns we're approaching, including this one. He's daring and clever with that bird of his, and he gets me reports nobody else can. The best way to anticipate an opponent's next move is to kill him. With enough information, we'll do just that."

Gerald fumed over not having Adrian's crystal from the castle vault so he could do some spying of his own. Someone, probably Draken, had it now. Without the crystal, he had no way to know which camp Adrian Albin and his ruffians used, and he didn't have time to visit them all. It was sheer foolishness to misplace the crystal when he first left for the conference, and he cursed his carelessness.

To add to Gerald's frustrations, the king's decision to pillage the town without detailed scouting rubbed him the wrong way. The town was a significant resource, but they were prepared for an attack. King Ithan would pay for his foolish decisions, fueled by his quest to conquer the entire kingdom in one pass. Gerald saw the signs of the king's overreach, partially due to Gerald's own failure to have supplies waiting.

He couldn't confront the king or challenge his decisions without risking his safety. "It will be as you command, Your Majesty. I'll pass along the order to attack once everyone's in place."

On the road, Gerald waited as the last of the hunters and patrols formed up with the rest of the animals and footmen. Their timing wasn't perfect, but Ithan's men showed good discipline. He could make good use of them once Ithan was out of the way.

Gerald passed the wagons where several of the hunters and scouts were already in controller trances with a heavy guard while the large animals they controlled ambled forward as shock troops. Gerald moved to follow behind them, connecting with the bear who had long been his crystal-trained companion.

Once everyone was in place, they proceeded over the last hills obstructing their view of the town. The closest chimneys showed lazy trails of smoke. Gerald wondered if the refugees had passed through without disturbing the town. Perhaps this would be easier than he had feared. It pained him to think King Ithan might be right.

A man on the road turned and fled as Gerald's bear and the other animals came over the last rise. Nobody ever outran the animals for long. Despite Gerald's disagreement with the king's goals, it was satisfying to see the people on the streets flee as the animals pounded down the road and adjacent fresh-plowed fields in a coordinated wave.

Gerald watched from the rear through his bear's eyes as the front wave of war animals, twenty-five wide and two deep, moved in. When they neared the outskirts, they hit a shallow, covered trench in a line perpendicular to the road. Thousands of sharp wooden spikes lined the trench. Most of the front rank hit a spike with a paw. Many animals fell, and more spikes drove into legs and chests as they landed. Screams of animal agony and fear reached back to the rear of the army. Those noises were echoed by a handful of men who were yanked violently back out of their trances at the death of their animal.

The injured animals limped past the shallow trench. Gerald's bear and the remaining animals used the road to cross the area, with footmen coming up behind. The worst of the injured animals pulled back. They checked for more traps but discovered a handful of archers who let off a volley from behind the corners of buildings before vanishing into the town.

The war animals eased forward to the first buildings and took shelter while waiting for the footmen to catch up. Without verbal commands relayed by the footmen, the animals regrouped to wait. To continue on their own would open them up to attack on all sides, and could split them into teams too small to be effective. The men came forward and issued orders to group up and gain some ground within the town. More men entered the homes and shops at the edge of town. Gerald joined the second wave into the town. The bear was one of his favorite war animals, despite it having lost an ear a few years prior. He inspected the trap as he picked his way past the spikes. The footmen came up empty in their search of the closest buildings. Gerald's curiosity grew as the teams found no half-prepared meals or other signs of occupation or hasty flight. The whole thing smelled of Adrian Albin's planning, right down to the decoy fires to make the town appear to be fully occupied. The man was too clever for his own good. He must have joined up with Draken. If those two were back together after all these years, it meant trouble. He'd gone to great lengths to keep them apart.

The animals slowed even more, advancing one home at a time until they caught sight of three dozen people in the town square. Gerald recognized the man standing in front as Reeve Baker, but the people behind him were only a small fraction of the population. Gerald loped forward to see what was happening.

"It wasn't us! We tried to stop them. We surrender to you. We open our homes to you."

The animals closed in on the people and did what they were best at, but Gerald had other plans. If the fools were going to butcher the people who could tell them about other traps, he wasn't going to get in their way.

He continued past the square to the far side of town to see several wagons race away to the south at a full gallop. Loaded in the wagons were a mix of mostly children with a few adults, but standing at the back of the final wagon was Adrian with his telltale metal collar. He pointed directly at Gerald's one-eared black bear and saluted. As an automatic response, Gerald raised the she-bear's right paw to return the signal. Adrian would know it was Gerald controlling the bear by his response. Perhaps there would be a way to make use of the spy later. Adrian had a way of showing up unexpectedly to deliver information, so Gerald must be ready to bring him back under his direct control when they met. You had to keep a firm hand to control your resources properly.

The wagons raced around a bend and were hidden from sight, leaving nothing but clouds of dust hanging over the road. Gerald had no way to chase them down. He returned to the town square and the grisly feast, letting his bear feed. Waste not, want not.

An hour later, Gerald approached the edge of town on his way back to the camp when he heard debris fall, followed by screams from the king's soldiers. A man in armor hobbled out of a nearby home. "The stairs collapsed. They've trapped the whole cracking town!" Rumors of danger spread among the men like wildfire, especially after a man was run through by a spear triggered by a tripwire. All told, they lost three more men to the traps and a dozen more were injured while looting homes.

Gerald knew Adrian took particular joy in projects like these traps.

Even though the traps were spread thinly around the town, they were frequent enough to make the soldiers suspect every building. It would be a pleasure to apply Adrian's skills on a whole new level once Gerald took the kingdom.

The downside was that taking the town was a disaster for the army. The only bright spots were the supplies left behind, and the feast in the town square.

Most of the subjects had fled with the group from the castle. Gerald picked his way through telltale campfire pits and latrines where the refugees had left them outside the town. A light autumn rain overnight made it difficult to tell how long it had been, but it couldn't be more than two or three days ago.

Back at his wagon, Gerald latched the bear's collar onto a special fixture designed to hold the animal fast once he released it. He pulled back to his body and stood on shaky feet and sought the king's tent. Ithan would expect a report.

Ithan raved as he glared at the town from their hastily formed camp. "We'll be stuck here for at least a day longer. We were close to catching your people, Gerald. Now we have so many injured animals and men that we will be hard pressed to find enough bandages. The men will want two days, but we're moving in one regardless. The injured will just have to keep up."

He pointed at the buildings. "Gerald, the men have heard noises from possible survivors hiding in the town. I want answers, and some of those survivors may have what I need. Go find me someone to question."

Gerald bit back a response. He knew what had happened, and the biggest traps would have failed if the king had trusted him. This arrangement had to change, but the king still had his uses. The king's men wouldn't follow Gerald when they were still this close to home. The ambush in the town had worn them down, but they'd retreat all the way to the Graven Kingdom if the king died here. Gerald still needed the army. Therefore, he still needed the king.

He nodded to Ithan. "I will organize the search for survivors. I've visited this town several times, and can speed up the search if it pleases you."

The king nodded a dismissal and marched into the camp muttering under his breath. His personal guards formed up around him.

Gerald walked back into the town and watched as two soldiers walked past a disguised storage cellar. "You two, follow me. The king sent me to direct the search. We'll start here." He pointed at the storage door decorated with shingles. Their expressions told him everything. They hadn't even seen it.

He stationed the guards outside the cellar, and then entered with a torch. "Hello? Is anyone here?" His accent would be familiar, even if they didn't recognize his voice. The first cellar held stacks of supplies set aside for winter but was otherwise empty. The third cellar was where his efforts paid off.

A voice in a dark corner shushed him. "They'll hear you. Get away from those stairs and put out your light."

Gerald made his way back, spilling light on a family hidden behind some storage crates. "Sir? Is it you? Baron Stoutheart? We thought you died with the king."

Gerald suppressed a smile. "Mere rumors. What happened to everyone?"

The man eased forward, leaving his wife to hug the children in the corner. "Your son, Gavin, took most of the people with him. Everyone's calling him the new baron now. He's doing you proud. We didn't believe an army would come, but we were wrong. Oh, so wrong. We should have joined the evacuation. A few of your son's men stayed and built the trench and all the traps. Some of them are still watching from a distance."

Gerald couldn't understand what this family hoped to gain by hiding. "You can't stay here in your cellar. The army will find you."

"I plan to peek out through the door when it gets dark to see if we can run for it. Will you stay here with us until dark, sir?"

Gerald said, "I'll send someone for you. You've helped me more than you will ever know." So, his son was leading the people. Maybe the boy was stepping up instead of dodging work. Gerald could always hope. Adrian and his men were still watching them, too. The news couldn't reach King Ithan, or it would turn his son into more of a target. He made his way around the storage and climbed back up the steep steps to where the soldiers waited outside.

He pointed down through the doorway with his thumb. "King's orders. Leave no one alive. Be careful not to ruin the supplies."

They emptied six hidden cellars of supplies and survivors by evening. The king would never learn of Adrian and his men watching from the woods. It was unfortunate to kill the two families he found, but the new information on Adrian's men gave him an edge. Gerald met with the king once more, this time in the nicest building not destroyed by the army or by saboteurs. "This is a good choice, Your Majesty. The Dragon's Plate was a fine inn. They served great food, but the hostess was too nosy for my liking. I see the fresh supplies made it to you." The king sat at a table set with a small feast.

"Yes. You did well in finding more than my men did on their own. Were there any survivors?"

"Unfortunately, everyone died or left with the evacuation." Technically, the statement was true. "With the lack of local opposition, I recommend you leave a minimal detachment of soldiers here. It will be trivial to hold against any locals who might come to town from nearby farms. We can use this town as a storage depot for the extra weapons we've found, along with those of the dead footmen. There is no threat here, and there's nothing at all behind us." Gerald hoped his lies all sounded reasonable, given what the king knew of the town.

The king steepled his hands in front of him. "I agree we must take as many men as we can with us. We'll leave the seriously wounded men and a few others. We can't lose sight of the goal to get to the capital with a large force and take control. Everything else is just a part of that goal."

Gerald smiled. A small garrison would be easy work for Adrian's men to cut down, and the extra weapons would arm them better. That should send a clear message to Adrian to prepare for a fight under Gerald's direction. Having the larger army with him would be important as they closed in on the capital.

King Ithan said, "We will travel east of the main road before we close on your refugees to claim their supplies. Not only has game been scared away from the main road, but my scout has reported back on the surroundings, and you somehow forgot to tell me about some of the smaller villages within easy reach."

Gerald pursed his lips. "I hoped to keep a more direct path, and to preserve some of the smaller farming and ranching communities for you untouched."

"I shouldn't have to remind you that you are the source of information, and I am the source of decisions. I expect a report from you on these villages as we approach them."

THE ARMY WAS BACK on the road after a day of delay. Gerald saw the king's growing anger and complaints at each setback. The army diverted to the east away from the main road and into the hills.

"We haven't brought down a deer for two days. We're advancing like an old crippled hag because of the injured men and animals. You assured me when we made our plans that supplies were the least of our worries, and now it turns out to be the greatest obstacle. I'm much freer with rewards to those who keep their commitments."

They walked along a ridge overlooking a now-deserted hamlet surrounded by freshly harvested fields. The people had been unable to haul the entire harvest when they fled, which left the army with some grain and vegetables, but it was a meager improvement.

"You're right, Your Majesty. The shortage of supplies is my failure, yet we still advance. Our successes have been limited, but we still succeed. I shared a great deal of information about the villages and what we can claim from them. The refugees ahead of us chose to burden themselves with a large stockpile of supplies, and they have many women and children with them."

King Ithan nodded. "My spy says they have heavily loaded wagons. They also have thirty or more head of cattle which, per your promise, belong to me."

"Well, that's our herd then. Is this spy the one with the bird? What kind of bird does he control?"

King Ithan peered up into the evening sky, a mottled mix of oranges and reds as the sun set. "I'm getting tired of reminding you that information goes *to* me, to share as I see fit. At least the garrison can hold Greenvale. We'll need it once we start running a full supply route."

Gerald smiled. "I think things will work out exactly as planned in Greenvale."

———

THE NEXT DAY, the army moved farther off the main road and came across the village of Spice Run, nestled in the forested hills. Gerald watched the farmers working their fields as he stood under brown fall trees at the edge of the farmland. Things were improving. The hunting parties had brought down some game as they ventured into more remote forest roads. It had also led them to an area that had received no warning of their approach.

"Your Highness, this village isn't overflowing with crops and herds, but they can contribute quite a bit to us." He tried to steer the king away from destroying this particular village. Gerald's second cousin, Phineas, lived here and would be useful. The man was an easily manipulated boot-licker and had gladly given resources to support Gerald in the past, in the hope of some unnamed future reward. At least he was dedicated and consistent, and that meant a lot to Gerald.

Gerald continued, "All we need from them is their extra food so we can cut our hunting time and get back to a fast advance. They'll have a lean winter, but they'll survive."

The king snorted. "You're going soft, Gerald. There's no room for the soft in this army. Are you up to the task? Will you still be useful to me, or do I cut you out like the runt of the litter?" The king glared at Gerald for a long moment as if evaluating him. "Gather all the people together. The rest of us will collect supplies while you keep them busy in the lodge in the center of the village."

———

PHINEAS and the other locals were grateful to see Baron Stoutheart and eagerly followed his instructions to gather together inside the central lodge to hear him speak.

"Our army needs supplies. You've been generous with your support in the past, and I will see to it that your support is rewarded." The footmen from the army had been commanded not to speak lest their accents betray them, and many of the war animals were held back to preserve the illusion it was a small baronial defense force.

"To make it fair, our forces will take a tax from each farm. We fight to defend you, and we need to move quickly. Thank you all for your help as we work to avoid a war." He wasn't specific as to which army they would help, or the size of the tax as King Ithan's forces spread out to pack everything they could carry. He approached Phineas with small talk. "How's the family these days? The children have grown since I saw them last."

A soldier peeked into the room, so Gerald broke off from the conversation and met the man at the door. "It's time to leave, sir. Please come with me."

Gerald turned to say a few last words, but the footman interrupted with an urgent whisper. "No, sir. It's time to leave now. The king insisted."

Unsure about the change of plans, Gerald followed, preparing a mental list of information gained from his subjects in the village. The messenger kicked a wedge under the door to secure it as they left. Gerald and the messenger reached the king who stood away from the central building with a small group of men. "What's all this about? I thought you wanted me to keep them distracted."

Archers let loose with flaming arrows, which stuck in the log walls and the thatched roof of the hall where the people of the village waited for their baron.

"No! There's no need to kill them! They won't even know you passed through." He took two quick steps forward, but the king's guard tackled him and held him down.

A few moments passed with the rising sound of flames before voices called out in fear.

The yells turned into screams. Two men inside managed to knock the stout door down after a few tries. Thick smoke poured out as the men collapsed to their hands and knees outside and coughed. Archers shot them and the building became an inferno with the improved airflow to feed the fire. The flames expanded and cut off any chance for those inside to flee. The sound of the roaring flames overcame the sound of screams, and Gerald felt the heat wash across his face.

Gerald clenched his jaw. "I promised them I would help them. You've made a liar of me."

King Ithan snorted. "You made a liar of yourself long ago, so don't blame me for that. I'm not taking chances with locals spreading the news about us, and we have no time or guards for prisoners. As I said, you're weak. Still useful, but weak. I did those people a favor. They would have slowly starved to death and turned on each other this winter with no supplies. It was unwise of you to question me, so you've been given a hard lesson."

Gerald planned to show the king exactly how strong he was, but would wait for the right moment. His burning resolve to destroy Ithan was fanned to an inferno, just like the burning lodge, but it wasn't time yet to act. His long-term plan to control the kingdom was more important than petty vengeance, but vengeance would come in due time.

CHAPTER

FIFTEEN

The rear half of the caravan had stopped. Gavin couldn't see the cause, so he signaled for a short rest stop, and then marched back with Tover on his tail to investigate. The people waved, bowed, or curtsied as he made his way past. Their nervous looks to the rear matched his worries. Every small failure brought the enemy army a little closer, and Gavin was afraid he wouldn't know how to save them if it came down to a confrontation.

Shouts brought Gavin's attention to a wagon, broken down and blocking the road. The shattered axle dug into the dirt where it had come to rest. The entire back end of the wagon had twisted and split under its heavy load. It wasn't ever going to roll again. The rocky terrain here made it too difficult for wagons behind the broken one to go off the road and get around the mess.

A woman stood at the corner of the wagon leaning against a tilted front wheel, her gaze to the ground. Her cheeks were wet with tears.

A man in his late twenties yelled, "You said my things would be safe on your wagon! What can I do now? I'm holding you responsible for replacing the lot of it."

She glanced up. "It's only the wagon that's broken. You're welcome to take your things and find another place for them."

The man backhanded her, leaving a red welt on her cheek.

Gavin came up behind him, placed a hand on his shoulder and said, "Hey, now that's not necessary."

The man whirled around and hit Gavin with a wild swing, full on the left side of his jaw. The blow knocked him to the ground and stars filled his vision as his head bounced on the packed dirt road.

When his sight cleared, he saw Tover step between Gavin and the man who had hit him. A human wave took his attacker to the ground, knives pointed at him from all sides. One of the men raised a long sword to strike. Gavin yelled, "Hold! Stand down."

The swordsman lowered his weapon to a rest position and stood, waiting. He moved with the practiced ease of a soldier. Gavin wondered who he had served under, and was grateful for the man's training to respond to commands. Despite the prompt response, the swordsman glared at his would-be target. "We all saw him attack you, sir. The old baron's killed men for far less. We're yours to command."

Gavin struggled to his feet and gingerly touched his jaw, feeling for loose teeth with his tongue. The world wavered back and forth, and he blinked a few times to clear the tears from his eyes. He tasted blood as he opened his mouth and shifted his jaw side to side to make sure everything lined up as it should. Aside from biting the inside of his cheek, things seemed to be in about the right place.

How had he gotten into this mess? The man's life was in his hands. How was that right? If he let the people have their way, the man's blood was on his hands just as if he'd killed him himself. If he dismissed the incident, it would lead to an erosion of authority. He needed some middle ground, and he needed it fast.

He had to occupy the people while he thought the issue through, so he bought time by asking, "Are you hurt, Goodwife?"

"No, good sir. I've had worse." She placed her fingers to her red cheek.

"What?" Gavin glared at the man on the ground. "From him?"

"No, sir. It's sometimes been difficult since my husband died." She looked down and didn't continue, letting Gavin fill in the blanks of those who might hurt a widow.

Gavin took a closer look at her. From her smooth face and dark hair, he judged she was young to be a widow, no more than thirty years of age. He saw no children with her. She'd already had a difficult life, and now this. Was this level of disrespect a common thing among his people? It was time to change expectations.

He softened the tone of his voice, hoping to ease her concern. "What was the problem he spoke about?"

"Sir, he asked me if I would haul his personal things back in Greenvale. The combined load was too heavy for the old wagon, and it gave out. Truth be told, I feel it would have given out a'fore long even without the extra load." She kicked at the dirt and brushed at her skirt. "Now I've lost it all. It's all I've got, and I can't carry it all on my back. Will I have to leave the caravan?"

Gavin heard the tremor in her voice, and her fear of being cast out for not keeping up. The army would overrun anyone who couldn't keep up. It was clear she expected to be yelled at and punished for her failure as she had been in the past. Being left behind was a death sentence, which would put *her* blood on his hands.

How widespread was this fear and desperation among the people of the caravan? He had to come up with something, anything, to solve the problems and inspire the people to work together instead of turning on each other. He had so many different issues in front of him, he struggled to separate the problems from one another. The combined problems of the caravan turned his thoughts to mush. Could he break this down into a list of smaller challenges?

Tover touched his arm and whispered, "Good sir, we must move soon. What would you like me to do?"

Gavin twitched as all eyes centered on him. "Right. One problem at a time." He would have to pare off challenges until the remainder was small enough to deal with. He wiped a streak of blood from the corner of his mouth and studied the people who waited on his word.

"First, the wagon. Tover, I need a wainwright. I doubt we can repair this, but we need to salvage anything we can from it."

Tover tapped one of his ever-present messengers and sent a girl named Izzy on her way, her skirts flapping as she ran to fetch a wainwright. Gavin had seen her running the length of the caravan on errands as they travelled.

"Second, the attack." The people rumbled and aimed their blades at the man still prone on the ground. At least Gavin's attacker had the common sense not to struggle.

"Is there anyone who believes he sought to assault me as his baron?" Gavin looked around as people reluctantly shook their heads. "Of course not. Therefore, I will treat this as a simple assault, and exact a penalty to match. We're in a war not of our making. I'm not going to waste the life of someone who can fight for our barony and for Riland, no matter what my father might have done. Release him." He walked over to the man on the ground and helped him up with an extended hand. The crowd grumbled.

"Do you have experience with the king's army?" He wasn't old enough to have served during the last war, but Gavin plied him with an easy question in a hope to find something to work with.

The man hugged his arms close to his chest and nodded. "Yes, sir. Never with the animals, or fighting on the field, but I was a swordsman's errand boy."

"Very well. You know a little about military discipline. You will forfeit your goods to the widow who willingly offered you space to carry them, assuming there is anything worth keeping. You will eat with the servants from the castle. You will train under Master Draken each morning and evening to fight as a footman."

The man blanched at the mention of Draken and objected. "But he's ... I ..."

"You think I'm being unfair?" Gavin raised his eyebrows. "Should I leave your fellow-travelers to choose your punishment?" He gestured to the glowering mob and paused to look at the swordsman.

"No, sir. You are fair and just. More than fair. Tonight, with the guards." The man swallowed hard and watched his boots, his arms still wrapped tightly around his chest. Apparently, the people had a lot more respect for the guards and for Draken than Gavin did. Perhaps a little fear, too, for those who were trained to wield death as a profession. Gavin's heart pained him as he thought of the people who endured hardships he had never known in his protected and pampered life.

He gave a final look at the man he had just assigned to the guard. He felt dirty for having threatened the man with death at the hands of a mob, but he saw no other way out. "I expect nothing less than your best efforts, and I will check with Master Draken on your progress. You are dismissed."

The man ran up the road.

Gavin saw some of the people nod in satisfaction at his verdict. Maybe it would be good enough.

Gavin worked his sore jaw a few more times as he looked at the wrecked wagon. His priorities had been served a painful and public reminder. His responsibility was to his people, singly and as a group. They might consider his safety, as they did when he was attacked, but they hadn't leapt to the defense of the woman when she was struck.

What were the people's priorities? Were they heroes waiting for a chance to be heroic, or did they only want a safe place to call home? They weren't heroes any more than he was.

The silence was broken as the wainwright stepped up and cursed at the sight of the twisted wreck. One of the bystanders nudged him and pointed to Gavin, at which point his eyes widened and he mumbled, "Sir? I, ah, didn't see you there. So sorry for the language. I'm Master Vanwagner."

With no target in sight, the people stowed their blades in belt sheaths and boots as if nothing had ever happened. Gavin pointed at the wagon. "Is it possible to fix this? We have to get back on the road as fast as possible."

The wheelwright tugged at his short beard as he thought, then said, "The only way to fix this is with a bonfire. It's ruined. I suppose we could take the yoke, and maybe the wheels if they aren't twisted. We've got a little room on a supply wagon for things like that."

Gavin was so used to finding a solution to problems that he stared for a moment with his mouth open before he found the right words. "Then we salvage what parts we can from the wagon, but what about the goods on it?"

"Begging your pardon, sir, I don't know much about handling cargo. I just build wagons."

Gavin accepted the comment with a sigh. "What are your thoughts, Travel Master?" He hoped mentioning the title would jog an idea out of Tover.

"If we have to remove the rubble and distribute the goods, it will slow us. We'll lose hours of travel time. I dislike the idea of leaving half the caravan behind to wait, but I'll stay with them if I must. They'll need help to catch up."

Gavin muttered a curse unbecoming a baron at the lack of good options. "I'm not leaving people behind, even if it's only for a few hours."

He needed to adapt if he was to have any hope of protecting these people, and they needed to adapt as well. He climbed to the wagon seat and drew a deep breath. "Listen, everyone. I need every able set of hands to clear this mess to the side of the road. Master Vanwagner will supervise. If you can find room for anything useful, we keep it. Otherwise, we leave it. Make a place somewhere for all the food."

Gavin turned to the woman. "Once we camp, we will work out how to keep track of your things somehow. I promised that man's belongings to you, but I can't see how we can save all of your own things, let alone his. I'm sorry. These people will help you, but they only have so much to give. They're good people."

He felt like he was shattering her dreams as a few small belongings were bound together for the crying widow to carry on her back.

The bystanders swarmed the broken cart like ants and tossed it aside piece by piece, along with most of the common items inside. They stored a few small household things on other nearby wagons.

He hated himself for forcing her to leave her things. She deserved better, but he had no idea what else he could do.

The work proceeded quickly with so many hands to focus on the problem. With the debris moved, the tail of the caravan lurched back to life. At least they hadn't lost the rest of the day.

Tover followed Gavin up the line, quieter than normal. Perhaps he also felt the load of the caravan's failures, despite everything Tover had done to keep people moving. Ultimately, the responsibility was Gavin's.

They passed Lindy, and she curtsied to him. "Good day, sir. What was the delay?"

"We lost a wagon. I'm afraid we'll have more breakdowns as we travel, too. What resources do we have when things break down? I heard you recommended getting all the wagon replacement parts stored together, so we have a good start."

Lindy wiped at a spot on her sleeve, giving the matter some thought. "I've seen plans for this sort of thing, adapting to breakdowns and such. I'll have an answer for you this evening, if that works for you, sir."

"That would be wonderful. Tover, please meet with us tonight as well. As the Travel Master of this evacuation, we'll need to coordinate resources with you."

"Of course, good sir. I met with Lindy on the way out of Greenvale, as you asked." Tover gave her a bow, a bit more generous than the ones he offered even to Gavin, which broke through Gavin's sour mood and made it hard to stifle a grin as the two traded ideas. Tover and Lindy were hitting it off well.

High above, he saw an eagle riding on the mid-day thermals. What would it be like to be so carefree and confident? He cared about the people and was afraid he would disappoint them through his ignorance.

All he had accomplished at the broken wagon was to get punched in the face and make a few obvious choices to get people back on the road. Was that what counted for leadership? With luck, things would change when they reached Richland, a day and a half away. The town was big enough they could erect defenses and repel the invasion, or at least divert the invading army with the addition of the people and animals following him. They would no longer have to worry about outrunning the army on their tail.

With the threat of attack gone, he might even be able to spend more time with Saleena. He knew their friendship could never become romantic, no matter what they wanted. He was still the baron, even with the barony in ruins. He was responsible for everyone. There would be expectations and politics, and he would marry for some alliance or trade route once they turned away this blasted invasion. Nothing in his personal life was his to choose. His father would have said it was for the best.

Unless things got worse and they had no barony at all to go back to. Then he would be free. His heart took him down an imaginary trail of hopes and dreams until reality stepped in, and he saw how foolish such dreams were. Wishing for the failure of the barony? He had real issues to deal with, and couldn't afford such daydreaming. He couldn't abandon the people for Saleena or for anyone. He banished the dangerous thoughts from his mind. There was work to do. Maybe he would have time later to dream.

He looked up again. The eagle was gone.

GAVIN CONSIDERED the people who sat around the fire, and how they looked to him to lead, each for their own reasons. Draken, the masters from the barony, even Saleena, Tover and Lindy looked to him for decisions.

Draken arrived in a foul mood and fumed about his unexpected recruit. "What am I supposed to do with this untrained hothead? We can't train a proper army as we flee from the invasion. We don't even have weapons to issue."

Adrian melted out of the shadows and dropped a bundle on the ground with a loud clatter. "Sure, we do. We found twenty longswords and about as many long daggers, and an even dozen bows along with other assorted smaller blades. I can bring the rest later. Do you need anything else to expand your training program, Master Draken?"

Draken pulled out a blade and inspected the edge. "We'll always need more time to train, but this will help. This is nice workmanship. Northern make?"

Adrian nodded. "Some northern, some local. I liberated them from the garrison King Ithan left in Greenvale. I'm sure the king will be disappointed his men aren't holding the town as he planned."

Gavin's mouth hung open. He tried to wrap his head around the information and its implications. "They overran the town as we expected, then? What about the people who refused to leave?"

Adrian's eyebrows pinched together and he frowned. "We lost a few families who stayed behind with the idiot reeve who stormed out of your dinner meeting. The ones we convinced to leave arrived with me an hour ago. The army took no prisoners. Everyone who stayed behind died."

Draken shook his head. "Filthy butchers." He focused back on Adrian with a piercing gaze. "Did you recognize any of them?"

Adrian shrugged. "I didn't get too close while the main army was there. I didn't know any of the garrison men we killed." With an abrupt change of subject, Adrian continued, "Because of our work to scatter the wild game, the army has gone off the main road to search for hunting areas and to take villages my men haven't had time to reach with a warning. I followed the main road straight here. We slowed them down with our traps, but not enough. They'll still gain ground on us if we don't pick up our pace."

Gavin looked to his side where Tover sat. "Tover? Is there any word on moving farther each day?"

Tover deferred with a polite wave to Lindy, who stood. "Thank you for allowing me to meet with you. We've worked out some details to get us on the road an hour earlier each day by grouping people into larger camp units with specific assignments, and we're working through some details on how to limit the mid-day delays like breakdowns. We can flag wagons with spare capacity so we'll redistribute goods as needed. We don't have a lot of flexibility, but we know what we have now." She sat back down.

Gavin thought of the woman whose belongings were left beside the trail. They might have had room to carry all those things, but it was no use second-guessing his past choices.

He wondered at the details of Lindy's and Tover's work to organize the caravan, but it was useless information in his hands. They were best at what they did, and he had to trust them to do their jobs.

Master Quincy piped up from the shadows where he sat away from the fire. "I noticed you redirected several of my wagons and rearranged their inventory. Was it too much to arrange it with me first?"

Gavin pursed his lips, and then answered. "I'm sorry you weren't consulted, but with the breakdown of a wagon, we were at risk of stopping everyone a half day early. I doubt anyone wants to be a half day closer to the army behind us. Lindy acted at my request, so you can address any questions to me."

Master Quincy took a long pull on a drink. "Well, it figures you would have your fingers in the problem." Belatedly, he added, "Sir. The people line up to eat out of your hand like trained animals. I have a hard enough time keeping the trade goods isolated and protected. The last remaining wealth of the barony is at stake."

Lindy stirred, but Tover put a hand on her arm and glanced at Gavin.

Gavin wondered what to say as Tover and the others watched with concern. It came down to sacrifice. "If we must choose between speed and secure supplies, then security must bend. If we lose our speed, they will overrun us. Nothing else matters. I'm ready to listen if you have any suggestions which do not slow us down. If you have no suggestions, then join in on the conversation and work with everyone else. Can you do that?"

Master Quincy gave a reluctant nod. "Of course. I can assure you I will work with the others so long as they use common sense."

Gavin had given him little choice on how he could respond without losing face, yet Quincy had still twisted it to be about the failures of other people.

"Tover and Lindy, would you be sure to keep all the Masters informed on what we need to do to move faster? This is especially important if we need cooperation on anything under their authority." He made sure he had everyone's attention. "Our lives are at stake. Speed trumps property, ownership, and everything else if need be. Remember that."

Both Tover and Lindy gave enthusiastic agreement that they could work together with the various council members.

Draken placed the northern blade back into the bag and spoke. "People got jittery with the slowdown today. Maybe some extra training will keep some of them occupied in the evenings, rather than letting them wander around spreading rumors. With these weapons, I'll be able to take a small group of beginners for training."

Adrian said with a grin, "I'll give you names of men who will be better off worn out with weapon practice. I've spotted a few men I wish would stop stating their complaints quite so freely. They are bad for morale. Speaking of rumors, sir, the people believe you're secretly building an army of war animals to take the fight to the invaders."

Gavin spread his hands in frustration. "How do these things start? We're slowly creating some new crystals. We have a herd of cattle, some oxen, three cats, a few dogs and a couple wolves and half-wolves. They trapped a badger yesterday to add to the list. Only two from the entire list have actual war training, and one of them is still recovering from an injury. It's hardly an army."

Draken said, "Those animals, a few guards, some retired footmen, a few shadow skulks," he nodded at Adrian, "and some beginning trainees are what we have for our defenses. I'll pull the men Adrian refers to me with Captain Zachary, but the men will never be more than a few minutes of delay if the army catches up to us. We can't fight very many with what we have. Five hundred footmen and fifty war animals would make quick work of us, even with our growing numbers."

A girl stepped into the light of their campfire and whimpered. She was gagged, and her hands were tied.

Tover leaped up and ran to untie the gag as Lindy joined him to untie her hands. They helped the girl to sit on Lindy's lap, her arms around the girl. Her wrists and face were rubbed raw by the rough cloth, and she had claw marks on her arms.

Tover said, "Izzy, what happened?"

She took a ragged breath. "He said to bring you a message or he would hurt Ma and Pa." She held out a coin, her face pale. "You won't let him hurt them, will you, Master Tover?"

Tover took the coin and handed it to Gavin. It had a man's face on it, just like the box of coins Gavin had found in his treasury. It was a coin from the Graven Kingdom.

Gavin clenched his jaw and held in his outrage, not wanting Izzy to think he was mad at her. He should have known of the danger to Tover's messengers because of the killed cattle, and should have sent the children to their families already. He regained enough composure to say, "Tover, the children are done running errands for you. Warn everyone to keep children close. We don't have any way to keep spies from walking into camp."

He turned to Adrian, his voice dead and cold as his insides churned. "Adrian, please check with Captain Zachary about his patrols. I've had him out searching since we lost the two animals. It could be a single spy watching us."

Someone watching. Gavin remembered the eagle in flight above the caravan, and his eyes widened. How could he have been so stupid? "Izzy, are those claw marks on your arms from a large bird?"

She nodded.

Gavin turned to the members of his council. "I've seen an eagle flying overhead. If it's crystal controlled, the spy can watch us from above and know more than any ground observer would. He might even know more about our overall movements and specific challenges than we do. I want this man found. He threatens all of us by threatening one of us."

Adrian stood to look at the horizon, his knuckles white as he held the hilt of his knife. Through clenched teeth, he said, "This wasn't a threat. He's *taunting* us, sir. Trust me. I know this game by heart. It's time we put a little hunting party together and put some pressure on our spy."

CHAPTER

SIXTEEN

Something about the grass seemed off to Adrian as he examined it under the light of a nearly full moon. Bent and broken stalks of dry grass among the low sage urged him forward to investigate, but this assignment called for caution. He held up a hand, stopping both Captain Zachary and Ruffian instantly. The guard, Otis, lay back in the camp controlling and directing Ruffian. Otis was the only member of the hunting party to enjoy any degree of safety.

Adrian signaled Ruffian forward to sniff out the trail. The half-wolf padded up to Adrian under the control of his master. Ruffian pointed forward, and then crept farther along the faint trail, low to the ground.

Adrian followed a few steps behind, nearly as silent as the wolf. At least Captain Zachary knew his limits and held back farther where his noise was less likely to alert their quarry.

Ruffian stopped and pointed his nose at a patch of flattened grass. Their quarry was already gone.

"Of all the shattered luck," Adrian said. "He was here, probably until just after sunset. Any eagle droppings around?"

The half-wolf sniffed around, then pawed the ground exposing eagle and human waste buried under a thin layer of soil.

Captain Zachary crunched his way through the grass to the hidden mini-camp. "At least we've confirmed what we're up against. How do you see so well in the dark, Adrian?"

"Stop looking at the cooking fires and the moon. It ruins your night vision, and the fires aren't going anywhere. Any chance we can track him by smell from here?"

Ruffian pointed.

Adrian said, "Good. Let's get to it, then. He might have just moved ahead and camped for the night. We can track for an hour or two before we have to return and report in."

The darkness slowed them, but they made steady progress, with enough scent for the half-wolf to track. Two false trails led them away momentarily, but they tracked back and continued. The man they followed was clever, but not good enough to hide from both Adrian and the half-wolf.

Zachary's part of this mission was to provide extra muscle if and when they caught up to the man. So far, there were only signs of one man. That would make him an infiltrator, a spy. Someone trained to sneak in, observe, take out targets of opportunity, and then escape.

The half-wolf stopped and circled. The trail was a dead-end leaving them out in the grass and brush with no more clues.

Adrian knew the job and the methods used, but never relied on the additional abilities of a war-trained animal. He could think the way this man did. The false trails and the faint tracks painted a picture of a man afraid of getting caught. But Adrian would have been much more careful and left no camp signs or trail at all. That meant the man was careless. Unless...

Adrian turned to signal Zachary to stop.

His voice pitched just above the gentle wind, Adrian said, "The trail ends here, with no sign of backtracking. He's better than I thought. He must have known he was being followed and led us out here on purpose."

Zachary said in the same hushed tones, "Ambush, or trap? I always prefer to know how I'm about to die."

"He's almost certainly solo. That means it's a trap. Let's back out on the trail we came in on. Slowly."

Even Zachary could follow the trail he'd left through the grass, so he led the way.

Fifty paces along their return trail, Adrian heard a snap at Zachary's feet and saw the tripwire.

Instinct kicked in. Adrian jumped forward and plowed into Zachary's back, pushing him to the ground. A small metal projectile whizzed overhead and into the dark, just missing Adrian's neck.

Zachary rolled onto his back and looked up, spitting out grass and dirt. "How about you give me a breather and go first for a while?"

"Right." Adrian had underestimated his opponent twice now. Not only was he good enough to lay a false trail or no trail at all, he watched them and booby trapped their return path. He was close, but he was also ready and waiting for them.

Was it worth risking the lives of Captain Zachary and a war trained half-wolf? His life was never on the scales when Adrian measured the potential cost. He would go to the beyond when it was his time, but his companions deserved more time to live, and he shied away from risking them against more traps with little chance of success. Perhaps Adrian could force his opponent into making a mistake if he played everything just right.

Raising his voice, he said, "I'm calling it. We're done chasing for the night. He's outfought me in my own head. He might still be watching, so get ready to sprint this way, and not right next to each other." Adrian pointed perpendicular to the trail, and slightly toward their camp.

Switching back to a subdued whisper, he continued, "I'm not running with you. Go out two hundred steps, then straight back to camp at your best speed. If he's still watching, he may take a shot. Otis, weave as you run Ruffian to camp. Zachary, you just run. You'll weave just fine on your own. Whatever you do, don't fall."

Zachary gave a crooked grin. "Your confidence warms my heart. You have my candle promise."

"And you have mine." It was an old army phrase, a promise to burn a candle if you came out alive where others didn't.

Adrian nocked an arrow in his horn bow while still on the ground out of sight, then counted down for them. "Three, two, one, run."

His two companions took off, and Adrian eased into a bush to watch along the optimal viewing path to where he would have hidden to watch this spot. Would the spy make a mistake after such a flawless performance? It was worth waiting to find out.

He settled his aim on the most likely clump of brush and counted out until his friends were at close to maximum range for a bow or crossbow.

There. A slight movement in the brush, out of sync with the wind. A glint of moonlight catching on something besides branches and leaves.

Adrian's ploy to send just his companions had kept the man from firing and exposing his position. His friends were safe because the tables had been turned momentarily. The watcher was now watched. Adrian expected no hesitation if the spy showed himself in the moonlight.

Adrian held his breath, aimed, and let his arrow fly through the night air.

He was rewarded with the sound of splintering wood and a grunt from the brush. He might have hurt his quarry, but the arrow could have hit a branch or glanced off the man's armor. Adrian whispered, "Tag. You're it."

Adrian crept toward the man's hiding spot in the brush, staying below the tops of the grass. He never saw his opponent leave, but his enemy's last known position was empty when he got there.

SALEENA WATCHED over Willem while he lay in a trance on his bedroll. The Cats of the Apocalypse ran through an intricate training routine to learn new techniques for hunting together while she rested. She had spent far too much time today controlling the cattle to keep them from slowing the caravan.

She peered out into the field searching for Willem's small predators, but was unable to catch a hint of the cats as he directed them to their prey. A raven sat on a low branch a couple of stone throws away from the edge of the camp. It had followed them for days and swooped in to pick up left-over food whenever it found something unguarded. Willem's job was to capture the bird, rather than allow the cats to follow their instinct to treat this as a food hunt.

A flutter of wings caught Saleena's attention as the bird showed interest in something on the ground. Saleena let out a dejected sigh. The bird saw the danger and was about to fly when Skull Crusher ran up the rear of the trunk and launched herself from directly behind the raven. The calico wrapped her front paws around the distracted bird and dropped to the ground with it.

Despite her exhaustion, Saleena leaped to her feet and made her way out into the field. She pulled one of the smaller crystals from a pouch on her hip. The cats held the bird down so it wouldn't be hurt, and she gently eased past the extended claws and teeth to attach the crystal via a special harness. A simple collar wouldn't work on a bird, so she used a set of tiny straps to hold the stone in place against its breast to keep it near both mind and heart. The crystal might work strapped to a leg, but they didn't have a lot of time to experiment. Once the crystal was on, she wrapped her hands around the raven and held its wings close, then said in a soft tone meant to calm the bird, "I've got it. Great job."

Saleena marveled at how well the cats accepted training hints and directions from Willem as a team while Willem provided their high-level tactics. Over time, the cats filled in more and more of the details to match what Willem wanted them to accomplish. They didn't need to be told to use a particular swipe of their claws or to crouch down while stalking. Willem had advanced to where Saleena had nothing to teach him.

The Cats of the Apocalypse backed off. She saw Willem drop his control over them and noted the change in behavior as they turned to trot back to the edge of camp, ears forward and tails held high like flags announcing their pride at the victory over the raven.

Willem sat up as the cats arrived to settle in on his blanket for some much-deserved attention and praise.

With the crystal attached, it might have been safe to let the bird go, but Saleena wanted to keep an eye on it and begin its training up close. Her makeshift cage of willow twigs and string would hold the bird, at least for the start of its training.

Saleena placed the bird in the cage along with a generous crust of bread and a small plate of water. Once she secured the raven, she reached for the matching crystal and was about to put it on when Willem stopped her with his hand on her forearm. "You're too tired to train it. You can't do every-thing. We can find someone else, or I can train the bird."

"But I so want to fly, to view the land from above and see things from a whole new direction. It sounds beautiful."

Willem grinned. "You could fly up there and poop on the caravan."

Saleena scowled. "You have a chance at the ultimate freedom of flying, and all you can think of is poop? Boys."

"No, really. Swoop in on the new baron and let loose from above. He's avoided you for days now, so you can get even with him and put a new stain on his leather armor."

Her scowl increased. "Gavin hasn't avoided me. He's been busy. I've attended his council meetings to tell them about how crystal training is going. He has all these people to lead, and I'm only one of them. There will be time to be friends again later when all this is over." She stared out at the fading sun as it approached the rolling plains to the west.

"Yeah, but what about the two of you? You haven't even been for a walk alone with him since before this all started, have you?"

She shrugged. "It's not like that. We're not as close as we used to be, but we work together for all these people." She waved her hand to include the whole camp. She hoped to convince herself as much as she hoped to convince Willem. "It's important work, and I've been busy, too. We've made saddlebags for some of the cattle so they can carry more, and we have litters they pull along behind. They take turns on the litters because they're heavier. They're used to the loads now because of the training I've done, so I won't have to control them as much anymore. I'm contributing in ways I never dreamed of."

Adrian sat next to Saleena, who let out a squeal of surprise. With her hands raised almost to her throat, she blurted out, "I thought you only jumped out at Gavin."

Adrian grinned like a jester. "Really, Saleena, I must keep up on my practice or my reputation as a sneak will be destroyed."

He inclined his head to Willem and said with a sly grin, "She's beating around the bush. She meant to say Baron Stoutheart won't chase you off if you wish to spend time together."

Saleena stared at Adrian, her cheeks flushed with embarrassment. Despite her open mouth, words fled and she failed to come up with a reply.

Willem looked away. "But I was only –"

Adrian held up a hand. "Don't ruin the moment. Anything you say will just muddy the water." He looked over to Saleena. "So, on a different subject. What's the farthest you've ever controlled an animal from?"

Saleena took a few deep breaths. Once her heart slowed, she said, "I've gone as far as a couple thousand paces. A better crystal could probably go farther."

"Good. Willem, your cats like bird watching, right?"

"They're cats, so yes. We just caught a raven."

Adrian raised an eyebrow, but let the comment pass. "Keep an eye out for an eagle when we're on the road. It's got a crystal. If we watch where it flies, we may be able to spot the center of its range and surprise a spy."

Adrian picked up one of Saleena's new saddlebags. "That's not bad. Where do you get the leather? Do you tan it yourself?"

Saleena nodded. "We managed to pack a couple of brine barrels, but those hides are from storage. We haven't had to butcher any cattle yet, so Willem's used the barrels to tan some smaller hides. Actually, several dozen smaller hides. The cats are good hunters now. It's scary how well they do. They can sneak and use each other for distractions as a team."

Adrian smiled at Willem and fingered his iron collar. "So, what do you do with the rest of the meat? The cats can't possibly eat everything they catch with that many hides."

Saleena stood up and would have left, but Adrian said, "Please stay. I hadn't expected it to be such a delicate subject."

She pouted. How could he be so insensitive? He had to be doing it on purpose. "Some spy you are. I thought you knew everything about everyone by now. Go ahead, Willem. I don't mind." It was a lie to claim she didn't mind, but she would endure the conversation anyway.

Willem grinned. "She doesn't like the thought of eating small critters, particularly rats and other vermin. I'm not sure why. Big critters, little critters, they're pretty much the same inside. They're different flavors, but not too different." He shrugged. "I've fed Master Draken's wolf all she can eat for days. She's mostly healed now, so we've sent the cats out hunting with the wolf a couple of times already."

Adrian clapped his hands together. "That's wonderful. Let me know if you find something big out there and I'll assist you in catching it. We still have a crystal pair big enough to control a full-size war animal. Just don't go too far, or our little spy friend will see you as a tempting target."

Saleena said, "You mean to tell me that you aren't using the crystal from the bear yet?"

Adrian gave her a mock look of dismay. "You injure me! Of course, it's in use, but I would like to put it to better use if you find something good."

He looked at the cats and the raven and pursed his lips. "Maybe I should think small and sneaky instead."

He stood and strode into the shadows of the night. "No time for more questions. There is much to do, and many people to see before I sleep."

Saleena tried to track him as he crossed into the camp but lost sight of him moments later.

She whispered under her breath, "Secretive jerk."

Off to the other side of the wagons came Adrian's voice, "I heard that."

CHAPTER

SEVENTEEN

Gavin's excitement fell when he saw Richland. Smoke came from only a handful of the town's old brick chimneys. It took quite a bit of discussion across a large field before the guards believed they were not the invaders and let the front riders approach. With most of the town gone, except for a few outliers and those slow to pack, Gavin's hopes of joining forces had come to naught, and it left him in a sour mood. He came into town with Draken and Adrian to meet with Captain Haverson who led the remains of the city guard.

A large stone hall stood on the square in the center of town, its doors open. It combined city hall and barracks into a single structure that shared walls with its neighbors. Stone was a rarity in the plains, and the buildings on the town square were the only sign of such sturdy construction. Two guards nodded at the men escorting them. They entered and were led to a side room where the captain kept an office. It took a bit of effort and shuffling to get everyone into the small space.

Captain Haverson stood from his heavy desk. "Please sit, Baron Stoutheart. I hope I don't have to mention how anyone caught looting within my jurisdiction will be dealt with most harshly. We are beyond the borders of your barony, and we are not under your rule. You are a guest here."

Gavin sat on the offered chair, faced the Captain, and waved his hand to dismiss the worries. "Of course. If we wish to make use of anything within the town, we'll see your people first. We would be happy for any of your remaining residents to join us as we journey to the capital. Even combining your people and mine, we don't have enough to make a stand here. Speaking of jurisdiction, do you have a new baron?"

Captain Haverson nodded as he seated himself. "Baron Watterson is our previous baron's cousin. He decided to evacuate when we heard of the incoming army. I believe the messengers we received are from your group."

Adrian nodded. "We sent some men ahead. They've reported back to me."

Captain Haverson leaned back in his chair and pointed to a map on the wall. "The baron led them East through the hills to a refuge. Once they reach it, they should be safe."

Gavin drummed his fingers. "East? Adrian, what's the latest on the army behind us? Didn't you tell me they cut through the eastern countryside rather than follow the main road?"

Adrian's men had been in and out since joining the caravan, and they kept up a long-range view of the incoming army. If anyone knew where they were, it was his men.

"Our men should have warned your baron. They may run into the invasion force before they reach the refuge. I'm expecting a new report any time on the position of the army. My latest information is a couple of days old."

Captain Haverson stared at the table before him before he replied. "Your men told the baron about the dangers, and how the enemy could be right in his path. Your men did their job, but Baron Watterson felt a short trip to the refuge was better than a much longer journey to the capital, even with the added danger. However his trip turns out, it's too late for us to change anything. They'll either make it past, or they'll be ripped to shreds. They have a couple war animals and most of the city guard with them. The refuge has a steep entry that's easy to defend, but the entry defenses won't help if they're all dead before they get there."

Gavin stood up as a somber mood took over his thoughts. "Every day I hope I don't forget something that could save lives, and now every day I hear about people who die or are in danger. Some villages have it much worse than us. Those who stayed behind in Greenvale were butchered. I think we've learned everything we can here, and must keep moving. Let's hope for the best and prepare for the worst."

Adrian interrupted before anyone could leave. "There's one thing we're forgetting. If they catch Baron Watterson and his people, it will speed the army up because of all the supplies they will take. We can't spend more than one night here. We're a tempting target. I will send messengers when my eastern scouts report to me. As for your earlier assignment to watch for a spy, I've seen where someone's slept in the fields near us, but he's good at hiding his trail, even from a hound. Assume King Ithan knows where we are and what we're doing. That's a lot more than we know about him."

Several of Captain Haverson's men muttered curses and imprecations as they stood around the table, all aimed at the army that drove them from their homes.

They adjourned and left the town hall. Richland was in a more settled and stable area of the plains far from the border, so it had no defensive castle as Stoutheart Barony had. Instead, shops and homes made of wood filled the streets, and the town square had plank boardwalks that ran before the large buildings, attaching their porches and entries to one another with a common path free of the mud of the street. It was a luxury they had yet to achieve in the village at Stoutheart Castle.

The rumors among his people continued to paint Gavin as a great hero, but his own self-examination left him wanting. He wasn't what the people said he was, and spreading those rumors wouldn't turn him into something he wasn't. It was both maddening and depressing as he compared himself to the flawless version people built in their imaginations.

He cared for the people and wanted to spare them from destruction at the hands of the invaders, but his actions merely postponed the inevitable. He needed a better plan. He needed more help.

———

GAVIN EXAMINED the other large buildings in the town square with their plastered and painted fronts where they flanked the town hall. Most were abandoned and boarded up. He imagined they had held guild and trade offices before being sealed. One exception was the chapel, which stood with its doors open and lamps lit, indicating a Priest of Order was in residence.

Gavin stopped to inspect the white plastered building, the religious heart of the town. It had been months since he'd had a conversation with one of the visiting priests who came around to the remote baronies like his father's. No, it was his barony now, not his father's. He could use someone to talk to who might straighten out his thoughts on what he must do.

He stepped through the door.

His personal guard had been such a universal presence that he often forgot he was there, always in the background. Some things were better done without his ever-present armed shadow. "Jase, please wait outside. I don't imagine this will take long."

"Of course, sir." Jase took position outside the door, standing at parade rest.

The large hall inside glowed with the flickering of lamps and candles casting their light on the polished stone walls. The oily smell of the lamps reminded Gavin of the castle back home. He walked to the front of the chapel and said, "Hello?"

A voice came from a narrow exit to the side. "Visitors? I thought the town was nearly empty. Welcome. Welcome." A short, muscular man dressed in a rough, gray robe entered and held his hand on his heart before extending it to Gavin for a firm handshake. "I'm Brother Cleo."

"I'm Gavin Stoutheart, new Baron of a land already overrun by King Ithan."

"Yes, we caught wind of the terrible news a few days back. My condolences on the loss of your father and brother. Well, then, I'll correct myself. I'm Brother Cleo, *sir*, unless you would prefer I call you Brother Stoutheart." His demeanor showed he was serious about the correction in addressing Gavin as was a baron's due. Gavin didn't respect his title enough to ask for protocol, let alone insist on it.

Gavin sat on the end of the nearest pew. "Call me whatever you're most comfortable with. The issue with titles and respect is part of my problem. Everyone looks to me and sees this great respectable person that only exists in their heads."

Brother Cleo nodded. "I see. Tell me about yourself. I'll set aside my preconceived notions and formalities."

Gavin took a deep breath and let his frustrations flow out. "I'm an ordinary man, barely more than a child. I skipped out on training through elaborate schemes. I dodged responsibility at every opportunity, and now I'm faced with the job of leading people when I'm not what they believe me to be. I feel so unqualified it's astounding they haven't rebelled and chosen someone better suited. I've stepped up because I want to help, but they deserve better than me."

Brother Cleo nodded and prompted Gavin to continue. It reminded Gavin of his technique where he asked questions and let others fill in the details while he weighed and considered his options.

"Most of the time I don't know what to do. I take my best guess, and luckily the only people to die under my command so far died by not following me. It still hurts, and they're still my people who died. As if my lack of skills wasn't bad enough, I've granted immunity to anyone who has experience using crystals and handed them out to anyone who can help. I'm using the people who violated the law and forged their own crystals as trainers and leaders. Everyone appeals to me as the ultimate authority, but I'm not. I'll have to go before our king, once we have one, and answer for my people, and for the things I've allowed. I've even violated some of the Accords of the Crystal Kings, all to keep the people alive and away from the army on our tail. Can you tell me where I'm going wrong, and what I need to do?"

Brother Cleo's face registered brief shock before he recovered with a genuine smile. "No, I can't tell you how to survive your trials. I'm sorry, but I've found telling people what to do rarely helps. Sometimes I preach, but mostly I tell stories. I'm afraid the best advice you'll get out of me is to learn *why* you do things, rather than to be told what to do. You will answer your questions for yourself once you are ready.

"I can tell the men and women to be good to their spouses, to be honest, and to do all the other things people should do. All those instructions are meaningless until someone *wants* to hear them. Until then I tell stories. When people are ready to understand the messages, they use those stories to tell themselves what they need to know, and why it's important. Like my regular visitors, you are responsible for your own choices and their consequences, even though you are influenced by your advisers and councilors. If they're good men, you'll get good advice, and it will help you to make good choices."

"About that. My current council includes a young woman barely old enough to marry, who was one of the first I had to pardon for violating two of the Accords. I've got a supposedly reformed criminal whom our dead king and my father forced to wear the animal side of a crystal set. I violated the third Accord right there, but I destroyed that master crystal once I knew what was going on. He's my source of intelligence. I've entrusted my supply chain management to a woman who owned an inn and tap house, and I've assigned a cattle herder as Travel Master to motivate the people to move forward each day. That's a good portion of my council."

Brother Cleo barely suppressed his laughter. "It seems to me you have no problem at all in deciding what to do. You've racked up quite a list of changes few are brave enough to make."

Brave enough? Gavin had never considered himself brave. "But that's not even the biggest issue. I want them to be safe and taken care of, and here we are running before an army that gains on us daily and destroys anything in its path. The people would be better off with an experienced baron who knows what they're doing, but it's my job. I'm doing my best, but I'm afraid my best is not enough to save them."

Brother Cleo's mirth became somber as he nodded. "So, it all seems to come down to why. It always does. A father asked his son, as he did every morning and evening, to milk the cows. There was snow on the ground, and the boy didn't want to get up. One morning, he gathered his courage and asked why he must milk the cows. The father, being the patient sort, explained how the cows must be milked or they would first become miserable, and then would stop giving milk. Not content with the answer, the boy asked not why the job had to be done, but why he was the one who had to do it. The patient father explained further how the boy was not yet big enough for the work the father did all day. The boy's mother was also busy with her workload of midwifery, spinning, weaving, cooking, and caring for the boy's little sister. The father, rather than force the boy from bed, gave him these parting words as he left to perform his labors. 'If not you, then who?'"

Gavin said, "You made that story up off the top of your head right here in front of me, didn't you?"

"Does it matter?" Cleo winked, and his smile returned. "Why did you pardon those people? What is more important than the Accords? Why is it you trust your advisers? Why are you even here, leading this evacuation? It must be deeper than their expectations."

Gavin considered before he replied. "I pardoned them to make use of what they know. I trust them because they haven't let me down. They know what they're doing, and they're good at what they do. Everything I've done was because I thought it was necessary. I led the people here with a hope of safety. Sometimes I wonder if they're in more danger because of me and what I do."

Brother Cleo ran a finger along the top of the old wooden pew. "They say the pookas did the same thing with us humans. Untold generations ago, a man was approached by a cat who said he could make him wealthy. The man agreed, and the creature transformed into a pooka and taught him how to create the crystals used to control animals. We have some ability the pookas lacked, or they saw something in us worth helping. But by giving us that power, they also put us in danger of each other when that power is misused."

Gavin had never heard a story about pookas before and was intrigued. "Why did they do it? Why give such power away?"

"Trust. Necessity. Vision. Fear. Some combination of all four. You said you've done what was necessary. I admire your good start, but it's only a start. The next step is to ask if you did what you knew was right. I think you know what's right for your people, but all those reasons you gave don't dig deep enough."

Brother Cleo pondered the wooden beams of the ceiling in thought before he continued. "You believe these advisers and all the others are worth something to you, as more than merely another subject of your barony. You've promised to stand up and represent yourself as responsible for their actions before the king. You've done much more than make use of people because of their skills. I see why they believe you are up to the task. What do your people say about you?"

Gavin balled his fists. "They spread wild stories about me, and how I'm this great leader who eats bears for breakfast and slays armies with my burning eyeballs. They see something I'm not."

"As a Priest of Order, I've been reduced at times to telling people that it's none of their business what others think of them. What matters is within them. In your case, I'll make an exception since you are responsible for your people. What they think makes a difference because of your position."

Gavin raised his hands in the air. "But I don't know what to do about it."

Brother Cleo folded his hands in his robe. "I know of two fathers who each had the same goal, to build a barn. One reached his goal through threats, bullying, and force, and soon his family finished the barn. The other compelled his family through love, sacrifice, and teaching. The second family built their barn about as quickly as the first one had. What might their families think of these two fathers? They both got the job done with the help of family, didn't they?"

"That's a false question, Brother Cleo. The barn isn't the important part of the story."

"Right, you are. Later in life, those fathers both grew old and frail, unable to continue their work. They each asked their children for a home in which to spend their sunset years."

Gavin said, "Let me guess. One got banished to his barn instead?"

"No. They were both given small homes in which they lived comfortably. The children of the first, you recall, feared him. When the end came, the one passed from this life huddled next to the embers of his lonely fire, while the other passed on surrounded by those he loved and who loved him."

"But this one doesn't match your other story. The two fathers show the importance of how you do things, where the first is about obligation."

Cleo leaned back in the pew. "Yes, on the surface you see what each story is about. Like any principle, there's infinite depth to the meaning of stories below the surface, and principles never stand in isolation. Everything is interconnected."

"If it will help us to stay ahead of the army, I'm all for changing the way I do things. I don't see anyone else stepping up to own the problem, or being pushed forward, like in your first story. If not me, then who? Then there's the second lesson; if not this way, then how? I think I see what you mean, with combining the two."

Cleo stood. "Then my work for the moment is done. I want you to become the leader they need. I want you to meet their expectations more than I want you to meet your own because I don't worry about your expectations. I want you to be wise, thoughtful, just, brave, and noble. But what I want doesn't matter in the least. What do you want, deep down inside? Search it out in your heart. There's no need to tell me your answer. I'm not the one who feels the need for change. I'm asked sometimes to judge matters of faith and the heart. You don't need either." He placed his hand over his heart.

It was a lot to digest. The people expected more from Gavin all the time, but Brother Cleo was right. They deserved a leader who was their champion and protector, and he was all they had. He had no choice but to step up and make whatever difference he could, because he cared enough to do what nobody else wanted to do. No, saying he merely cared enough was avoiding the truth. He loved his people.

He might as well admit it out loud where it would commit his course. "It's about love, isn't it? My love for the people."

Brother Cleo smiled. "You've found the greatest motivator. It's the foundation of what you do and why you do it in any trial." He set about blowing out all the candles, a clear indication that their conversation had covered everything the priest had intended.

The rumors inflated everyone's view. He would have to work harder to meet those expectations because it gave the people hope, something they needed as danger threatened. It would still be hard for both the people and Gavin, but it was the right choice.

Gavin thanked Brother Cleo and left the chapel only to find Brother Cleo following on his heels through the door. He closed and latched the door, then fell in beside Jase as they made their way back to the camp outside town.

"What are you doing, Brother Cleo?"

"I'm going with you, sir. I wouldn't miss this for the world."

As they left the town square, Gavin spotted the Cats of the Apocalypse running through the streets together, each carrying something. It must be another training run.

Near the edge of town, a man on a horse leaned over to talk with a man who looked familiar. Before they reached the two, the man on foot waved and ran off back to the camp. Gavin finally placed him as the man who had hit him in the face back at the broken wagon.

Gavin held a hand back to get Jase's attention. "Careful, we might have trouble here."

The man on the horse sat up and turned to leave, but pulled up short as he saw Gavin. "You're Baron Stoutheart?"

The saddle on the horse was cavalry issue, designed to allow for the rider to strap in and slip into a remote trance without falling off. The horse wore a crystal within a harness about its neck. This was no ordinary rider or horse. They were a crystal-trained pair. Nearly everyone considered it insane to take the risks cavalry riders took.

Jase tensed to Gavin's left, and Brother Cleo took a step forward on his right. "Yes, I am. Is there something I can do for you?"

"I've heard a lot about you." He gestured back to where he and the other man had spoken. "I want to hear about you firsthand."

Even though the rider breached several rules of etiquette, Gavin didn't care. He needed skilled people to join with the exodus to keep them away from the incoming army. Antagonizing people would not get him what he needed, and this man had military experience.

"Ah, I see. He and I had a problem on the road the other day. I don't know what he told you, but I stripped him of his property and assigned him to the guard for training to keep him busy and make use of his skills. He has quite a haymaker." Gavin rubbed his chin.

"Huh. The way he tells it, you saved him from getting sliced to ribbons by the people in your caravan after he assaulted you. Then you put him in a position of trust to be trained to defend the same people that wanted to stick him to the ground. It didn't make a lot of sense to me, and I thought he might have stretched the truth."

Gavin smiled, remembering the conversation with Brother Cleo. He needed to work to become what the people wanted him to be, and what they thought he was. This one seemed easier since both sides of the story were true, but colored by personal experience. "I gave him the benefit of the doubt. The people were ready to kill him, so I found a compromise. We can't go around killing people because the rules say we can. We need everyone we can get on our side. We've got to get these people to safety and combine forces if we're to have any chance of winning against the invasion behind us. We need to put things back together."

The cavalryman eased his mount in sideways and extended his hand. "I'm Rider Faven."

Gavin grasped Faven's rough hand. It would be a wonderful boon to get an actual cavalryman to join with them. "Will you join us on the road?"

Faven shook his head. "There's too much to do. I'll see you in the capital." He saluted, turned, and trotted his horse past the edge of the town before he broke into a gallop.

Brother Cleo stood with his mouth open as Faven rode out of sight. "Do you have any idea what you've done? He saluted you."

"What's that got to do with anything? He was military. They salute each other all the time."

Brother Cleo shook his head. "No, the order of who salutes who is important among cavalrymen and works differently than you might expect. It's not just important; it means absolutely everything. Junior officers salute only the senior officers in their chain of command. He's accepted you as his commander. He took whatever you said to him as instructions, not as opinions or idle conversation."

Jase nodded. "I never worked with them, but I've heard the same of them. They're an interesting bunch, stricter about chains of command than any men I know."

Gavin ran a few steps forward and peered into the distance, but saw no more sign of Faven. Whatever he'd ridden off to do was out of Gavin's control now. He couldn't remember all the details of what he had said. Gathering people? Something about working together. If he'd known more about the way the cavalry worked, he might have built a better plan. It was a lost opportunity, like when he discovered most of the residents of Richland were gone. Plans were thrown out over and over as he discovered new information and made new plans.

"We're picking up more people on the road and from the villages, and they're all untrained refugees. I'm barely ahead of an enemy army, people think I'm here to save them, and I accidentally gave useless orders to our best chance at a real combat force, and I can't recall him to fix the problem. Keep an eye out to see where the folks of Richland gather to drink and gossip. There must be a tavern that hasn't been boarded up yet. Maybe a pint will make me feel less stupid."

Jase said, "Begging your pardon, sir, but strong drink doesn't work like that. You can trust my sad experience. The best it will do is make you care a little less for a few hours."

"Caring a little less will do for now. Ah, there's something." Gavin approached a building with a sign hanging from the eves depicting a frothy mug, but the tap room windows were dark. Wagons loaded near to capacity sat at the back of the building where men worked to place and tie down loads. Gavin overheard a man with a knapsack as he talked to the workers.

"We didn't leave Greenvale when he asked us to, and we nearly died. If not for the men he left behind to set traps and save us, we would have been fed to bears. I seen them myself, I did. The rescue was a mercy we didn't deserve, so I'm for Baron Stoutheart. You should come with us too. It will be a good bit safer than going south on your own. He's been right every time. He got us all moving to safety, those who listened or were rescued after our foolishness. We're training more people to use crystals for war animals, and we're training men to fight. Once we have enough people, he'll lead us to beat the whole Graven army."

The workers looked to the man tying the load. He nodded. "You make a good case. I'll think about it."

The man with the knapsack said, "We've got a little gathering planned tonight in our camp. Meet some of our people. See where you can help. I hear they're roasting one of the cattle."

Gavin scowled at Jase. "If I walk over there, they'll be disappointed I don't have wings and ride a unicorn. Did you know about this event at the camp?"

Jase grinned. "I've been with you the whole time, sir. I deny all knowledge of any party planned to improve the morale of a bunch of people who are tired of walking day after day. But it might help matters if I get this pack of herbs to Lindy soon." He patted a pouch tied to his belt.

CHAPTER

EIGHTEEN

Saleena had no choice when one of her herd came up lame. It wouldn't be able to keep up, so it was a matter of butchering it while they camped or losing it on the side of the road where they might not be able to make use of it at all. She was protective of Gavin's herd, but acknowledged they were there to feed the people.

Things were a little different on the road than they had been back home. They had no time for formal feasts while traveling, or all the racks and equipment to handle butchering. But what they did have was spare labor. A lot of people were able to help, so she assigned as many as possible to strip the animal down to the bone.

One of her volunteers, a young father of two with a wife, set some bones aside, not fully stripped of meat.

"No, we need to get as much off those as we can."

He gave her an apologetic look. "I was hoping to take those bones for my family if I could. I was going to ask."

She noticed his hollow cheeks and shaky hands as he continued to work.

"When was the last time you ate, Goodman?"

"You see, we only have enough to feed the children every day, so I've skipped a few meals. It's not that bad."

Her voice grew firm. "How long?"

He hesitated, and then said, "Only two days this time."

Saleena stared. "You've given all your food to your children? I thought we had enough to go around to care for everyone."

"I don't want to be a burden. We left home before harvest and had to carry the children. They're not big enough to walk all day. If I might just take the bones, we could make some soup."

"No, that's not how this will work." She pulled a generous slice from the growing pile of deboned meat and handed it to him along with the bones.

"Didn't you know we were doing this for a common feast? Bring everyone. And you take this for your family. The bones, too, if you want them still. I'll get you some flour tomorrow from the barony supplies."

The man said, "But what will Baron Stoutheart think? I've heard he's unpredictable. If he makes us leave, we'll starve."

"No, he's a different kind of unpredictable. He'll likely think I wasn't generous enough. My guess is he'll take a tour looking for more hungry people in the caravan. My only worry is that Master Quincy will get in the way until Gavin forces him into line. Don't worry about that. Now, go and get your family. You will all eat everything you can manage tonight."

A tear ran down his cheek as he placed a hand on his heart. He turned and hurried off.

How many were like him, who didn't dare, or were too proud, to ask for the help they needed? Saleena didn't know how much food the caravan carried, but if she hadn't gone hungry yet, there must be enough to share with those who had nothing.

Like that father and his wife, she would go hungry herself before she let another child go without.

SALEENA WRAPPED both fore shanks from the animal and packed them onto her back intending to drop them off with Lindy, who occupied a large kitchen in town to make use of the ovens and hearth. As Saleena approached, she saw a stream of people delivering things to or from the kitchen. She saw serving platters, fruits, vegetables, bread, and many packages. Lindy's children, Chase and Finney, were among the people in what seemed to be chaos, but everyone flowed through with a definite purpose.

Lindy waved to her as Saleena entered the kitchen. "Bring those legs right over to this table, dear." She waved a sizable knife to where she was stripping the meat from some small game and tossing it into a pot. "We'll put those to roast in the hearth right over there. They'll make a great presentation there while everyone's busy with all the coming and going."

Saleena said, "I can get them set up on a spit for you if you're busy." The small game in front of Lindy caught her attention. "You, ah, didn't get all that from the Cats of the Apocalypse, did you?"

She still unintentionally made things hard for Willem when they were together, despite enjoying his company and friendship. Their conversations had lengthened and ranged over a lot more than just the crystal training. She learned gratitude from him through his infectious positive attitude, yet she still held back. His occasional touch on her arm or hand as they talked sent a flutter through her. Maybe it was time she let her disagreements go and stopped silently expecting him to meet her ideals.

Lindy raised an eyebrow and gave her a stern glance. "Now don't pay any mind to everyone else's part here. We won't have anyone go hungry if I have a say, and I'll use whatever gets offered. Still, it would help if everyone believes we're serving beef stew.

"Salt everything you didn't bring here. We'll need it in about a week if I'm counting right. People will be tired of things we dig up in the wild if we're not to the capital by then. Everyone does their part, and we're better off for it. You might even say we're improving as we go. Oh, and be sure to make a show of tanning the hide, too. The presentation is half the battle for morale."

Lindy kept speaking to her, but Saleena's thoughts were still on Willem and she couldn't remember what Lindy had just said.

Lindy said, "See, there he is."

She waved a man over and spoke to him. "This is Saleena, the young woman I told you about. She can tell you about our cattle." Looking back at Saleena she continued, "This is Royn. He's a local tanner and leather-worker, and he'll be joining the caravan. He just got back from a trade trip and missed the town's first evacuation. He has a dozen head of cattle to add to the herd if you can manage the addition."

He nodded a greeting. "Mistress Lindy has told me about you and your father. I'll be glad to team up to manage the combined herd. She says you've done some interesting things with the cattle using crystals."

Saleena said, "The baron issued a pardon to anyone who can help with crystal training in any way at all. We're doing what we can." She remembered her work to put saddlebags on the cattle, and asked, "How many tanned hides do you have?"

"Quite a few. The sad part is only a few are supple enough for clothing or bags. I gathered supplies on this last trip for an order of armor for the town guard and have a lot of unused heavy boiled hides. They're not much use except for shoe soles if I'm not making armor."

Saleena had made things from similar leather before while assisting her father. Her skills had grown as she helped Tover and the local leather workers turn leather into breastplates like the one Gavin wore, as well as vambraces and greaves when steel was too heavy. It had to be split to be thin enough for anything else. "My father is busy with the caravan most of the time, so I'll make a spot for you in camp. I've got an idea on how to use your leather, but it will take a lot of work."

He waved and headed out as he called back, "I'll see you there."

A woman in a dirty apron came in with a large load of cattails, and another with a sack of tubers which had been harvested from along the road. Lindy waved directions to them and called out to some volunteer cooks to dive into the preparations on the new deliveries. The room had several wash basins as well as piles of fruit and vegetables in various states of preparation. Saleena had no idea how Lindy kept track of so much all at once, but it was clear she knew where everything was and what needed to happen next as everyone prepared for the impromptu feast.

Willem entered and dropped off a lidded basket. Saleena tagged along behind him when he left, and grabbed his arm once they were out in the street. He jumped at the unexpected hand, but let out a sigh of relief at the sight of Saleena. "Oh, it's you. That's quite the kitchen she's running there."

Saleena thought of what Lindy had said to her about each person doing their part, and how it helped the camp to not only survive, but thrive. "Willem, I wanted to say something to you."

"Say away." He eyed her suspiciously.

She clasped and released her hands nervously and looked around, not sure how to begin, and then stopped and met his gaze. "I'm sorry I looked down on you when we started working together. I thought less of you, thought bad things before I got to know you. I've learned a lot, but sometimes I'm slow at it. I'm glad you're my friend. You've done great things with the cats and in training others. We're doing things nobody's ever done, as far as I know. I've held back because of the first opinion I had of you. It wasn't fair of me, and it's time I let it go."

He smiled at her. "That's the nicest thing I've ever heard. I bet you'll still skip Lindy's stew no matter how good it smells." He grabbed her hand and laughed as he pulled her down the street.

She bared her soul, and he made a joke out of it. Then again, that was his way, to stay positive and light hearted despite problems. How could she complain when his positive attitude was one of the things she liked about him?

Once they reached camp, Saleena adjusted the lines where the extra cattle were to be staked out for grazing while Willem took the cats back to where he rolled out his sleeping pad a short distance from the cattle camp. Most of the Crystal Cabal camped within earshot of each other, which made it easier to gather for training. Royn arrived as she finished adjusting the lines, so she showed him the crystals on both the cattle and on her large necklace.

Royn looked but didn't touch the stones. "I never used magic before, and I don't plan to start now. Herding and leatherwork are good enough for me. You get told long enough something is best left alone, and you believe it."

Saleena pursed her lips together and looked at him.

"Well, I mean for me. Nearly thirty years I've been at this. I'm pretty set in my ways."

She tapped on a barrel strapped into one of the wagons. "We're tanning the new hide here. We'll use some of our salt to pack the rest of the animal we butchered. We've got everything we need for tanning on the road, as long as you don't try to get too fancy."

She spotted her father on the far side of the herd and waved to get his attention. A minute later Tover leaned against the tanning wagon to rest with Runner plopped down at his feet.

"Da, this is Royn. He's the local tanner."

Royn offered his hand. "Sir, it's good to meet you. I've heard you're Travel Master of the whole caravan."

Tover glanced at Saleena with a smile. "Are you telling stories on me again, girl? There's no need to give me any 'sir.' I'm only doing the job the baron asked of me. Speaking of which, here are the last of the new crystals. The tinker lost the rest to damage and couldn't recut them."

Saleena had counted on more stones. "I won't be able to cover the whole herd with the new animals Royn brought. I can add even less of the new cattle if the cats and the wolf trap any more badgers."

Royn took a step back. "You're serious about this crystal work, aren't you? I thought it was all stories, or using crystals so weak they wouldn't do much. You're putting together an army of war animals made up of cattle, cats, and badgers? You're crazy, the lot of you."

Tover set a hand on Royn's shoulder. "Yet here we are. The baron has kept us safe. We're growing. We'll be to the capital before long, and with the army there we'll beat the Graven army with whatever we got, cats and badgers right beside the rest of us."

Royn said, "You sound like Brother Cleo. He still tells stories of the last war, before he retired from fighting and returned to the Priests of Order. Cautionary tales, he calls them. I think something bad happened to him. You think this ragtag group of yours will make a difference against a trained army?"

Saleena pulled out a sheet of parchment, sat down and spread it on her lap. "Not alone, but we'll do it. I have an idea for how we can make use of your boiled leather to build armor for the cattle. They're most vulnerable when they charge, so anything we add up front will help."

She sketched out the armor pieces she wanted to make, noting how they might help when she controlled the herd. The armor on the front and across the shoulders would help when charging, while the rear half didn't need as much protection.

Royn looked over the sketch. "Isn't it a big risk to leave so much uncovered?"

Saleena nodded. "We don't have the time or the leather to do more than that, and cattle aren't built for it. Your heavy leather can protect the herd even if it's not perfect." If she and the herd did their best, they might save someone from being killed.

After she shared the details of her plan with Royn, Tover spoke. "Saleena, if this Brother Cleo was in the war, see if he knows what to do with the raven. I reckon there's a chance he's been around war animals, even if he's been away from it for a few years."

It was a sheer coincidence Gavin backed into the man whom he had over-heard recruiting the Richland residents earlier in the day. The man juggled his plate and barely avoided dumping his meal on the ground, but then he saw it was Baron Stoutheart behind him, and the plate bobbled again despite his best efforts.

"Sir, I'm sorry. Let me make a path for you. You know, I need to thank you for saving my life despite my foolishness. I stayed behind in Greenvale and barely escaped with the men you left behind. Without them, I would have been bear food."

Gavin held his plate of meat and vegetables one-handed to pat the man on the back. "That's why some men stayed behind." Since they had few first-hand accounts of the invasion, Gavin pressed for more information. "How many animals did you see?"

"Well, I saw the whole front line attack. It was a beauty to behold when they tripped into the spikes. There were too many to count, but it was dozens. Up close, I never saw more than a one-eared black bear as we left in the wagon."

Gavin didn't notice his plate had hit the ground until those around him scrambled to help clean up the mess. "A one-eared bear?"

"Right. I might not have noticed if your man hadn't saluted it as we fled. The bear even waved back."

Adrian would recognize his father's bear if he'd seen it. Why wouldn't he report it to Gavin? Was there a chance his father was still alive?

Gavin mumbled, "Thank you for your speech earlier today to rally the locals. It means a lot to me. If you'll excuse me, I have someone I need to talk to."

As he left he overheard the whispers behind him. "I never told him I was out to convince people to join up with us. How does he do that?"

Gavin turned to face the man, tension building as he said, "I listen, and I care, just like you. There's no magic to it. No spy network, at least not to watch *you*. We're in this together as we run before the enemy. If you feel the need to tell hero stories, make them about the people around you instead of about me. They're all heroes in their own right."

He ran his hands through his hair in an attempt to disburse the raw emotions churning through him. "Jase, I need a private meeting with Draken and Adrian. Now. I'll meet them at the town hall."

Jase said, "Sir, if you're sending me on errands, be sure to take another guard with you. With spies about causing trouble, not everyone here is your friend."

"Apparently, we can't guarantee I'm among friends anywhere. I'll find someone to go with me." Gavin paced through the crowd, oblivious to the light mood all around him as people waved or gave stiff bows as he passed through the throngs.

Gavin heard rushed steps behind him and glanced back to see Brother Cleo approach. "Well done, sir. I wouldn't have thought anyone could change the mind of all those who wanted to stay behind, but it looks like we'll be emptying the town."

A concerned expression grew on Brother Cleo's face as he considered Gavin's demeanor. "What's wrong? Something has changed, hasn't it, sir?"

Gavin nodded as Brother Cleo matched pace beside him. Gavin wasn't in a talkative mood, so he let the silence draw out as they walked together until finally, Gavin said, "Trust. Honesty. What are they worth?"

"You like to ask hard questions, sir." Brother Cleo clasped his hands behind his back as they continued down the street. "It might depend on whether we're talking about the cost or the value. The cost of honesty is what you give up to be honest, where the value is what you gain from being honest. I consider it a worthwhile exchange at any cost."

Gavin nodded. "I believe you. It might even help tonight. I need to find out if I've been lied to."

"So you know, sir, I believe you've made a lot of people more honest with your efforts. Your decision to not enforce crystal restrictions has shown people a path from hidden darkness into the honest light of day, and, from what I've seen, they thrive at the opportunity to be useful. You are either wise for your years or one of the luckiest men I've ever met."

"You sound like Master Draken and the way he gives out backhanded compliments, like when he told me I wasn't nearly as lazy as he had supposed I was."

"That wasn't my intent, I assure you. I received training to control a war animal years back with several of the Priests of Order. I understand the temptation to keep training when sent back to a normal life, despite the law. You've given a lot of people a chance to step up and be useful, including me. Did you know your Crystal Mistress offered me a raven to train and control? It's rare to strap a crystal to a bird so small. I accepted the bird, and you have my respect, sir. I was right to tag along after we spoke at the chapel. I'll have dozens of new stories to tell when we're done."

Gavin snorted. "So long as you don't buy into *all* the wild tales about me."

Brother Cleo put his hand over his heart. "I promise every tale I tell about you will be true to the best of my knowledge, so help me. At least when I use your name."

Gavin shook his head in mock dismay as they came to a stop in front of the town hall. "I guess I can't ask much more than that. This is where we part ways for the moment. I have a meeting I would rather not attend. Thank you. If you could wait here until we're done?"

Brother Cleo smiled, but his eyes showed concern. "I'll be here."

Gavin stepped into the building and lit the wall lamps while he waited, idly peering out one of the small glazed windows. It would have been nice to have more windows like this at home, to be able to see more of the world from within the safety of the walls. The distorted view caused by the uneven glass was better than no view at all. Likewise, he wanted windows into what people thought and did in his name. Even a partial understanding was better than ignorance.

He didn't have to wait long. He knew by sound alone it was Draken who entered, his boot heels hitting the wooden floor in what sounded like a military precision march until he came to a stop with a scrape in the center of the room.

Gavin waved an arm over to the chairs without bothering to face him. "We're still waiting on Adrian."

A shadow came through the door and resolved into the form of Adrian as he came into the light of the lamps. "I'm here."

It was clear to Gavin from Draken's formal posture and Adrian's subdued voice they knew he was upset, so he decided to dive in with no preamble.

"Draken, you saw the army approaching before we left the castle back in Stoutheart Barony. Adrian, you saw my father's bear in Greenvale. I know both of you may have hidden things from me on purpose. Did you see my father? Is he alive?"

Draken lowered his gaze. "Yes, he is. I thought it best to spare you the burden, sir. I spoke with Adrian when he joined us, and again after his escape from Greenvale to encourage him to withhold the information until you were ready for it."

Gavin paced back and forth across the hall, fuming. "You thought it was best I not know my father is a traitor to everyone I know, and to the kingdom? How could you think this wasn't important for me to know? Do you have any idea how bad it would be for morale if the people saw him fight alongside the Graven King's army after what we've been through?"

Adrian deferred to Draken with a slight hand gesture, leaving Draken to answer the charges.

"You were untested and had too much to accomplish in a short time. I didn't want you to be distracted or do anything foolish like trying to reach out to him."

Gavin stopped in front of Draken. "I've had responsibility thrust upon me ever since Father left to the council with the king. I didn't want any of this, but I've done it because I saw no one else able to do it, and it was the right thing to do. My only hope for these people is to have enough information to keep them ahead of the army and get them to safety. And you, Adrian, asked me once about whether I wanted to be knowledgeable or honest. I don't like the idea, but I've got to know everything that might be important to save my people. They're my people, and my responsibility, and I'll do whatever it takes to make this work. I'll figure out how to stay honest afterward.

"I'm disappointed, but not so much by what you kept from me. I'm disappointed in myself for being the man you couldn't trust. I still feel like a child inside, but I have to be a different person on the outside for everyone else to see. I have to be what the people need, and I need your help to do this. Tell me things, even if it hurts. I know you can both make hard choices. I expect myself to make hard choices as well. How else am I going to learn?"

Draken gave a more formal bow than Gavin remembered ever seeing from him. "I am at your service, sir. It won't happen again."

From many other men, Gavin might have taken the gesture as mockery or a weak attempt to placate him, but he had never doubted Draken outside of this one problem. Draken had been right to worry about Gavin's possible reaction. It was enough.

Draken paused a moment. "You should also know your brother died as a hero, defending our king."

Despite his distant relationship with Stephan, Gavin's heart filled with gratitude to know his brother had not been in league with his father and the invaders. He blinked away tears before they betrayed his stiff posture before his advisers.

Adrian leaned with a hand on the back of a chair. "You're not the baron I expected. I thought I knew things about you, and you're nothing like your father. I suspect that's a good thing, and we can work well together. I've learned I can trust you, and I hope you can learn to trust me. I'm not sure your father ever did." He tapped a finger on his collar, which showed a new groove.

Gavin leaned in for a close view of the collar. "Did you find a file? It's going to take a while, but I suppose it's better than cold chisels and hammers at your neck."

"I wasn't going to mention anything, since it was the king's court that put the collar on me on behalf of your father, truth be told. I suppose I will need to save my conniving and deceit for later when I'm spying."

The murmur of voices reached them from the street through the open doorway, and Brother Cleo poked his head around the corner. "Sir, this man claims to be a messenger for Adrian. He's injured."

Both Gavin and Adrian said in unison, "Send him in." Adrian shrugged at Gavin and turned to the door as one of his spies stumbled in with a forearm wrapped in a crude bloodstained bandage. He fell to his knees on the wood floor with his good hand holding another wound in his side.

The spy breathed in quick, ragged gasps. "The army took out one of our patrols and advanced on us before we knew where they were. They found a large cache of supplies somewhere and picked up their pace. They know you're here and they didn't stop to camp. They'll be on us by morning."

Gavin wondered how many poor villages had given their all, or if the army had run across Richland's people before they got to their refuge. It wouldn't change their plans, but he wanted to know who to burn candles for when he could take the time. Mourning would have to wait. The caravan and the city would be destroyed if the full army caught up with them here. They had slowed the army before, but it was temporary, and they wouldn't fall for something like the trench trap again. There were few options to choose from, but he had an idea.

"Adrian, I need you to work out a distraction to draw off their army. Lead as many as you can away from us. We need more time."

Adrian pursed his lips for a moment. "Any ideas on how?"

"You know your team's resources better than I do. You probably know *my* resources better than I do. Take whatever you need. If we can't make it work, nothing else will matter. You need to give them something worth chasing. If you can distract them, we'll take care of the rest."

"Whatever I need? In our spirit of newfound honesty and trust, I must admit I used those two salted hams to feed my men in luxury while we waited in Greenvale. I didn't need them to build the traps."

Gavin said, "Don't you ever take anything seriously?"

Adrian smiled. "I take everything seriously. Can't it be fun, too?"

He leaned out the door and gave a piercing whistle. One of his men repeated it back to him in the distance. "I'll keep you informed. I'll send someone with fresh bandages for my man." He darted off into the shadows.

Draken asked simply, "Do you want me to send out runners to the locals and the camp, sir?"

"I'll go back to the celebration and ruin the mood for everyone there, myself. Get the message out to everyone else." It would be a long, sleepless night.

CHAPTER

NINETEEN

Adrian dodged around and through swarms of people until he finally found Lindy. She pointed, yelled, and directed what seemed like an angry anthill. He approached in the shadows out of habit before remembering he needed her to notice him. Even after he stepped out into plain sight, he had to wave to get her attention.

"What can I help you with, Adrian?" It was as if he was her only concern, even amid the chaos and interruptions. How did she do it? Such focus and attention to detail gave her a palpable sense of purpose. If he could learn the tactic, it would complement his other skills.

"I noticed you had all the wagon spare parts for repairs loaded onto one wagon with a team of oxen. Can I have it?"

She gawked at him as if she hadn't heard correctly. "Why do you want to take over the repair supplies? You don't strike me as the type to corral wagon parts."

"Not take over. I want to use them, and then burn them in a glorious funeral pyre. I'll leave nothing behind but a pile of ash."

"I'm sorry, you lost me." She waved a couple of people past and pointed them in the right direction as she watched Adrian. "We need those supplies. The road from here to the capital isn't long, but it has some rough spots. Things will break."

Adrian grimaced. He leaned in close and lowered his voice for only her ears. "That's where my job becomes critical. The army will catch up to us before we can get to the capital, no matter how fast we move. I'm going to convince them to chase me instead for a while, to give the caravan a chance for survival. I'd appreciate it if you not spread how the caravan may be nothing but a pile of bone and ash within two days if I fail in my assignment."

He hated to manipulate her, playing with her emotions by divulging just the right amount of information. He was in too much of a hurry to convince her it was her own idea to give him the wagon.

She raised an eyebrow at him. "You know you're insane, don't you?"

"But I'm good enough it doesn't matter, right?"

"Sure, we'll go with that. You can't have them because they might make all the difference if we have a breakdown."

Adrian sighed. He would have to play his trump card. "I may have forgotten to mention this is at Baron Stoutheart's request."

Her lips formed a thin line and her eyebrows lowered. "Fine. Take the supplies, but don't make me regret it, even if I only live to regret it for two days."

Adrian turned to leave, but glanced over his shoulder to ask, "Can I also trade the oxen for two matched pairs of horses? Those I'll bring back to you."

"Yes! Go, before I change my mind. I'll tell Tover what you're taking."

His next stop was the Richland farrier's shop. The owner had already left with the earlier evacuation. Adrian slipped in through an unlocked second story window, barely large enough to shimmy through, and packed all the horseshoes he could fit into a bag. He looked around for nails and found none.

He had no use for the shoes without nails, but searching through boxes and cupboards turned up nothing. Nails weren't something a person would hide. The farrier must have taken them with him.

"Splinters. Now I have to make an extra stop."

Adrian dropped the bag from the second story window and cringed at the clank it made when it landed. He eased out and dropped to the ground in a roll.

Within minutes he found Master Smith from Stoutheart Barony and came up behind him. "Hello, Master Smith."

The smith spun around with a start. Adrian was only a pace away with his hands spread out and empty. No need to alarm the locals.

"And who might you be?" Master Smith squinted and reached for a handy hammer.

"Sorry, I'm Adrian. I didn't visit Stoutheart Barony's castle often, but I hear you're the best smith around."

"I'm the only smith around, so best is a given." The smith lowered his fists a touch.

"I hate to bother you, but I need a sack of nails. Farrier nails if you have them. Baron Stoutheart has charged me with a special project tonight."

"Gavin, eh? He's a good boy. He used to be a bit of a wastrel, but he's taken some great strides stepping up as the baron. I'm right proud of him for the improvement. Nails, you say? They're a rare thing on the trail, but we're not stopping to build anything, either." His hands lowered at the mention of Gavin, and he rubbed his nose as he thought.

"They should be right over here." Master Smith led the way to a wagon where he hefted a crate that outweighed Adrian twice over. The man was an ox, his arms as thick as a man's legs. He pulled a much smaller box from the next crate down and handed it over.

"They're not farrier nails, but they're close in size."

Adrian flipped the lid off and saw nails as long as two knuckles. "Yes, these will do wonderfully. I can't thank you enough."

He shook the smith's meaty hand to seal the deal. "You'll see my hand-iwork outside of town. I hope I don't disappoint you too much, but this will be a bit of a rush job. I'm likely to disappoint the carpenters and wheel-wrights as well with my workmanship. They may disown me for the sin I am about to commit against both good skills and common sense."

As Adrian walked away from the wagon, he gave out two coded whis-tles to get the rest of the team headed in the right direction. He met them at the supply wagon, where one of the men swapped the oxen for horses and set up a different yoke to hook all four horses to the spare parts wagon.

They left camp shortly after midnight with lanterns blazing on the front of the wagon to light the road for the horses as best they could, comple-menting the moonlight. It was dangerous to ride at night, especially as fast as Adrian pushed them, but it was better than death at the hands of the army. His emergency construction team rode on the wagon behind him. He leaned back and said, "We'll ride to the first main crossroad about a half hour out and build there."

He kept an eye on the stars to track the time. He nodded to himself thirty minutes later, gratified they reached the crossroads when he'd estimated. "Right here to the side of the road. You two, we need shovels and pine branches to smooth out as many of the caravan's tracks as possible after most of them pass us. Recruit some of the caravan's stragglers to drag the branches behind them. Cut a small evergreen and tie it behind their last wagon as well. The rest of you, I have a rough drawing here, and we haven't got much time to build these beasts."

He laid out the plans on the seat of the wagon where the torches cast enough light to see by. "Divide up the spare parts. Wheels there, axles there, and leave the lumber in the back since it's on the bottom of the stack. I have more nails, and the repair tools are in this box." He pointed as he issued each command. The men swarmed the wagon and pulled supplies out to distribute and stack them as directed.

"Good. Once we have the two frames built, you can attach the extra axles and wheels. The horses will be used as two pairs rather than as one large team of four. We'll use the supply wagon for one team, and build a new front axle for the other team."

Again, the swarm of men pulled lumber and hammered boards into place based on the rough sketch. The contraptions came together with startling speed as they positioned parts and attached them together with rope and nails. Adrian acquired a hammer and pounded horseshoes onto boards attached to the outside of the wheels.

Soon they were tweaking the final production. Each team would pull eight axles, most of which had horseshoes attached around the wheels at varying offsets. The wagons would ride like an unbroken colt and wouldn't last long before falling apart. He hoped they would last long enough to draw part of the army away from the main road.

Adrian laughed. "Behold, the wagons of doom! Won't this be fun? Once we get moving, I'll need a pair of you to watch this crossroad to see how many of them we draw off. Trail whoever follows us and take out their rear scouts. You two with the pine branches, that will be your job since you'll be here doing cleanup anyway. The rest of you will be with me and the wagons. Walk behind. If you have spare boots, put them on the bottom of walking sticks. Your tracks will be on top of the wagon tracks. It might obscure enough that they won't see the telltale patterns the wagons will leave."

The vanguard of the caravan passed them in the dark as they finished their work. Adrian's men rested while they watched the caravan hurry past. The caravan wagons carried as many people as possible to gain a little more speed, but there was no way to move everyone quickly. Most of those riding were children unable to walk through the night.

Adrian waved cheerfully to Lindy as she gawked at the monstrosities created from her spare wagon parts. He yelled out, "Douse as many of your torches as you can from here until sunup. We want them to follow us, not you."

Lindy came over and fastened her torch to a bracket on Adrian's supply wagon. "Like I said, you're insane. Take care of yourself and your men. I want to hear your tale at a full taproom in the capital. Standing room only."

Adrian gave her a bow with a great flourish of his arms. "As you wish, my Supply Mistress. You're my favorite person—at least until tomorrow. Beyond that, it depends on if you're buying."

When the smith led his wagon past and saw the result of Adrian's efforts, he raised a bushy eyebrow, shook his head and kept moving.

The trail of refugees died down, and Adrian sent out shovelers and sweepers to erase as much of the caravan's trail as they could. They wanted a few tracks to still head forward, but it had to appear as if only a few fled straight while most tracks led off to the side road. The wagons of doom had to look like a significant threat, or they would be ignored.

A quick survey showed only a few families hadn't already passed them, so he climbed aboard the reworked supply wagon. "I think that's all we can do here. Head out, boys." Under his breath, he continued, "If this doesn't work, we'll all be dead soon. But no matter."

The city behind them gave off a glow as burning buildings filled the night sky with smoke. His men rolled their creations into the main road to set the start of the trail, then veered onto the path which would loop to the west and back past Richland. He suspected Gavin ordered them to burn the city to buy them a few precious hours. Adrian laughed. If Gavin could destroy an entire city to give people a better chance of survival, he was the right man for the job to lead them.

The mass of wagon tracks, hoof prints, and boot prints was impressive, though the ride was even rougher than he had anticipated. The two wagons crossed each other's trail as they rolled so as to break up the patterns they inevitably left for those clever enough to inspect the trail closely. Once daytime came, the risk of discovery would increase.

An hour into the ride, Adrian called two of his men up onto the wagon for instructions. "It's trap time. What can you do to their wagons to slow them down as they go past here? Without getting yourselves killed."

A straggle-haired older man with only a few teeth said, "Getting a mite picky about getting killed now, ain't ya? I got an idea. Can we spare a crossbow and two lengths of light rope?" He glanced at the sky, not dark for much longer as the morning constellations shone down on them. "They'll pass here a bit after sunrise. Dark would be better, but sunrise will do."

Adrian dug into the few remaining wagon supplies and handed off the rope. "What's your plan?"

The toothless man answered, "Set up a crossbow to fire a bolt through their spokes trailin' a rope. The other rope will be my remote trigger on the crossbow, so I don't have to be right there. By the time they can get the wagon stopped, the ropes will be all twisted up in the axle. The longer they don't notice, the better it gets. Y'all ever tried to back up a wagon with a tied-up axle? They'll have to either abandon the wagon or cut the knots out by hand to get 'er running again."

Adrian pulled a bag from his belt and tossed it. "Nice. I'll have to remember that one. Toss a few of these caltrops out on the road before they get there, too. Good luck!"

Farther along the road, he pulled four more men, cutting his team in half. "Now is when the real fun begins. If they've lost their rear scouts and been slowed, this is where we make it hurt. Burn whatever you can of their supplies and get away fast. The rest of us will take these wagons as far as we can and burn them as well. They're coming apart already, so I don't think we'll get too far. Then we'll loop back to take out any scouts we find on our way back. Once we regroup, we will move in as rear support for the caravan. We'll be between the two halves of their army, so keep a sharp eye out. Is everybody clear?"

The men each nodded to confirm their orders.

"Drinks are on me at the capital when we're done, unless Lindy is buying."

He wondered how many candles he would burn for those killed today. He'd lost one man to the enemy before they evacuated the town and nearly lost the messenger who escaped to warn them. Without their sacrifice, the whole town and caravan would have been overrun. They all knew death was possible, and anyone in the spy business, or in the military, knew fate caught up on occasion, but his men cheered and labored at their tasks with a single-minded intensity that always amazed him.

"Can you boys remind me again why it is you follow me? It's certainly not for the soft beds and gold coins, since we've seen neither in an age."

One of the men looked up from beside the wagon. "I'd still be in the mines if not for you. What's not to like about seeing the light of day regularly? Besides, we have a pool on how long we go between crazy ideas. I lost the bet this time."

Adrian's motivation was different. Was Sharise alive still? The baron had used her to get Adrian's best efforts and had kept them apart for the past two years, except to show Adrian she still lived on each marriage anniversary.

Every day had been a gift since his pardon, but it was a two-edged sword. He lived each day as if it could be his last, yet he still planned what he would do when he got Sharise back. He also plotted what he would do to those who had kept them apart. Even so, the joy of living was too important to miss out on, no matter if you were serving someone else, or even if you were never free at all. Everything could still work out, so Adrian smiled as he got the horses moving again, drawing the rickety contraptions forward.

One of the wagons collapsed a half mile short of Adrian's goal, but it was useless to split up and leave one behind. Once the enemy found either wagon, they would know they had been tricked.

Adrian's men unhitched the horses, and then butted the wagons against each other in the middle of the road. He noted the dry grass and considered using a wildfire as a tool, but the light wind wasn't blowing in the right direction. It made no sense to start a grass fire without good purpose.

They lit the wagons on fire, parked as a barricade across the road. The smoke would surprise the enemy and make them curious. Adrian's hope was to draw them even farther forward. The fire would seem to be a last-ditch obstacle to slow the men following them.

They split up into hunting pairs and scattered. Adrian's partner was Van, a young man with a short black ponytail and an old leather jacket that had seen better days. They tied their horses on the far side of a hill and crept around to watch for advance scouts as the sun rose. A trail of dark smoke rose from where he had left his ambush team, matching the smoke from his barricade. His men must have set at least one supply wagon ablaze. The smoke was thick enough they might have burned several wagons. If the enemy sent out advance scouts, they should arrive any time now. He crouched down and blended into the brush to wait.

It didn't take long. There, across the other side of the road and up into the sparse trees he spotted a pair on foot. They moved without a sound, eyes dodging back and forth to scan the area. He tapped his partner and pointed, whispering, "I'll get them. Watch for more on this side." He ghosted his way from shadow to shadow until he came up a few steps behind the rear man.

The first one was easy, since he trailed a few paces behind his partner. Adrian grabbed him across the mouth and slipped a knife between his ribs and into his heart. The man tensed and sighed out his last breath, and it was over almost before it started. Adrian crept up within a few paces of the second man when his target turned, saw Adrian and pulled a short blade.

He took a deep breath to yell, and Adrian threw his knife. It hit the scout at the base of his larynx. His eyes widened as he dropped his sword and reached for the protruding dagger, but he fell over before he could remove the fatal blade.

Such a pitiful waste of life made Adrian's heart ache. This was why he preferred sneaking and spying to killing. So much potential, so much life to live, snuffed out before it was due. In other circumstances, the two dead men might have told war stories to their children and grandchildren. It wasn't fair Adrian got to decide so many fates, but it was the job he had been given, and his actions gave his own people the chance to see their children and grandchildren. He would take the exchange.

Adrian was almost back to Van when he heard the rapid clash of steel on steel. The trees thinned as he approached their hiding spot. Van circled, armed with a cutlass, facing a man with a longsword. The opponent's longer reach didn't bode well, but Van held his own defensively, stalling for time. Stalling for Adrian's return.

Adrian was almost there when he saw the swordsman's partner down on the ground with a cut across his thigh. The injured man fired a crossbow into Van's back before Adrian could draw a breath to shout a warning.

Adrian watched Van crumple with blood coming from his mouth and held silent his rage. The swordsman lowered his guard, not noticing as Adrian came up behind him and ran a knife across his throat. He dodged to the right, past the collapsing man, and reached the crossbowman, who tried to reload with shaky hands. Adrian kicked the crossbowman in the face, breaking his nose with a crunch and knocking him unconscious.

The crossbowman's leg injury hadn't hit an artery, so there was a chance he would survive. Adrian had to preserve their ruse, so he killed the man and set the stage with dozens of footprints as if the man had been ambushed by a large armed team. He packed up the dead man's weapons.

It was time to gather the rest of his men and get between the two halves of the Graven army. A few trees felled across the road might help, once he got around the force that had followed him. With a bit of luck, the pursuit would continue down the road for a while before they found there was nobody to chase. Forcing luck was his specialty. He hoped his team had delayed these men enough to make a difference for the caravan.

CHAPTER

TWENTY

G erald Stoutheart was in a delicate position, and it had little to do with riding on the wagon beside King Ithan. He knew he had to act soon, but the timing had to be perfect.

King Ithan said, "I want both groups of refugees destroyed. We'll make an example of them."

"Are you sure it was wise to send so many men to chase the group that broke off? Based on the tracks going this way, the group that split off may be smaller than we thought."

King Ithan scowled. "I know what I'm doing. The footmen will have their hands full. I saw the shod hoof prints mixed in with the wagon tracks. They could have found some cavalrymen. I know the reputation of Riland cavalry. If you want to help, then tell me why the devil they would try to get behind us."

"But a full third of our army, Your Majesty? The refugees must have a plan. Lacking more information, I can only guess what it might be. The men are about to drop after marching for two days and a night."

The men with crystals were exhausted. The king had ordered many of them stacked in wagons or strapped them to their animals for the past thirty-six hours. The losses in footmen and among the war animals were unfortunate, but acceptably small. The forced march had brought them up within striking distance of the evacuation.

"Very well. Increase the rear guard. We haven't seen anyone else break off to the sides, so pull in the side patrols and reassign them."

Gerald nodded and climbed off the wagon without waiting for it to stop. "I'll see to it immediately."

They were burning through their supplies quickly, but it paid off in speed. All they had to do was reach the remainder of the caravan, and their supply woes would end. With luck, Gerald would find his son and save him from the slavery or death others would face. His plan hung in a delicate balance, but he held the critical parts all in his mind as the time of action approached.

He pulled himself up onto another wagon to sit beside the master of the duty roster. The duty schedule was usually out of his control, but this was an opportunity Gerald hadn't counted on, and he wouldn't pass it up. "The king needs a few of his trusted men to keep a larger watch behind us."

He dickered back and forth about various names until he had what he wanted, with the king's most trusted men sent back out of Gerald's way. The king hadn't asked for his best to hang back, but a little exaggeration worked wonders. He sent the order, and several of the king's guard stepped off to the side of the road to wait for everyone to pass. Gerald smiled at how easily fate could be bent to his will.

He had seen the king mobilize the full army of war animals only for the attacks on Greenvale and Richland, but those two instances gave him the information he needed to make his plan. The king kept guards at his wagon, but would be short-staffed with the guards Gerald had sent to the rear. Gerald would throw his loyal men at them at just the right point near the end of the coming battle. He would lose several men, but sometimes you had to make sacrifices to succeed.

Gerald listened in on scout reports that confirmed the location of the enemy camp on an upcoming rise.

The march ground to a halt, and some soldiers took the time to set up camp while others collapsed where the march left them. Such blatant lack of discipline annoyed Gerald. At least those caring for the animals managed to organize the cages.

The effort to travel two days and a night with no rest left both the refugees and the army with no option but to camp. Reports were that the refugees had no large war animals at all, which meant this was to be one of the most one-sided fights he had ever been part of, despite his son's people having the advantage of high ground. Perhaps the king would get sloppy about his security and make things easier for him.

Their animals needed rest before combat as much as the men. King

Ithan ordered the men to eat and prepare for battle the next day. Food was one of the few motivators the men still responded to after the march. Once the camp was settled in the valley below the refugee camp, Gerald visited his bear and checked on her battle armor. It was mostly leather, but had some steel scales sewn into decorative patterns. Armor wasn't needed against peasants, but the rumors of cavalry had spooked the men. They were taking no chances on this ragtag caravan.

"Gerald. I figured I would find you here." King Ithan and a pair of armed and armored guards had approached before he was aware of them. "The rear scouts haven't heard from our footmen. They spotted smoke at two locations early in the day, so it's clear they've seen action. We'll move early enough tomorrow that they won't be back, even under the best of circumstances. We will need every animal except for my reserve team on the front line first thing in the morning. I realize your son is with this rabble, but I expect your best effort, as always."

Gerald understood the undercurrent of the comment to mean the king had a critical eye on him, even more than normal. The king hadn't asked him a single question. The entire purpose of the visit was to keep him in line. The king wouldn't need him as a guide through this territory for much longer, and Gerald hadn't provided much information since leaving Stout-heart Barony.

"I understand how the outcome tomorrow is critical. I'll give this fight my absolute best effort, Your Highness."

CHAPTER

TWENTY-ONE

Saleena listened to Draken's plan for a night raid involving all the small animals in the slim hope of finding a way to weaken the enemy. They all stood to stave off sleep.

Draken said, "If the raven can get us the camp layout, we still have to worry about their guard patrols. Once we're past them, we need to get to their war animals. Assuming that works, our task is to take crystals from them. Any failure in the chain and our whole plan falls apart."

The longer Draken spoke to the assembled Crystal Cabal, the worse the plan sounded, but Saleena couldn't think of any other way to help.

Draken said, "We sent a rider ahead to the capital on horseback when we left Richland, but the people at the capital may not be able or willing to help us. We don't know what state the capital is in, or how organized they are. We could use the horse here, but Baron Stoutheart felt it more important to send the messenger. We must plan with whatever we have. The baron will be monitoring the battle to issue orders, and won't be controlling an animal. It turns out that he's got a gift for strategy, which makes up for his other, shall we say, missed educational opportunities."

Despite the seriousness of the mood, Saleena giggled when she saw Gavin roll his eyes. She'd heard Draken berate Gavin for years, but Gavin didn't rise to the bait as he had in the past.

Gavin took a cue from Draken and said, "Adrian's decoy has bought us better odds, which is a chance. It's still only a slim chance, so we're going to do our best to even things up a little more. At the top level, the plan for tonight's raid is straightforward. We have to do something to disable their fighting force. The only way to do that, without losing most of our people, is to take some of their war animals out of the fight. As Master Draken so eloquently put it, I'm not equipped to tell you how to do that. You are. All of you as a group. You each have valuable input because of what you can do, especially in the areas the enemy doesn't know about. You are our secret weapon. You know what each of our animals is capable of and how you can play your part in the plan."

It made sense, but Saleena was still unhappy at the risk. "What's our final count on animals we can use for this?"

Draken pulled out a paper, sighed, and read from the list. "Our assault team consists of the three Cats of the Apocalypse, one raven, two rats, two badgers, and a squirrel. They'll either never know what hit them, or they'll die laughing as they squash our team like bugs."

He waved over at a second group. "The medium-sized animals will be at the ready as well, but they need to hang back where they won't be spotted. Those are my wolf, Runner, four other farm dogs, and two half-wolves. Does that account for everyone here?"

His gaze swept over Saleena and the others as they nodded. He continued, "The rest of our crystals are for larger animals like the cattle and oxen. The dog-sized group can get in close, but not close enough to do the actual work tonight. They are the backup and distraction in case things go horribly wrong. This sounds cruel, but getting even those small, weak crystals back is more important than the life of any of our animals.

"Shards. I'd trade a person's life in an instant if it saved more lives. Some of you are not used to a military point of view. To be blunt, lives are a resource. Sometimes they get spent. It's your job to minimize the losses of your families, friends, and neighbors through your actions tonight. It's also your job to minimize those losses during our sneak attack. Don't waste a life, but don't hesitate to spend it if it will save the caravan."

Draken's practical outlook on spending lives shocked Saleena, but war was a new experience for her. Saleena followed up, hoping to clarify some of the details. "If you need to relay information, Gav— Baron Stoutheart and I will be here watching over you. We won't wake you from your trance unless it's critical, but if you notice anything we need to do, wake yourself to relay the message to us. We can't approach the men and take crystals from around their necks, so your best option is to take crystals from the animals and bring them back here. Your second-best option is to take their crystals and hide them."

Saleena mentally reviewed the emergency military training from Draken. It was little more than a few simple tactics and hand signals designed to work while controlling animals. Failure would doom the entire camp, and even if they succeeded beyond their wildest dreams, it would fall to her to provide their biggest offensive and defensive wall with nearly forty head of cattle tomorrow.

Fear of failure was new to her. She had always found a way to succeed. When the cattle had been threatened by wolves and mountain cats, her family had made crystals and trained the cattle into a defensive force. This was the same, wasn't it? Just another threat, but deadlier. She understood threats.

She and her friends were going up against people with trained war animals and experience in combat. Her friends knew everything she could share on using animals as a team, but fear lurked in the back of her thoughts over their chances for success. She was tired to her bones, and her friends showed shadows under their eyes. She couldn't let her doubt show, or it would spread to the others. Gavin trusted her, and the Crystal Cabal trusted her. She took a deep breath to steady her nerves.

Saleena said, "We can do this. Is everyone ready? Like we planned, Brother Cleo, you go first and report back on the location of our best targets. Then everyone else will join in once we make the final assignments."

The first time Brother Cleo entered a trance with the raven he'd done an odd meditation with his bare feet and hands all pressed together as he sat and hummed. He was able to control the raven a short time later, so it must have done some good to help him focus as he attuned to the crystal.

Today, Brother Cleo lay back on a bundled blanket and closed his eyes. The tension grew as they waited. The plan was for him to be gone for no more than ten minutes, but the trip stretched to fifteen, then twenty. Soon he would cut into the time they needed for their ground-based expedition.

As Saleena was about to force Brother Cleo awake, the raven flew in and dropped a chain next to the lamp hung from the side of a nearby wagon. Brother Cleo stirred, and then sat up. "Sorry for taking so long.

Nighttime isn't the best for a raven, so I had to get close. Then I found that even in the dark, ravens are exceptionally good at spotting shiny things. Once I had the information on patrols and positions, I found this." He grinned and he leaned over to the lamp, picking up the crystal on a chain.

Brother Cleo continued, "It was set aside while one of their men performed some cleansing ritual or other. I never did study Northern practices, and I couldn't stick around to watch."

Master Draken swore. "They'll know something is up as soon as they see this master crystal is missing. We need to go now, or the whole thing goes into the latrine. At the first sign of alarm, get out. The only exception is if you find something worth losing your animal and its crystal to accomplish. Once they figure out what's happening, they will spot you, and they will kill your animal. Then they will go after the rest of us."

Brother Cleo sketched out the camp and gave his report. "Their animal cages are set up on the east side of the center of their camp. They have regular patrols all along their perimeter with no more than five minutes between passes. The enemy campfires make it easy to see." He continued with details on the timing and location of guard patrols. The patrols would be tricky since he didn't have a lot of time to watch them. Master Draken broke them down into teams with specific assignments.

With the overview complete, Saleena inspected the group as they settled into comfortable positions, waiting for the command to begin their assignments. Their stern looks let her know they understood the burden they bore. Everyone wore a crystal for tonight's mission except for Gavin and herself. She joined him, standing near the lamp and picked up the crystal on the chain. "I'll try this crystal to see if I can acclimate to it fast enough."

Gavin said, "Hold on. It might take too long, and we need you here."

"Well, if it takes too long, I won't be able to go into a trance, and I'll be here to help anyway." She slipped the cord over her neck. "I'm the best choice. It might be the bit of good luck we need to succeed. I'll switch back to wearing the cattle crystals as soon as the mission is done."

Gavin nodded, but he didn't look convinced.

The bare beginnings of a new connection formed rapidly in the back of her head. "The other end is there. I'll let you know how it goes." Saleena's experiments with other crystals showed that acclimating to a crystal took longer for the beasts that were either a lot larger or smaller than herself. Size mattered. It was likely common knowledge among those accustomed to training with different sized animals.

A few minutes later everyone wearing a crystal except for Saleena entered a trance. Their first offensive action as war animals was on.

Saleena watched the animals scurry down the hill together, splitting off from the main group as their team's assignment required. Some of the smaller, slower animals rode on the backs of the faster dogs and wolves until they got close to the enemy camp. They were out of sight in the darkness almost immediately.

Brother Cleo went back out with the raven to watch from above. He had taken to the raven far more easily than she thought he would. He attuned to it quickly, but there was more than that. He must have had more experience he wasn't talking about. As she considered the raven, the new connection in her mind blossomed unexpectedly from a hint to a full window all at once, ready for her to take control of whatever was on the other end.

She spread out on her blanket and turned her face toward Gavin. "I'm going in."

"How can you be attuned so fast?"

Saleena shrugged and closed her eyes, dropping through the mental window. She opened her new eyes and saw stars through the bars of a cage above her. So far, so good. She sat up and reached for the bars of the cage door, realizing she was in a human form. She had taken control of a slave. A meat puppet. That explained how she had made the connection so fast. The slave woman was about her size, and the physical similarities made the connection easier.

A man outside the bars glanced in. "About time. The baron needs you to get her chained up in his tent, and can't do it himself. He said something about wanting leverage with one of his men." The accent was from home, which didn't make sense. This man wasn't a northerner.

She scooted to the door and gave what she hoped was a convincing nod.

He unlocked her cage and swung the door open. The cage sat on a wagon, so she scrambled out and down to the ground. Her new body cramped with the movement. She stood to her full height and flexed, adjusting a loose robe, her only clothing. Raw sores covered her elbows and knees. Saleena had seen them on animals when they weren't allowed to run free often enough. The way this woman had been treated made her stomach turn. Her jaw clenched as she studied her surroundings with an intensity built by her loathing of the man in front of her.

He wore the uniform of a man-at-arms, maybe part of a private guard, with a metal breastplate, a sword, and dagger on his hip. He released some straps on the wagon and hefted a small box. "He'll need this if he keeps her long. She gets pretty wild without the sleep juice if nobody's controlling her." He gave a mean laugh. "Of course, I don't have to remind you of that. You still carry a nice scar where she bit you that one time."

He set the box down and walked up close. "You know, there's not that much of a hurry. We got time for a quick peek, I think." He reached for her robe.

Saleena's seething rage boiled out all at once. She leaned forward and kneed him in the groin as hard as she could. He doubled over in pain with a loud grunt, fell to his side, and curled up in a ball. She pulled a dagger from his belt. She could kill him, but she'd never killed a man before. In tomorrow's battle, she would probably kill several men, but she hesitated before coming to a decision.

She kicked him again to assure he would not walk normally for at least a week, then ripped a sash from his clothing and used it to gag him. He turned his head, bloodshot eyes wide with pain and an unspoken question. She grabbed a loose set of leather reins from the wagon and hogtied him while he was unable to defend himself.

Despite long confinement and abuse, the body she occupied was strong. She hoisted the loose end of the reins and tied it to a hook on the wagon, nearly lifting the man off the ground. She slipped his dagger into her rope belt and carried his sword.

Saleena grabbed the box in her free hand. If she made it all the way out, they would look closer at the contents. With the box safely tucked under her left arm, she oriented herself from Brother Cleo's landmarks and headed off to the nearby animal pens.

Twice she ducked back into the shadows as someone walked past, but eventually, she found a dark spot between some boxes and sat to watch the approach to the pens. A few minutes later, she saw a tabby cat wandering her direction as if he hadn't a care in the world.

She shifted position, and the cat's eyes were instantly on her. She formed her hands into one of the prearranged signals for danger, and then pointed back the way she had come. Death Claw tapped his paw three times on the ground. End the Trance.

She shook her head, no. Leaving would put this woman, whoever she was, back at the mercy of the monsters she escaped from. If the mystery woman became awake and aware, Saleena had no way to predict what would happen. The woman would probably remember Saleena's conversation with the cat. Maybe the drug would prevent that, but she didn't know.

The three cats appeared with her between the crates and boxes. Doom Bringer, nearly invisible in the darkness, crossed his front paws. Guard me.

She nodded and huddled with all three of them in her arms while Willem disengaged to report about the change in the situation. Less than a minute later, all three tapped her on the arm to let her know he was back. They signaled in unison for her to wait, and then they stalked to the pens and animals tied to wagons.

The cages came in various sizes. They were the same sort she had appeared in. Saleena's keen eyes picked out two rats as they scurried up and into one cage after another. Some were empty, and they came right back out. Others were not. A growl sounded from one cage as they approached, and they backed off to try another.

She lost sight of the cats and rats for a time, but soon felt a light touch on her bare foot. A rat held a crystal out to her. It was a relief to know the word had been spread. She took the crystal, which had been chewed free from its collar. She placed it in the box.

Death Claw brought her another prize, a smaller crystal on a cord with chew marks where it had been cut.

A half hour passed, and by the end, she held eight crystals. Other animals on her team would carry or hide their own haul of stolen crystals. She watched the cats climb to the largest wagon cage and slip through the bars.

She heard yelling in the main camp behind her. Whether it was because of her escape or for some other reason, it was time to retreat. She crouched and prepared to move. Her eyes darted back to the enemy camp at every noise. If the cats didn't come back soon, she would have to make her own way out.

A low rumbling growl came from the cage, and three cats darted out in different directions. The animal continued to make noise. A guard to the far side of the cage grunted and said, "It's your turn. See what His Majesty's beast wants."

Skull Crusher ran up to check on her, and she gave a quick signal of retreat. The calico acknowledged the signal and led the way into the darkness. Saleena's night vision was poor, so she relied on the cats to keep her from being seen as she followed them. They were faster than she was, so they waited and watched as she hurried from one spot to the next through the enemy camp.

The cats diverted her to a space between two tents as a man marched back the way they had come. She held her breath and waited until the man moved out of a direct line of sight. Eventually, she stood again and crept along behind her guides.

Some of the less dangerous animals were tied along her path, so she pulled her dagger and cut the hitch lines free as she passed. It might not be much, but anything helped.

Soon, they were clear of the wagons and tents, but the open fields made it much easier for her to be seen. They hadn't planned on having to hide a human crossing the gap between forces. She crouched down as low as possible and followed the cats out into the open. Her bare feet were not used to rough ground and gained several new cuts and scrapes.

The cats crossed a game trail in a flurry and vanished into the grass on the other side. Saleena crept out and stepped on a thorn. She let out a tiny yelp and fell to her knees.

"You there! Don't move." Two men in armor melted out of the darkness beside a large boulder where they had been hidden. She was ready to make a run for it when she spotted Skull Crusher in the grass. The cat gave the signal to wait.

The men split up and approached her from two angles with swords out. The same one commanded her, "Now stand up, slowly."

She left the sword on the ground out of sight and stood to face him, seeing recognition on his face. "Sir, she's the prisoner!"

Before the men could react, Runner, along with the wolf and two half-wolves, sprang into action. The two men fell under the weight of the attack, but pulled their arms in close to guard their throats. This left their legs exposed, and Runner, under Tover's control, bit through a boot and into the tendons at the back of one man's leg, refusing to let go.

The men screamed. Whether as a warning or from pain made no difference. The camp would come alive within moments, no matter how tired they were. Saleena gave up on stealth and ran through the empty field as snarls, yells, and yelps filled the air behind her. Sharp rocks cut her feet, but she didn't dare stop. She clutched the stolen box desperately to her chest as she struggled up the gentle slope.

Two cattle dogs appeared at her sides as an escort. They were too small to do more than guide her, but that was enough. The yells and howls of the fight died down in the background, and they fled across no-man's-land and made their way up the hill to their own camp through the darkness.

Guards at their camp called out a challenge and trained bows and spears on her until the dogs came forward to be recognized. She said, "I'm Saleena, controlling this woman. Help me get to my team." The voice she spoke with was low and rough, as if she'd spent a lot of time screaming. She gave her escort a set of hand signals for emphasis as she said, "Go watch for the others. They will need more help."

The closest guard nodded. "A messenger told us to expect you."

The dogs turned and ran back to the fight as it progressed slowly up the hill.

The perimeter guards handed her off to two other guards, along with the box and crystals. They carried her with her arms around their necks so she wouldn't have to use her blood-streaked feet.

Saleena saw herself, stretched out on a blanket. The sense of oddness had never gone away at seeing her body through another's eyes. She held out her arms and said to the guards, "Bind these hands now. We don't know who she is or what she might do when released. She was kept in a cage and has this vile collar with a crystal built into it like Adrian's."

Controlling another human gave Saleena a creepy feeling. It was a forbidden thing she had believed was an abomination all her life, and here she was, using a vile and forbidden connection to rescue a slave. The noble cause didn't make her feel any better as she broke the last of the three Accords.

Once the prisoner was bound and leaned back as comfortably as the ropes allowed, Saleena pulled back to herself and worked her way to her feet. The wobbles faded after a few seconds, and she stepped over the others, still in their trances, to examine the woman. She was unconscious now, which was strange. Anything that kept her asleep should have kept someone like Saleena from taking control.

With guards watching the woman, she took the box and crystals and set them aside. There was still work to do. The two men who controlled the small farm dogs sat up as their dogs ran into the camp. They lavished the dogs with attention and treats for a job well done.

Next, the badger crew came back. They had been due to return last because they didn't move as fast. Saleena cast a worried glance at the remaining sleepers. Otis, the gate guard who owned one of the half-wolves sat up with a start and swore as he stumbled to his knees. "Archers. They have archers following us. Some are hurt bad. I lost Ruffian!" He stifled a sob as Saleena and the guards intercepted him before he could run off to help. He was still dizzy, so it was easy to steer him back to his blanket.

Gavin said, "We have men on the perimeter. They'll get all the help we have if they make it close enough." He put a hand on the guard's shoulder. "I'm sorry about Ruffian."

The guard sat back down. "The cats must be half demon. I've never seen anything like it. Their claws and teeth were everywhere. Men were screaming and thrashing on the ground, their faces covered in blood. The cats popped up out of nowhere, attacked, and vanished over and over, like little maniacs. We hamstrung the men to keep them on the ground where the cats got to them. We almost got clear before the archers got there and shot at anything that moved, even their own men. They couldn't see as well in the dark as we could." He peered at the rest of the team where they lay on the ground, still in their trances, and chewed at a knuckle. "Come on, you can do it. Get out of there."

It was a good sign their trances had not ended yet. They were still in control and working their way up the hill.

A raven fluttered in, and Brother Cleo opened his eyes. "They just reached the perimeter. Most of them made it, but they've been hurt. The worst are being carried here." He sat up and caressed the back of the bird with a fingertip, then moved the bird into its cage with all the care he could manage with shaky hands.

Saleena put a hand on Gavin's arm. "Gavin, we're going to need people to treat the wounded."

"Oh, of course." He gazed at her with a lost expression which was quickly replaced by determination. "We need help for wounded animals!" He turned with a pleading expression to his personal guard who gave him a nod and sprinted off into the dark. Gavin was distant, occupied by some weighty matter. "Saleena, will you give me the master crystal for her now, please?"

She removed the chain from her neck and reluctantly handed it to him, then watched as he stepped over and set it on top of a large rock. He picked up another rock the size of his fist and yelled as he slammed it down on the crystal with such force splinters scattered all around the large stone.

"This is the second time I've seen this, and I will choose to free slaves every time. Our animals serve us, but they serve as guardians, companions, and friends. This?" He pointed to the collar around the woman's neck. "This is slavery to a level beyond mere servitude. Tell me, Saleena. Do your cattle hate you?"

"No, of course not. They'll follow me around like puppies if I let them. They did even before the crystals."

"But you've trained them to do hard things. You've even forced them to work hard at times. Like when you taught them how to defend themselves from predators."

Saleena nodded.

"Saleena, I think this whole camp would follow me around like puppies. And tomorrow I have to send them, man and beast alike, to a fight that will kill some of them, maybe even most of them. Tonight's losses will be nothing compared to the sacrifices we make tomorrow. What makes me different from the men who did this?" He waved at the woman's collar. "Have I helped the people enough that I deserve what they'll do in my name?"

"Of course, you have. You've saved the lives of more people than I can count." She thought of all the things he had done. Most of the rumors were rubbish, but that didn't take away from who he was and what he had done. She knew why he asked, but she had never hesitated or worried over her own actions and motives as she and her family chose to break the law. They made and used crystals in the service of the old baron, a man who would have condemned them for it. "There's a reason people have confidence in you. You're a good leader. They will follow you and die at your command if it saves others."

She reached toward him, but paused as heavy footfalls approached from behind.

"Make way!" The perimeter guards carried the injured animals in, disrupting her thoughts.

Draken's wolf could walk, but not well. Then Saleena noticed the wolf had lost most of her tail. Draken woke and immediately reached for his travel pack and pulled out a strip of cloth. He patted the wolf gently as she lay down with a whimper, but after a few moments of attention to bandage her tail, Draken was off to tend to the others.

Saleena's eyes fell on Runner. Her father held control to keep him still, but she saw her father's breathing was fast and shallow. He was barely holding the trance in place. An arrow ran in Runner's left side through his ribs and back out on the right. She couldn't imagine the pain both Runner and her father must be in. She knelt beside Runner as he was set down. "Da, let him go now. We've got him. He'll want to see you as himself before he goes."

Runner's head shook in faint denial.

"Da, this is too bad. We can't save him. You can't take the pain to hold him still for stitching his wounds, and he won't know to hold still on his own."

She dashed tears from her eyes and glanced around at those surrounding her in an appeal for help.

Then she saw the box liberated from the enemy camp. "Wait. We might be able to do this." She stood to intercept a man who arrived with bandages.

She grabbed him by the arm. "Sleep juice. Will it let Runner be sewn up?" She pointed at the dog.

"Nobody has that stuff out here. It would take more than a week's pay for just the one dog, even if I had some."

She grabbed the box and thrust it toward him. "Use it on any of these animals if it will help, but please try it first on Runner. He won't last long if he's bleeding inside."

The man uncorked a bottle from the box and gave it a sniff, then noticed there were a dozen bottles, with ten already empty. "Someone's already spent a king's ransom on this stuff. Are you sure you want to use it on the animals?"

She nodded, and he set to work on Runner.

Soon, Tover pulled back from his trance, leaving Runner in a deep sleep. He said, "I'm so sorry. I shouldn't have risked it." He rubbed his sides.

Her speech to Gavin still rang through Saleena's head. Was it true? Was the sacrifice worth it? She had to convince not only herself but her father as Runner lay near death.

Saleena had one hand on Runner's head and one on her father's shoulder. "No, Da. You did right. You and Runner hit them hard. You helped save us and the woman. You and the others gave us a chance to survive tomorrow." Tears ran down her face and dropped onto Runner's fur. She ran her fingers along the top of Runner's head to comfort herself as the dog slept through the work to patch him up. "We're all sorry about how it turned out, but don't apologize for doing the right thing. Runner deserves that from us. He helped save us all."

Soon, the job was done. Runner was left with her, bandages encasing his ribs.

The animal surgeon said, "He might make it, but there's no guarantee. As the drug wears off, it's normal to wake and sleep several times."

The words rolled past her without meaning. Everyone around Saleena was in a rush that never quite touched her. She and Da sat with Runner and held him close. Time passed, and the rush subsided. Runner still breathed.

GAVIN KNELT BESIDE SALEENA, concerned she hadn't moved the whole time as the other animals were attended to. The rest of the creatures were resting easily now. "Saleena, it's time for you to get some sleep."

She gave a nod and crawled over to her blanket where she had lain while bringing the mystery woman back. She put her cattle crystals on, then curled up and took a few deep breaths.

Satisfied she was all right, Gavin returned to Draken who inspected the small wooden chest from the enemy camp.

Draken pulled the cork from a bottle and sniffed. "This is a lot of sleep juice, even for training. Ten empty bottles could knock out an army." His eyes grew wide, and he swore a stream in a language Gavin had never heard before.

A puzzle piece fell into place in Gavin's mind. "The Baron's Conference. They were drugged. No wonder. They must have used it on her as well." He pointed at the woman bundled head to toe in blankets, nothing but a shock of hair showing in the moonlight. Her feet had been cleaned and bandaged, and they had done what they could to make her comfortable.

Gavin said, "She hasn't woken up at all, even when Saleena woke up after controlling her."

Draken said, "Sleep juice will do that. It's used when training particularly difficult animals, and it's horribly expensive. This might explain the barony's empty treasury. While using this, you can control an animal even when it's out cold. It normally lasts only for an hour or two on a large beast. They must have given a lot of it to her. I don't know how long it will take to wear off."

Gavin's eyes drooped as he nodded. "We'll wait and deal with her when she wakes up. We'd better get a little rest before it gets light. It's been a long night, and it will be a lot worse tomorrow."

CHAPTER

TWENTY-TWO

Saleena faced Willem with her hands on her hips. "If we get overrun, it will be too late. You need to wear some armor, at least."

"I don't have any. Don't need it, don't want it."

She shook her head and bit her tongue to hold back a string of names which would have been both accurate and childish. "Look. I think I have at least an old spaulder from when Gavin beat the two men."

"And a bear. Don't forget the bear. You can't forget to idolize him for that, too."

She climbed the wagon to rummage through her things and mumbled, "I don't have time for this." She understood his response was because she had been short with him, but she was still annoyed. Finally, she came across the layered leather spaulder, still near the battered camping pack from what seemed like forever ago. She tossed the shoulder armor down to Willem. "The buckles should let you adjust it to extra small." As soon as she said it, she knew it was a mistake. It wasn't fair for her to take out her frustrations on him. Runner's brush with death had hit her hard, and the smallest things were setting her off this morning as the sky lit up with orange-tinted clouds.

The pack tipped as she dropped it, and the contents spilled out. An old case with a lock on it landed on one corner and broke open. With a sigh of exasperation, she sat down to ram everything back into the pack and came across a letter with a wax seal. It had Gavin's name on it. "Willem, why would a bandit's letter have Gavin's name on it?"

"Don't ask me. I don't read. Too stupid and too little." He twisted the armor this way and that, working out how to adjust all the buckles.

"I need to get this to Gavin."

Willem glared at her where she stood on the wagon, holding the note. "It's waited a long time with no problem. It'll still be there later. We need to get going. We're already late since you made me get this." He shrugged into the shoulder piece and fastened the iron buckles.

She nodded and tucked the envelope into a pouch on her hip. "Fine. There. Now you can only be stabbed on *most* of your body instead of all of it." She jumped down and rapped her knuckles on his new armor. "Let's go. They've set up a guarded perimeter around where we'll spread out."

Most of the team was already gathered. In addition to the regulars, she saw Royn, the leatherworker who had taken over most of the day-to-day herd management. "What are you doing up here, Royn?"

"I had to show you what I finished. The armor is rough, and it doesn't fit well, but every head of cattle with a crystal now has a neck guard and some heavy leather to cover their, um, chuck, brisket, and ribs."

She nearly burst out in laughter at the use of meat cuts to describe the areas he'd armored, but it told her what he'd done faster than any other description would have. They would have armor on the front, and a little past their shoulders. Anything would help. "Thank you, Royn. I hope to make you proud today."

Behind her, Willem sniffed, then said, "We about ready? I'm heading over to spread myself out now. There's a shady spot under the wagons."

Saleena hadn't seen the cats arrive, but Willem assured her they survived the night without serious injury. She hadn't been aware of much last night after the fight. Thinking about it made her alternately sad and angry, wanting to weep, and then wanting to rip the enemy to shreds over Runner's injuries. The cattle might pick up on her mood as she controlled them. She needed to gain focus for the coming battle, or they would become too aggressive for their own good and endanger themselves and her.

Her blankets lay under a cloth pavilion with most of the others. Willem could hide away on his own if he wanted, but she needed to be part of the team. She slipped into a trance and became aware of over three dozen views of the hillside as she took control of the herd mind. Several of the cattle had a view of the space between the camps, and she saw the enemy animals and men forming up below. This would be a messy, deadly day.

GAVIN GAZED over the open field as the sun's first rays lit the sparse trees. There was no sunlight advantage either way since the enemy was to the north. Their night raid had sown some chaos, but the force below them still fielded an impressive array of bears, mountain lions, wolves, a couple of moose, and some more exotic northern animals he hadn't seen before.

Carnivore or not made little difference. If they were large and had antlers, horns, claws, hooves, or teeth they were of use in a fight. Most of them wore metal or leather plates of fitted armor. He'd seen Saleena use her herd to take out a single bear, but now they faced a whole line of trained, armored war animals. Rather than overwhelming one opponent, they would need to rely on strategy and tactics to push the fight in their favor. Aside from the high ground, they had a few advantages the enemy didn't know about. The herd performed more precisely under Saleena's control than any group of people could manage. They would have to use that to their advantage, and it would only surprise the enemy once.

A hundred footmen formed up in front of the enemy animals in the valley below. This was a change. In the past, they'd always run the animals in first. Maybe they had hit harder than he gave his team credit for, or, more likely, they were wary of traps.

The army was smaller than the original estimates of five-hundred men, and Gavin was thankful Adrian had the rest running a merry chase. They still had too many men ready to fight compared to his forces. Success seemed a remote chance, but they had to try.

Saleena had brought back several crystals, and their squirrel had come back with cheeks bulging to capacity. The war animals had left some of the stolen crystals hidden in the enemy camp for lack of hands to carry them. All of the crystals they had taken, aside from the one, had been the animal's half of the pair. Gavin had no way to make use of those animals or crystals for the battle, but the enemy couldn't use them, either. The animals could be set free, but there was no way to tell who or what they might attack, or if they would flee into the countryside. Those animals were useless now unless they rounded up spare crystals, and spares were always rare.

It was a waste of time to second-guess himself. Everything had been set in motion, and, as usual, precious few of the final details were up to him. He came up with the main strategy and then let the individual experts figure out how to make the tactics work. If this was what leadership was like, it was overvalued.

His own forces were meager. He had the cattle and a couple of oxen, as well as the wolves and dogs who remained. They had switched a few crystals to uninjured animals, but those animals had almost no training. There was no time. Draken's wolf was in good enough shape to make a difference, even without her tail. The smaller creatures had escaped without serious injury, probably because they were so easy to overlook.

Gavin smiled at the thought of how such small creatures had made such a big difference. It wasn't so much what you had as how you used it. He saw himself in the same category, small and usually ignored, but thrust into the line of duty to perform unexpected and heroic miracles. So far, those miracles hadn't included winning a head-to-head battle.

He caught a hint of movement near the top of the hill as the cats and badgers picked their way through the tall grass. In moments, they were lost to his sight. He never saw the smaller ones at all. He had little idea what a rat could do against a bear or moose, but their job was to get behind the enemy and hit targets of opportunity, and then get out of the way as fast as possible.

The enemy forces slowly advanced up the hill in formation. It was hard for Gavin to pick out details at this distance, but the men up front seemed to be pointing at the cattle at the top of the hill. Gavin retrieved a spyglass, borrowed from Draken, and put it to his eye. Draken had threatened to break his fingers if harm came to the spyglass, so he held it with care. The men below pointed at the cattle and laughed, making rude gestures. That would change soon. Because of the raid, Gavin's unconventional war animals accounted for more crystals than those of the enemy's army. The enemy still had far more training in war.

The men below formed into lines two deep, with bows in the back and pikes up front to destroy any direct charge. The cattle wouldn't survive if Saleena had to face them head on, but she said she had a plan. The cattle's armor would help, but not enough by itself. If those men diverted by

Adrian had made it back, the fight would have been quick and deadly. Now they had a slim chance if everything worked in their favor.

His men had no front row of pikes, but he did have archers and swordsmen armed with a mix of their personal bows and the weapons Adrian had brought back from Greenvale. They stood behind the cattle. Women were mixed in among the men, everyone taking their place to defend those they cared for.

They had several swordsmen deployed to guard the Crystal Cabal, yet many had little or no training. An old, retired army bugler stood to Gavin's side, ready to send signals out to the field, but each group was responsible for their own actions now that the larger strategy had been laid out. They only needed a signal from him to put the battle plan into motion.

The enemy footmen below reached a predetermined location, and Gavin said, "Now."

A horn blast echoed across the field, and the cattle turned downhill, moving as one. Gavin's archers held back until the enemy pike men came into range. Their volley fell among the rows of men far downhill. They didn't have enough men to do a real rain of arrows, but every little bit helped.

The cattle gained speed until they were at a full run, straight at the pike men who stopped and braced their pikes directly up the hill, ready to receive the attack. The men of the enemy front line were brave, he'd give them that. Few men would stand in the face of a full charge of any animal. The archers behind the enemy pike men let loose with a volley, and to Gavin's disappointment, a few of the cattle now had arrows rising from their backs. None fell.

At the last instant, the cattle shifted direction, turning hard to the left in a wave so they could hit the front line almost sideways. It was a move nobody could coordinate if you had individuals each controlling each animal. The enemy had no way to predict it or protect themselves from it — the first time. A few of the pike men turned their weapons to receive attackers at the new angle, but they tangled their pikes when most remained in the useless forward position. The cattle hit the pike men, then ran down the row, tossing them aside like rag dolls or crushing them whenever beast and man collided. A few cattle swung wide to threaten the archers, reducing their attacks. Several archers dropped back out of the way, but they moved back up as soon as the wave of cattle stampeded past.

Because of the direction change, more of the damage hit the left side of the pike line. The cattle peeled to the left again and retreated up the hill. Gavin supported Draken when he denied Saleena's request to plow straight through and go head-to-head with the larger war animals. A normal charge would lead to the destruction of the whole herd and the loss of the battle.

The cattle charge missed most of the enemy archers. The archers fired at the retreating cattle, hitting where the animals had no armor. Gavin's archers were useless. They risked hitting the cattle if they tried to shoot that far. The enemy war animals behind the archers closed the gap, moving forward to prepare for a counterattack. The enemy force of war animals had been reduced by their night raid, but they still formed a great animal army, able to kill any who ended up in their way.

The cattle appeared to be in disarray as they ran back up the hill, but that was part of the plan. The enemy wouldn't know they were controlled as a single unit and would, hopefully, misjudge their readiness for their next attack. Gavin spotted the men below shouting orders to the animals. Gavin gave no orders since the plan was still mostly intact.

A lucky archer lobbed a high, indirect shot and hit one of the cattle in a rear leg, taking it down. It got back up but limped as it moved. The armor did its job, deflecting much of the attack against the herd with the poorly aimed pikes and the sporadic arrows, but Saleena had to be in a lot of pain. Gavin glanced at her and saw she was drenched in sweat even in the cool morning air.

Gavin had given so much attention to the movements of the men that he had paid little attention to the war animals behind them. With a sudden rush, the animals ran through gaps in their front line, intent on reaching the cattle now that the field had been shown to be free of traps.

Some of the enemy animals howled and turned rather than charge. Tiny shapes darted away into the grass while the remainder of the animals came up the hill at full speed. His team of small animals did their best, but it wasn't enough to make a real difference as most of the force charged up the hill.

As one again, the cattle turned in place and aimed at one of the largest enemy animals out front, a huge brown bear. It was a repeat of Gavin's first sight of the cattle fighting together. They streamed in from all angles with perfect spacing to barely miss each other. One after the other, they hit their target until it dropped. Saleena took opportunistic shots at others with horns and hooves as the cattle sped past. Without the concentrated power of the group, they took as many swipes as they gave on those secondary targets. Three smaller war animals were taken out by the cattle, while four of the cattle collapsed when their legs were taken out from under them. Several animals pounced on the fallen cattle to make sure they stayed down.

Gavin spotted his father's black bear among those shredding a fallen animal. Was his father controlling the one-eared bear, or was it someone else? It was impossible to tell.

After breaking the charge, the cattle fled back up the hill among a scattered hail of arrows. Again, more of Saleena's force failed to make it back up the hill. The enemy war animals reformed outside of Gavin's archer's range. Even the strongest and least injured of the cattle struggled from all the running. Those that remained needed a rest.

Apparently, the enemy saw the same thing as the men and animals charged again. The animals loped along easily behind the men as they waited for a signal to break into a charge.

Gavin turned to the bugler. "We need the archers to hit them as the animals cut between their men to come forward. It's a more concentrated target."

The command didn't work well. They barely had enough archers to wear the enemy down as their war animals surged. It wasn't enough. Gavin's animals were falling faster than the enemy's.

Gavin spared a glance back at Saleena. With the damage her cattle had taken, it amazed Gavin that she kept control of her herd. He had never considered the pain she and her cattle endured in their initial training against mountain predators, just like he had never considered the pain of those who fought in wars with trained animals. Now people fought, suffered and died at his command.

Saleena ran the cattle down again to meet the approaching war animals and then broke into another formation aimed at their front rank. A moose formed the tip of a triangle formation charging at full-speed. Gavin heard the collision from his vantage point on the hill when horns and antlers tangled at high speed. Saleena sacrificed at least three animals in full speed collisions to pierce through armor and take out the largest animals at the head of the enemy's charge in a one-for-one trade.

The enemy's momentum broke, but the field was strewn with corpses and injured bodies of both men and beasts. Two enemy bears broke all the way through to the hilltop where they crashed through some swordsmen and attacked the archers in a desperate bid to reach Gavin's position near the Crystal Cabal. Men and women screamed in rage and pain as the fight was joined.

Without warning, the mystery woman looked around, and then leaped toward the two bears. She ran her wrist bonds against the sword of a fallen guard to free herself, then grabbed the sword as she raced forward. She screamed two men's names at the bears who both turned to face her. She spun in place, swinging the sword in a great circle, then let the sword fly like a giant throwing knife, piercing the leather chest armor of the lead bear to sink a hand span into its flesh. The bear batted it free, only slightly injured. Gavin's forces and the woman shared an enemy, and that was good enough for him. She now had the full attention of both animals.

Jase said, "Don't move unless I fall," and sprinted forward. Gavin ignored the command and drew his short blade as he ran behind Jase.

Women and children charged to join the men to attack the bears. Gavin shouted, "Jase, go left! I'll come in on the center." The strange woman jabbed a spear she had found at the injured bear as it stumbled. She continued her assault in a rapid series of thrusts and jabs forcing the bear to focus on her.

Gavin and Jase arrived too late to save the first rank of defenders who fell under great swings of the bear's claws. Jase slashed at a left rear leg as Gavin leaped, with both hands on the hilt of his blade. He landed on the bear's back and drove the blade between its ribs just below its shoulder.

It bellowed in pain and rolled on the side Jase had hit, throwing Gavin to the ground. He hit his head, and his vision filled with blackness shot through with stars.

Something pinned his leg. He shook his head clear and saw the bear crumpled half on top of him, but still swinging claws at anyone who approached.

The handle of his blade protruded from the bear's back, within his reach. Clenching both hands together, Gavin pounded sideways on the blade hilt, forcing it to cut through the thick fur and muscles beneath.

As the bear struggled and fought, everyone who could get their hands on a weapon swarmed in until both beasts stopped moving.

Jase glared at Gavin and pulled him free. "I told you to wait, sir. We can't risk losing you."

"I refuse to stand by and watch as men, women, and children throw themselves at the enemy to defend me. I don't deserve their lives if I'm not willing to join them."

The mystery woman stood over the animal corpses with the other defenders, breathing hard. She collapsed, and two guardsmen set her back onto her blankets, fast asleep once more due to the waning effects of the sleep juice. The bandages on her feet showed fresh red stains.

One of the bears had attacked a member of the Crystal Cabal. A badger controller bled from a head injury and looked around, dazed. Gavin hurried over and pulled the crystal cord from the man's neck and dropped it around his own.

The man was in no shape to go back into a trance, but it would likely take too long for Gavin to do any good either.

The enemy reformed out of range of the archers and waited. Gavin took stock of their resources as the remaining cattle gathered. More than half of the cattle had fallen in the attacks, and all were wounded. They didn't have enough animals to keep another enemy charge away from the dwindling swordsmen and archers, the last line of defense for the main camp.

A runner approached, waving at Gavin. "Sir, the archers are running low on arrows." Desperation seeped into Gavin as he watched his army shrink by the moment.

He cast his eyes about and saw hundreds, maybe thousands, of used arrows pin-cushioning the battlefield. Reaching them would take care and a good guard to avoid exposing his men to the enemy below, who still had enough archers to blanket the battleground.

Brother Cleo stepped up beside him and pointed behind the main force.

"That's the king's animal. See the big grizzly bear? He's holding back to watch. We nearly got his crystal last night, but the collar was too heavy to chew through. It's got to be barely hanging on. I'm going to take the raven in close to take a peek at it. I've seen some of the small animals down that way, too, trying to flank them."

Gavin nodded. "I have one of the badger crystals, but it won't do any good. It takes too long to attune to it."

Brother Cleo said, "Take your boots off, quickly!"

Gavin gave him an odd look but complied.

"Now sit like this." Brother Cleo sat with his feet together and pulled close, with his hands pressed against the tops of his feet.

Once Gavin was in position, Bother Cleo pushed his hands and feet a bit to adjust their position, and then said, "Now hum. No, higher. Good. Hold just like that as long as you can."

Brother Cleo continued, "We have to do our best to take him out of the fight. If he brings his reserve force up now, we've lost. He has to know that. If we work together we might have a chance."

Brother Cleo ran back and collapsed onto the ground without taking the time to settle into a comfortable position.

Gavin felt the link forming, but it wasn't ready yet. He watched the army below as he hummed, an odd resonance filling his mind.

The enemy paused in their attack, so Gavin issued the order to march the cattle down part way to give the men some protection so they could gather arrows from the upper field. If they had an actual fighting force, things might be different. Most of the armed men were farmers, traders, and craftsmen who had been faced with a choice of defending themselves or being killed. Many of the women insisted on helping with the defensive wall as well. They stood beside their husbands, sons, and brothers, and had come up with all kinds of improvised death-dealing weapons. The people performed admirably given they had less than two weeks of training, but it would all be for naught if the enemy combined all their forces and pushed.

The defensive wall had Draken's wolf among them as an additional guard, running back and forth among the cattle. Two oxen also stood guard with their bulk between Gavin's men and the enemy archers.

Jase borrowed Draken's spyglass to look at the rear enemy group. "An eagle is chasing Brother Cleo's raven away from the enemy's reserve group. It must be the one they used to spy on us."

Gavin could see the two birds engaged in battle, dodging and swooping. Three times the raven barely escaped the eagle's claws. The raven's advantage was its maneuverability as they twisted and looped through the sky.

The birds danced their way gradually up the hill, until they were within range of the archers who let a volley fly at the eagle. An arrow pierced its left wing, and the large bird spiraled to the ground.

A cheer rose from the archers, but the main war animal force below began to advance. Jase stepped in and told the trumpeter, "Sound a retreat. Get those men back up now!"

As the bugler put his lips to his horn, a different horn sounded from behind their camp. The bugler's eyes widened. "That's a cavalry call!" He turned and blasted out a series of notes, then listened for a response.

A call came back, and the bugler said, "There's six of them. That's a good bit of help."

Gavin tried to figure out if the man was serious, but saw the bugler's relief. How much could six riders possibly do? He hummed as he thought. The crystal echoed the hum back to him.

It was hard to see much from the ground, but he took a quick inventory of both sides and came up short. The cavalry men weren't enough to even the odds.

Jase turned to Gavin. "Bluff? Maybe we can make it look like we have a lot of cavalry."

Gavin nodded as he hummed, trying to keep the pitch Brother Cleo had shown him.

Jase continued, "Split them up, three on each side. Wait out of sight below the ridge until we signal them to come up and look as big as possible right on the ridge where they'll be the most visible. Lots to see and lots of noise. We might be able to use the terrain to convince the enemy they're the front rank of a larger force."

The bugler scratched his beard. "You've got to be kidding. Not even the cavalry buglers can put that much detail into their orders. I'll tell them to form up." He turned to face away from the fight and traded bugle commands back and forth.

Gavin's men retreated, but not quickly enough. In less than a minute the enemy would overrun them.

The link to the badger appeared in Gavin's mind, and he dropped into control. Brother Cleo's odd trick worked. The priest was a man of surprises.

The view from ground-level disoriented him. It was dim, almost dark. The animal had found a hiding place after its master had been pulled from his trance.

Gavin crawled out and spotted the enemy king's reserve force nearby, along with a few animals from Gavin's force of small creatures.

He let out a yip then made a paw signal, telling his friends to attack his target. Then he charged up to the King's grizzly bear.

The bear saw him and raised a paw, ready to squash him with a deadly swing. Three small creatures bit its rear legs, causing it to turn and bellow.

Gavin hopped to the top of a rock and leaped into the air, grabbing the bear's crystal in his teeth. It didn't break free. The collar had been repaired. He dangled from the thick leather and clamped his jaws tighter as the bear swung its head back and forth.

Every time the bear tried to stand to use its paws against him, the smaller animals darted in with teeth and claws. A squirrel ran up the bear's back and latched onto an ear, one of the few places it could get a good hold.

The bear turned his head with a mighty jerk at the squirrel's attack. Gavin twisted, his teeth shearing through leather. He flew free to crash through a bush and land on his back with a thump.

He choked on a small object and reflexively swallowed. Was that the crystal? A glance at the bear showed the collar no longer held a gem.

He rolled to his feet and yipped again, hoping everyone knew enough to get out of the way. Once he was out of immediate danger, Gavin found another hiding spot and released control.

He put his boots on, too dizzy to stand. "We got the king's crystal off the bear."

Jase lent an arm and handed him the spyglass with a grin. "It's getting lively down there."

Gavin turned the spyglass back to the enemy as the grizzly, previously harassed and pestered on all sides, was free to act on its own. It lashed out at anything close. The rest of the king's reserve force scattered to get out of the bear's reach.

He would never get a better shot than this. "Forget about having the cavalry form up. Sound a full charge. Everybody all the way in, including the guard wall. Including us. It's our only chance. It's victory or death. Get the cavalry out there with us to see what they can do."

The bugler let out a blast and Gavin grinned like a maniac, watching the enemy reserve team break. His ragtag army ran down the hill, screaming at the top of their lungs. The meager cavalry force came over the hill on both sides and charged down into the arena of combat.

Gavin stumbled as he ran, shaking the trance tremors away as he gained speed.

The enemy front ranks of men and animals stopped, stared, and held to a slow retreat for a half a minute. Then they turned and ran. The cavalry cut in on their flanks while Saleena's remaining cattle plowed forward through the center where the pike men were now in disarray. Draken's wolf and some farm dogs bit anyone who tried to dodge out of the way. The oxen rumbled through after the cattle and stomped anything still moving. The front wave of cattle ran straight over the fleeing men and beasts and into the enemy camp, leaving injury and death in their wake. Gavin's footmen and archers screamed and followed. They swarmed anyone who didn't flee fast enough or throw down their arms.

Gavin ran with them, losing his hilltop view of the field. He had given his last order, and the rest of the fight was in the hands of his people. Jase and the bugler ran at his side, keeping pace, screaming a battle cry of "Stoutheart!"

Two men from the cavalry force, one on each side, were buglers. They directed the other four who maintained a trance to control their mounts. The buglers coordinated their flanking maneuvers to devastating effect through the edges of the routed forces. If the enemy had seen the cavalry was only six strong, they might have ended the fight with a renewed attack.

The confusion and chaos sewn by the rampaging grizzly played into the hands of the amateur soldiers under Gavin's command as they flooded down the field of battle.

Again and again, men and trained animals fell to the cavalry, lacking orders to organize against the three fronts they faced. Soon there was a path through the enemy to the camp where men, many of Northern noble blood, lay helpless in their trances.

Rather than be butchered by the cavalry and the approaching footmen, they surrendered. War animals lay out flat on the ground in the common signal for surrender. The remaining Graven soldiers threw down their weapons, kneeling on the ground with raised arms.

It was over.

They'd won.

All that remained were an angry, injured grizzly bear and a few animals that fled back through the enemy camp.

Gavin looked out across the wreckage and carnage. It was a victory, but it had cost them nearly everything. People swarmed him and cheered, making their slow way back up the hill to their camp in his wake.

"Sir?" Brother Cleo was once again at his elbow, breathing hard. "I spotted Adrian and six of his men at the rear of the enemy camp on horseback, but I lost them. Outrunning the eagle seemed more important at the time."

"Thank you. I'm sure they'll show up soon." Gavin checked to make sure Adrian wasn't already standing beside him.

Gavin wandered around the top of the hill in a daze and ended up standing where the bears had broken through to savage their defenses. He heard weeping and cries of pain all around him. On the ground was a boy's red-stained shoe, torn loose in the fight. He fell to his knees and squeezed his eyes shut to block out the sight of the bodies as he clenched his fists. He'd failed to save them all, with more lives lost than ever before. They deserved better, and he could only make it up to the survivors.

———

ADRIAN MOTIONED his men to stand back, two in the far corners of the tent and two inside the entrance. He didn't want any interruptions. Gerald Stoutheart's guards lay lifeless, their blood soaking into the ground. Stoutheart himself sprawled on a low cot in a trance. Adrian fingered shackles that had been attached to a tent pole as he waited. He had seen the baron's shackles before.

Outside, a large animal ran up to the tent, and Adrian heard the clinking sound of a latch as it slid home. The baron often used the bear to lock itself up before releasing control. Adrian smiled at the Baron's predictability.

Baron Gerald Stoutheart sat up and glanced around the room. "Adrian, those were my men, not the king's. I think you, of all people, would recognize them and ask before killing them." He sat up, all poise and confidence despite the shakes from his recent trance. "I've hoped for you to catch up to me for some time. That was brilliant how you led a third of the army away on a wild goose chase. Did you buy more than a day?"

Adrian said, "They might be two days. Three if they search all the false trails. It was some of my better work, but I wasn't after your approval. You see, your son's done an admirable job as the new baron."

Gerald grunted. "It sounds like he'll make a fine figurehead if things don't work out as I planned. We need to get to King Ithan before my son's ragtag crew gets there. Help me up, will you?" He stretched out a hand.

Adrian stood still. "She's not here. When I first thought you were dead, I hoped she was released or had escaped. She never showed up. How long was it before you killed her?"

"Oh. I see where you're going with this. I still have her. She'll be fine as long as you continue to serve me as you have in the past." Gerald struggled to his feet, still shaky.

"You forget I know how you work. You're not subtle with your messages. If you had her, she'd be here. You're at a disadvantage now." Adrian tapped his collar with a groove worn where he had worked to remove it. "Do you know what your son did when he found out your crystal controlled me? He smashed the master crystal right there in front of me. No discussion. No threats. No putting my own knife to my throat. Do you know why? Because he saw right through me and accepted me for what I was, and for what I could become. He has honor you'll never understand."

Adrian turned his back on Gerald. "I only came for one thing, and you don't have it."

Gerald drew a dagger and slashed through the back wall of the tent, but before he had so much as taken a step to escape, an inconspicuous but deadly snake struck from its hiding place near Gerald's leg. It pulled back and struck again as he jerked back and tumbled onto the cot. The striped snake had one of the fastest acting venoms known, and it wore an over-sized crystal, fastened behind its head.

"Right. Small and sneaky worked out pretty well." Adrian placed a sack on the ground, and the snake obediently climbed in. Gerald gasped in pain and surprise, his skin turning ashen. A few moments later, two more of Adrian's men came into the tent, one of them wavering as he walked, steadied by the other as he recovered from his trance.

"No kingdom for you today, sir. You'll never see family, never watch your son marry and have your grandchildren. Never even see another sunset. You've taken everything from me, and now I'm taking everything from you."

Adrian looked at the old baron and shook his head. "Some would call this justice. Others, vengeance. I can't really tell the difference."

"She's ..." Gerald held a hand out to appeal to Adrian as paralysis spread through his body. It would take an hour or more for him to die, but there was no stopping it now.

"Goodbye, sir. I'll watch over your grandchildren." Adrian walked through the door flap and handed the bagged snake off to the man who wore its matching crystal. He gestured behind him at the baron. "Please bring him along. The new Baron Stoutheart will want to know about his father."

CHAPTER

TWENTY-THREE

Gavin sat down to rest and catch his breath near the Crystal Cabal's camp when Saleena approached him tentatively. "I don't know what this means, but this was in the gear of those bandits you fought in the canyon. It has your name on it. There wasn't time to bring it to you before."

She offered the wax-sealed envelope. He stared at it and then pulled out a knife to break the seal as Adrian hopped down from the wagon behind him to peer over his shoulder. Gavin held the knife out defensively and then gave an exhausted grimace. "Must you do that every time?"

"Sorry, old habit. I need you to see something." Adrian stood and held out a hand to Gavin, then stopped as he looked past Gavin to the freed slave woman who sat wrapped in a blanket.

He ran and skidded to a stop on his knees. "Sharise?"

She swallowed and squinted at him. "Adrian? Who are these people? I think they rescued me." Her voice was soft and slow. She pieced the words together, as if through a thick mental fog.

"You were dead." He gazed at her as if to absorb her through his eyes. His hands reached out but he hesitated, as if afraid to touch her, lest she break.

"I guess it didn't work out." She blinked and rubbed her eyes.

He pulled her into his arms and kissed her, caressing her hair. Neither of them said a word until Lindy cleared her throat. "Adrian, let her breathe. She can spend all the time she wants with you after she's got a little more strength back. She's not going anywhere and needs this broth more than she needs you draped all over her. Now git!"

Adrian leaned back, holding Sharise at arm's length. "Right. If I go for a few minutes, will you stay here? Of course, you will. How stupid of me."

Gavin smiled at the unexpected reunion, a splash of joy among a sea of sorrows. "We didn't know who she was. We stole the crystal used to control her and walked her out of their camp. I'll be ready to go with you if you give me a minute, Adrian."

He opened the letter and recognized his father's handwriting.

Gavin,

I'm sorry to have sent such ruffians to take possession of you and the cattle. The king of the Graven Kingdom is invading. There is nothing we can do to stop it, but I have a plan to lead him into our lands and destroy him. Your brother is dead. All of the other barons are dead as well, and there will be a lack of leadership throughout our kingdom. Once I kill the Graven King and take control of his army, we will be the only ones strong enough to lead Riland.

He didn't finish the letter. He didn't need to. He folded it up and put it into his pocket.

Adrian cocked his head. "Is something wrong, sir?"

Gavin shook his head distractedly. "No, it was a message too late to make a difference. Has there been any sign of my father?"

Adrian said, "Funny you should ask. Come with me."

Adrian's few remaining men stood guard outside the tent as Gavin and Adrian approached. They held the flaps up to let Gavin in. Adrian gave Jase a quick shake of the head. "A moment of privacy first, please."

Jase peered in and saw a wrapped form on the ground and nodded as he took up position outside with the others.

Gavin gestured to the wrapped body. "This is what you needed to show me? I've seen enough bodies today already."

Adrian lifted a cloth to show Gavin the face of his father, still breathing in shallow gasps with his eyes wide open. "He will be dead soon, but he can hear you."

Adrian stepped back as Gavin sat next to the man he loathed, yet loved.

Gavin wept.

They had disagreed on almost everything. His father had intimidated and belittled him. He had thought for days that his father was dead, then learned he was a traitor to everyone and everything the kingdom stood for. His father's plan was heartless and cruel, and was a personal grab for power to take over the kingdom through stealth and betrayal. Doing it for family didn't make any of that any better, and now his father was dying, and his plan with him.

"I finally saw your letter. You're wrong. The people don't need you. I'm sorry." And he was sorry, to the deepest recesses of his heart. Sorry for those he failed to save, and sorry for those who had chosen betrayal over devotion.

What would a baron do in his place? He wasn't a scared child facing his father's death. He wiped away his tears and pushed the heartache away. "You're right that there will be a struggle for power. I will do what I can to find and support a new king. I will take these people to the capital and work to restore stability."

He looked into his father's wide eyes. "I will do my best to see the sword of justice prevail. Only now do I see how similar we are, both rebelling against authority. Only our reasons are different. You sought to take power, where it was thrust upon me. I sought to save lives, where you spent them as currency."

Gavin had no choice but to keep going in his efforts to save his people. Anything else betrayed their trust, and he'd seen enough betrayal. He would accept a formal surrender and lead the remaining people to the capital to finalize a treaty. The whole situation was a messy assortment of assumed authorities and power by consent.

His father's plan bypassed some of that confusion, but it had been no more than the ravings of a power-hungry madman. Yet, through all that, his father's plan succeeded almost to the end.

He sat beside his father, then said, "I'll burn a candle for you and see you're remembered as an enemy of King Ithan. May you rest eternally in the kingdom you most deserve, whatever that may be."

His feelings burst to the foreground again, and he wept at the senseless loss on all sides. So much death and pain, all of it haunting him. What could he have done better? Who might he have saved if he were a little faster or cleverer?

Gavin wiped his tears and stood to face Adrian. "I found a note from my father. King Ithan spared him because they worked together, but my father planned to betray the king. If it makes any difference, the note proves this is all true. He was misguided, but his long view was for a stronger kingdom. Now I have to find a way to have him put to rest publicly."

Adrian nodded. "Everyone believes he died in the first attack. It's a workable fiction."

"No, it's not. King Ithan knows better and believes my father betrayed us all to serve him. I can't have him holding it over my head. I need a way to make the information in my father's note public to keep his actions from being used against me later."

"It's simpler to kill King Ithan."

Gavin shook his head. "I won't be the kind of baron who would do that. I'll come up with something. Can you help?"

Adrian frowned. "Only if it's for your sake, and not his." He nodded at the barely breathing form of Gerald Stoutheart.

Gavin placed his hand on his heart. "It's for me, and for the people lost in this battle."

Adrian looked thoughtful. "You need a big splash, then. The surrender."

The spymaster grimaced, and then continued. "One more thing, sir. You said you wanted all the information I have, unpleasant or not. My men and I poisoned him." Adrian handed the black bear's master crystal to Gavin. "This is yours. The bear is tied up with the other captured animals."

Gavin wanted to lash out at Adrian, but it was pointless. Adrian hadn't known of his father's plan, and his father would have received a public execution for treason if he had been captured. There was no closure, no sense of justice or finality to the events his father had set into motion. Even if he couldn't resolve everything, there was one thing he could do.

He bent down and removed his father's signet ring and put it on.

"Please bring Saleena here to see me. I made a promise to her. You can have this note after she's seen it." He spread out the note on his knee and waited.

THE TENT DOOR was open when Saleena peered in to see Gavin standing with a paper in his hand. Adrian had said nothing more than that Gavin had something important to tell her, so her imagination had run wild. She stepped into the tent at the beckoning of Adrian. "Gavin? What is it?"

He handed her the note, and she began to read. Her emotions flew through curiosity, rage, hatred, and despair as the pieces fit together, but her face stayed rock still from exhaustion. "Why? Why do you show this to me now?"

What could Gavin hope to gain by showing this letter to her?

"I made a promise to you, Saleena. I promised to let you see who was responsible for your brother's death." Gavin tugged the cover back to expose his father's ashen, sweating face, his eyes still staring upward.

He continued, "He will die soon. I know it won't bring your brother back. Ned died because he was in the way, just like you and your father would have died. Knowing all of this won't change anything that's happened. The only thing it can change is the future. I'll do whatever I can to save everyone I can. Nobody deserves to die as an inconvenient pawn. As people, we can be better than that."

Saleena didn't scream. She didn't cry on his shoulder. She wasn't tempted to do either. She understood Gavin wasn't to blame for the actions of his father, but she also saw Gavin had become distant and formal. He was in every way her baron now, rather than her childhood friend. He was the trusted and respected leader, and she was one of his advisers.

Her brother was gone. Many friends and fellow travelers had died on the field of battle. All these deaths left blood on the hands of an invading king and the man who lay on the ground gasping and staring at the ceiling. It would be a mercy to kill him and free him from his lingering death, but mercy wasn't something she could offer to the old baron.

She nodded, turned, and left the tent without another word. She wiped tears on the sleeve of her red blouse, deciding she would grieve with her father once they had the time. Maybe Willem would like to join them.

GAVIN HAD NEVER SEEN a formal surrender nor had one been described to him, so he called Draken to fill him in as they formed up on the bloody battlefield.

Draken said, "It's quite simple. He offers his sword by stabbing it into the ground, and then he hangs a bag from it with his personal crystals. His most valued commanders and crystal users do the same by seniority. At that point, you and your best step forward and – Oh. This will be interesting. Normally, you and your command staff would represent us. Just for fun, rank your people from most critical in the battle to the least. Tell me when you see the issue."

Gavin gave it a moment of thought. "Oh, he's not going to be pleased, is he?"

Draken said, "Those laws banning commoners from crystal use, and from using more than one at a time were set out by the Accords ages ago. You've flouted those rules. Technically, there's no rule against women using them, but it's far from normal."

"As baron, I can authorize who uses them. That's one Accord violation he can't pin on me."

"But sir, there's the unwritten rules as well. The gentlemanly agreements of how things are to be done. You and tradition really aren't on speaking terms. You never have been."

"Well, then. The day's early. Let's go ahead and flout some more rules and procedures. Tell the cavalrymen, Saleena, Willem and the rest to mount up for a show of force, rather than following the ritual forms. Bring the cats up from the rear, and cattle and horses behind me in a line. Tell our crystal team I want a salute of some kind from each of them when I call for it. I want you and Jase to flank me."

An hour later, everyone was in place. Gavin searched through the cavalrymen and was unable to find Rider Faven among them. When he asked after the man, one of the riders responded with a salute. "Faven is at the capital, sir."

Gavin didn't have time to ask for details. The cavalry men were maddening in their obscurity. It would take all his skill and patience to figure them out later.

Gavin took one last look up and down the line to calm his nerves and stepped into his designated spot at the head of what could only loosely be called his army. It wasn't really an army, and it was debatable as to whether it was even his. Not everyone was from his barony.

Ithan Talandor, leader of the Graven Kingdom, stepped forward, rammed his sword into the ground and hung a leather bag from the hilt. Each of his men, in turn, did the same, leaving a row of swords in the ground tip first.

Once they all stepped back, Gavin stepped forward and motioned Jase and Draken to come up behind him. He whispered, "Hold your arms out. This will get heavy."

Draken murmured, "Nobody will believe us when we describe this surrender. I hope this works."

Gavin knew to take credit himself was wrong. His people deserved the credit for their win, yet he had to still show respect for his conquered enemy to have any hope of creating a treaty they would honor.

At the king's sword, Gavin raised his voice to carry and said, "My force salutes you for your effort, and we respect the honor you have shown in a surrender that has saved lives and allowed a chance for peace." He lifted the first bag and grasped the king's sword. "On behalf of the cavalry, salute!"

Behind him, horses reared and whinnied as Gavin handed the bag to Draken, then pulled the sword and handed it to Jase to set it across his outstretched arms.

He moved to the next sword and repeated his actions. "On behalf of the cattle shield wall, salute!"

The king and his men glanced at each other. It was clear this wasn't what they expected.

From behind he heard a stomped rhythm. At first, it was a soft thump, but it gained strength until it became a synchronized drum beat rhythm felt through the ground. They stopped all at once and let out the loudest combined moo he had ever heard. The solemnity of the event vanished as he struggled to keep a straight face.

At the next sword, he regained his composure and gave the next line with a special effort to be a bit vague as to what kind of cat he talked about. "On behalf of the Cats of the Apocalypse, Doom Bringer, Skull Crusher, and Death Claw, salute!"

A haunting trio of dissonant yowls from the tall grass put a chill up Gavin's spine. It was impossible to tell the noise came from three common, rat-chasing cats. The king and his men darted glances to the side but stood their ground with nothing more than a few murmurs.

Gavin removed one more sword and again called out, "On behalf of the canine patrol, salute!"

A series of overlapping howls rose from behind Gavin. Mixed among the animal sounds was one human voice, that of Otis, who had lost Ruffian. As the pitches rose, dropped, and contrasted with each other, it felt like a cry of despair for the fallen. The sound cut off all at once, and Gavin stepped over once more.

"On behalf of the airborne, salute."

The raven drifted down and settled on his shoulder, gave a nod, and flapped back into the air.

"On behalf of the smallest and cleverest of the ground-based army, salute."

The badgers were the loudest of the animals as they set up a growl in the grass near Gavin, who subdued a nervous twitch at the unexpectedly close noise. The king also flinched at the noise. Gavin had growled like that at the throat of his bear during the fight.

Gavin held his hands over his heart at the next sword. "On behalf of those who were lost." He didn't call for a salute, and didn't even specify which army he spoke about, but continued down the line pulling swords and pouches until only two remained.

"On my own behalf as the one who must answer for our losses." He pulled the next to last sword and handed off the sword and crystals.

Now that they were off balance with the odd ceremony, it was time to hit them with his best shot.

"Finally, on behalf of my father Baron Gerald Stoutheart who died in today's battle. He led you here to betray and destroy you. Without our intervention, he may have succeeded. You owe him your life, and he will be remembered as your closest enemy."

Gasps were heard from behind Gavin on the hill. Gavin wondered how long it would take for the king to realize he owed his life to Gavin twice over. The king's clenched jaw and white knuckles told Gavin all he needed to know.

Perhaps now his father could be buried with honor despite his failings.

King Ithan opened his mouth, but he held his peace as he folded his arms and glared at Gavin.

Gavin gave a nod to the king as one would to a peer then he pulled the last sword and handed it off with the accompanying pouch.

A wild roar of applause erupted from the hill. The animal salutes joined in once again as everyone from his camp chanted, "Stoutheart! Stoutheart!"

Gavin marched back to face the king and waited for the noise to die.

King Ithan took one step forward and spoke loud enough to carry across the field. "You are not the man I expected you to be. You honor us even after you beat us through luck and shrewd cunning. Your people give you fanatical devotion when you demand none at all."

King Ithan lowered his voice so it would only be heard by those nearest them. "Despite all that, this entire kingdom will be nothing but a smear of soot within two years, once the remaining Crystal Kings discover your breach of the Accords. That is, if your people don't put you down themselves. I don't know how you managed it, but I can tell you've set someone up to run that entire herd solo. I know what to look for. You will stand alone, and you will be overrun and destroyed to prevent the world from descending into chaos. It's only a matter of time." He returned the same nod Gavin had given to him, that of a peer.

Gavin mulled the king's threat. How devoted to him were the people? Devoted enough to follow him into a larger war? Weren't they only doing what it took to survive under trying circumstances? Gavin felt no guilt for what he had done for his people, but had no desire to push them into a war that King Ithan implied was already on its way.

With a start, he realized King Ithan waited for a response. "You pushed desperate people to defend themselves against your unprovoked attack. They have been forever changed, and not for the better. As for the Crystal Kings, if our dead King Vargas was any indication, then I'd say the kings have their share of guilt. Can you tell me you've never violated any of the Accords? Was it to save your people from destruction or for your personal gain?"

In his mind, Gavin ran through the short speech worked out earlier with Draken, and scrapped it. In old times, enemy commanders were often executed on the field of battle, and while tempting, both Draken and Gavin rejected execution as an option. The king was more valuable as a bargaining chip, and Gavin didn't want to be responsible for his death when there were other options.

There had been no time to discuss how to put a treaty together, even if someone was available to represent the whole country. Nobody in the camp had the sort of expertise needed to write a treaty.

Their plan was to delay with a touch of bluff, so he skipped to the final bits of his scrapped speech. "We will escort you and your advisers to the capital for negotiations. I give you and your men my personal assurance and word of honor that you will be safe under my care. When discussions are complete and fully satisfied, you will be returned to your borders and released. The rest of your forces are to remain unarmed and under guard until discussions are complete and a proper escort can assure their safe return home. We leave for the capital in the morning."

Gavin made a mental tally of his opponent's forces. The rout at the end of the battle had cost them a great deal, mostly in injuries. Gavin's people may have missed a couple of crystals, but they had confiscated those used to control nearly all of King Ithan's war animals. He wouldn't worry too much about them as an organized fighting force when movement required every able-bodied man to assist those who suffered from broken bones and other injuries.

Gavin would take a few of his uninjured people to the capital with him to watch over the king and his chief advisers. They could make it in a long day of travel. The remainder would use wagons to carry the injured and to escort the prisoners to arrive the day after.

Facing the enemy army, Gavin said, "Your Highness, please join me for dinner at sundown. You may bring two advisers with you."

Gavin stepped back with Jase and Draken at his side.

Draken mumbled, "That will have to do, for now. I would have gone more traditional myself, but for you, it worked well."

Gavin whispered back, "I just did that thing you do that I hate so much. Remember the way you give an invitation to do something that's actually a command? I'm not turning into you, am I?"

The trio turned and marched back to the forces arrayed on the gentle slope.

"No, sir, you're not turning into me. You never have, and you never will. I've come to realize I was never your crucible or refining fire no matter how much I wanted to be. What I wanted from you, what I asked for, or even what I demanded never changed you. Look up there."

Draken pointed his chin at the people of the caravan scattered about the hillside and the camp above. "These people are your crucible. They've changed you. They did it by becoming your people. You helped by accepting them. They respect you because you care about them more than you care about yourself. That's something I never taught you."

CHAPTER

TWENTY-FOUR

G avin stood on his toes to see the capital city main gate in the distance. It was the largest gate he had ever seen, set into a stone wall higher and thicker than any his imagination had prepared him to expect. The wall reminded him of the main hall of Stoutheart Barony's castle, but it extended all the way around the core of the city. Where they had found so much stone was a mystery. Stoutheart Castle had been built from stone cut from the nearby hills, but here there was nothing but flat, slowly rolling plains for miles on one side, and sea on the other.

They passed through several outlying farms as they approached, then they passed more and more homes, shops, and other buildings whose purpose he couldn't deduce. The smell of the city grew as they approached; it was a constantly changing combination of smoke, animals, waste, and food which assaulted him in varying degrees.

An unfamiliar tang of salt, from the docks and sea on the far side of the city, joined with the other smells as a constant undercurrent. He had no idea what sort of reception they would receive, or who would give it. Gavin glanced back at the chain of people walking behind him. "We'll need a place to put everyone." One of the cavalrymen who rode alongside gave a nod and galloped off. Gavin held up a hand as a futile gesture for the man to wait but gave up.

"I didn't mean for him to ride off to make arrangements."

Draken shook his head. "Cavalry are like that. If their commander says something that might be instructions or a request, or I guess even saying you need or want something, they'll jump on it as an order. I've never heard of them doing that for a baron, though. Be careful what you say."

The city ahead of them was so large the entire evacuation could get lost within its streets and markets. Gavin doubted anyone from Stoutheart Barony besides the old military men and a few of the merchants had ever been to the Riland capital to see such magnificent structures.

People entered and exited between the stone columns flanking the open gate. Some locals came out and passed them, but the majority hurried in through the gate while casting looks over their shoulder. It was ridiculous to think that his team might be some kind of threat, and the movement mystified him.

They hiked to within bowshot of the wall before the sound of hooves echoed through the open gate and the tunnel beyond. Cavalry riders came out in pairs which split to either side of the road. More and more of them came through until Gavin counted twenty lined up on either side. All but the two lead men were leaning forward in their special saddles, in a trance controlling their horses. They formed up to face each other to make walls on either side of the road where they waited.

Gavin whispered over to Draken as they approached, "What's going on?"

Draken grinned. "It's an honor guard. I've seen it before. Once, a long time ago."

Gavin said, "It's nice to know they're not here to arrest the lot of us."

A man walked out of the gate and came forward to meet them, timed so he would reach Gavin before they marched between the cavalry riders. Gavin recognized Rider Faven and let out a sigh of relief as the man turned to face the gate.

"Cavalry, attention!" Every horse came to attention and stomped their hooves in place in crisp unison. The show made the cavalry's surrender ceremony salute seem like a sloppy accident.

Faven marched up to Gavin, stood at attention, and saluted. "Full order has been restored to the city over the past several days under the cavalry's direction with the assistance of the palace guard and other local forces. While some damage remains, I hope the state of the city meets with your approval, sir."

Draken's jaw dropped for a few moments before he recovered. "Oh, cracks and splinters. Your crucible is a lot hotter now." He turned to Rider

Faven. "Did I hear you right? Did you declare martial law in Baron Stout-heart's name?"

Faven gave Draken a level stare and a nod before he turned back to Gavin. "The cavalry chooses whom they serve. Baron Stoutheart has done more than any other baron during this crisis, so the choice to turn the city over to him was clear. We've prepared council chambers, and have representatives from twenty-four baronies present. Yours makes twenty-five. All barons are freshly appointed, while some areas have either no representative or a regent acting on behalf of a baron too young to attend. Three have sent a Baroness. Most representatives have at least an adviser or assistant with them. Unfortunately, several baronies have fallen into chaos, with nobody at the helm and are unrepresented."

It was like the early days of the march all over again, hearing stories about himself as if he were a larger-than-life hero of children's stories. They expected him to lead. There was no sense in stepping back now. Brother Cleo's story echoed in his mind. If not him, then who? More people than ever needed him. Some might be disappointed, and some would die under his command, but he would do his best.

Faven swept an arm forward. "If you and Master Draken would follow me, please? He is your primary adviser, yes? Good. Your evacuees and the Graven Kingdom guests will be directed to appropriate temporary lodgings as they arrive. The king and his men will be housed in a wing of the palace with both sufficient security and a pleasant environment."

Good. At least the king wouldn't be held in the dungeon, wherever it was. He would still need to find out about the old king's prisoners as a favor to Adrian's men.

They walked to the gate where Faven gave a quick hand gesture to set the cavalry into motion, each to their assigned task with the rest of the caravan.

THE INSIDE of the city boggled Gavin's mind. Stone buildings three and four stories tall stood to either side with red tile or gray slate roofs, separated by cobblestone roads with gutters. Some buildings were whitewashed with dark wooden beams exposed, while others sported more interesting shades of red and brown.

Draken leaned toward Gavin. "Stop gawking. They'll think you're some country bumpkin, sir."

Gavin smiled. Draken was still himself, using the proper forms of address, but still thinking of Gavin as his wayward student, always in need of instruction. So much had changed, yet the old reminders were a comfort. The group stopped at the bridge before the main castle gate, with an honor guard of six sword-bearing footmen, three to either side of the entry. They wore the dark blue uniforms of the royal guard.

Faven stepped forward and said, "I present Baron Stoutheart, the Capital Regent."

Gavin cringed at the new title. He hadn't asked for that and hadn't been asked if he would accept it, yet he accepted it for the sake of the city and its people. He had disliked the regent title while at the barony. What new tasks lay ahead of him here as Capital Regent? And what would he do about all the people? How could he possibly get to know a city of several thousand people like he had come to know his people from the barony?

With luck, he could assign Faven to continue administering martial law and not have to interfere until after they settled this whole mess. He had no idea how to see to the safety and success of such a huge city until they had a king. Like his barony council, he would find qualified people and give them the authority they needed to make things work.

Two guards formed up as an escort and took them to a lavishly appointed oak-paneled chamber large enough to hold all the new barons and their advisers. They argued with one another and milled about in small knots of three or four among rows of desks. Large fireplaces at both ends were laid out but not lit, since the fall weather was still moderate.

Upon taking a closer look, Gavin noted that roughly half of the gathering wore a formal red baron's sash and their ages ranged from at least forty to some who couldn't be more than twelve years old. There were a handful of black regent sashes as well, some escorting the youngest barons. From the doorway, flanked by both Draken and Faven, he mumbled, "It's going to take a huge common cause to pull this group together."

A flick of Faven's wrist brought one of the servants with a baron's sash for Gavin to wear. Gavin still wore his dirty leather armor with the stab holes, making the sash appear out of place with its clean elegance. The other barons were dressed in their best finery. Gavin had none. It was a miracle they hadn't all fled at his smell.

Faven gestured discretely at a clean-shaven young man, no more than twenty years old, and said under his breath, "That one, Baron Case Perandi, is the one to call on for procedures. He's quite a scholar, despite his age, and he has a sharp memory. We've set the Baronesses to the side as observers. Please take a seat at the head table." He pointed to an empty seat across the hall. "Do I have your leave to call this meeting to order?"

Gavin's attention snapped back to Faven. "Yes, of course." Faven's comment about the Baronesses echoed hints of his second-class status growing up. This would not do. He asked Draken in a whisper, "Does a baroness or regent have the same authority as a baron to represent their people in a council?"

Draken nodded. "There are a few limits, but not many."

The others noted Gavin's arrival and took their assigned seats as Faven stood at attention in front of the head table and clicked his boots on the floor. He gave a formal salute to Gavin, then pulled out a whistle similar to a boson's whistle and gave it a blast. "This council is now in session, with Baron Stoutheart presiding."

Gavin picked up on some derision from the seated men, along with a few curious stares. He brushed some dirt off his sleeve, and then wiped it from the table onto the floor.

Faven said, "Baron Stoutheart, as regent, has allowed me to conduct the business of this gathering. We have several concerns which must be addressed, some of which are much more time-critical than others."

Gavin interrupted. "There's a matter of fairness to consider first if you would. If you are a regent or a baroness here to represent your barony, please stand." Two young women and a girl of about thirteen stood to the side of the room, and some older men stood from their desks in the middle of the room next to their very young charges. Two regents stood along the wall near the baronesses, having no baron in attendance with them. Gavin stood with them.

"Are there any objections to making room for all representatives among the general body?"

One older baron raised his hand. "It's a waste of time, and I don't see what difference it would make. It's not like they will have anything to contribute to our discussions."

Gavin walked in measured steps to stand in front of the man's desk. He was an older man with gray streaks showing in his beard. "Sir, how long have you been a baron?"

"I've served the people under my brother the baron for –"

"No. I asked how long *you* have been a *baron*."

He looked down. "Almost a week."

Gavin pressed forward. "And how did you become baron?"

"By right of blood, when we received news of my brother's death."

Gavin saw one of the young women suppress a satisfied grin. He continued, "With the ambush of the barons having taken place at the edge of my barony, I will go on record confirming the deaths of all barons. My father was the last baron to die."

He laid out the steps within his mind, hoping against hope that he wasn't overstepping an obscure law. He'd bypassed laws to save his people, but blatant disregard for the law wouldn't work if it only suited his own needs.

He suspected at least the one young woman knew where he was headed, so he walked to her desk. "Baroness. How did you come to this position?"

"I am the oldest surviving child among three daughters of Baron Lightmore."

Gavin walked back and stood beside his desk. "By right of blood, then. Given the situation, and that we have among us barons as young as, or younger than, any of these women, I propose we recognize all representatives and seat everyone on the main floor."

The old baron spoke up. "You expect us to just welcome these girls and do whatever comes into their silly heads?"

Gavin slammed his open hand on the desk. "Whether Baron, Baroness, Regent, or indentured servant polishing your buttons, you will show respect in these chambers or you will be removed. I've had a lot of practice lately doing what had to be done to save lives despite rules and procedure. I've ignored policy, procedure, law, and the Accords to save *all* of our people from invaders. Don't doubt my resolve. Men, women, and children died under my watch defending Riland and defending you. You will not mock those who are here to represent their people. Am I clear?"

The room was deadly silent for the space of several heartbeats before the man said, "My apologies. Please continue." Despite the man's polite reply, his glare bored holes through Gavin.

With no other objections, servants shuffled desks around, and everyone sat on the main floor away from the walls.

Gavin sat and took a deep breath to restore his calm. "Rider Faven, you were about to give us an agenda."

With a wry grin, Faven said, "Thank you, *Regent*."

Gavin heard the emphasis on the last word and hoped no one else noticed, as Gavin had just increased the authority of every other regent present.

Faven turned to address the body. "First, we made you aware this morning of the surrender of King Ithan Talandor of the Graven Kingdom to Baron Stoutheart on the field of battle. We have no formal terms or written treaty yet. Who has expertise in this area?"

Baron Perandi raised his hand, and a few others made a tentative movement. Baron Perandi said, "It appears we have a committee." He took out a paper, dipped a pen and made note of those who knew something useful.

Faven continued, "When we break, Master Draken and Baron Stoutheart will tell your committee everything we know so far. Please add them to your list, Baron Perandi."

Gavin nodded, figuring that was fair. They would need to know everything about the battle and the surrender.

Baron Perandi raised his hand again. "Begging your pardon, but we have another issue. We have nobody to sign such a treaty since it must be done by a representative of the whole kingdom. By law, barons and Capital Regents are not qualified to represent Riland."

Gavin nodded, having come to the same conclusion at the surrender.

A stout, gray-haired baron let out a cynical laugh and raised a hand. Faven said, "The council recognizes Baron Pader Woed."

"We have a majority of baronies represented here. All we need to do is pick a new king and we'll be on our way. The king left no direct descendant, and the law gives a majority of barons the authority to choose. All that's left is to agree and swear fealty." It was clear the man saw the task as anything but simple.

Faven raised a finger to speak but was interrupted as a messenger skidded into the room, then slowed to a brisk walk and approached Gavin's table. Faven waited.

The messenger was, of all people, Mick, who had first discovered the attack on the king and his barons. He smelled of sweaty horse and breathed hard. He removed his fox fur cap and whispered to Gavin, "Sir, the prisoners due to arrive tomorrow rebelled and attacked the guards and the remainder of your caravan."

Gavin ran his fingers through his hair and took a deep breath. "Do we need to act on this, or is it too late?"

"The fighting is over."

"Then please give your full report to the assembled barons, Mick. This concerns us all, and this is as close as we have to a ruling body." Good news or bad, everyone needed to know where things stood with the army he had supposedly defeated. His failure to keep order among his prisoners endangered his people. He dreaded learning of the newly dead under his command.

Gavin raised his voice for all to hear. "This man has a report on a prisoner revolt among our caravan on the road. It consisted primarily of supply wagons, the slow, the injured, and many of our prisoners along with a guard detail." The council deserved the unvarnished truth, whether it reflected well or poorly on Gavin.

Mick turned and clasped his hands behind his back. Gavin watched Mick's hands shake as he began his report. "The healthy prisoners left the injured ones behind and broke through the guards, then rushed the caravan. They used small weapons they hid from us. I reckon they thought all our crystal users had gone ahead with Baron Stoutheart, or they'd ha' never done it. Captain Zachary put up a defensive wall around our injured, while Crystal Mistress Saleena Tanner, her father the Travel Master Tover Tanner and some of the common folk from the barony used crystals like they done with the big battle. I never saw who controlled what animals, but the whole cattle herd and half of the captured war animals turned on the army and killed every one of them what wouldn't put his weapon down. We had two guards and four townsfolk killed, and five others hurt too bad to walk. Everyone else can make it here on their own. I can't rightly say for sure that the ones who attacked the women and children were given a chance to surrender."

He lowered his voice a notch. "Without Baron Stoutheart and the people he chose to lead us, we would all be dead. That's two battles he's won for us, and the second he weren't even there. The surviving prisoners will get here with the rest of the caravan tomorrow. Tover writ me a list of the people who died." He unclasped his hands, reached into a pouch, and handed a crumpled paper to Gavin before going to one knee to wait while he caught his breath.

Gavin flattened the paper carefully on his desk, and placed a hand over his heart as he silently read the names of those killed. More lives lost because of following him. More candles to burn in remembrance. More heroes.

He breathed again, unaware he had held his breath as he read. His people knew what to do, despite being left behind on their own. Saleena had distributed the crystals he left with her, and they hadn't needed his leadership to pull through and survive. Somehow, they'd trained more people than he thought possible, or they'd taken a terrible risk to use multiple crystals. He couldn't fault them for doing what it took to survive. He'd done the same on their behalf. None of his closest friends were on the list of the dead, but that didn't make the tragedy any less personal, or any less his responsibility.

Baron Woed rose from his seat and came forward to stand before Gavin. He raised his hands in the air. "Female advisers? Peasants trusted to not rise up against you with crystal-trained war animals? You claim to have set aside the Accords. I can't tell if you're completely without guile, or if you're the shrewdest man in the room. Perhaps you're merely mad. For all I know, you're all three. One can only hope."

He turned to face the room with his back to Gavin. "The people need a person, a symbol to rally behind, and we have one at the ready. Crystals are useless lumps without pooka symbols. Likewise, people aren't worth much without a symbol to join them together. None of us have a chance to overcome even a portion of Baron Stoutheart's reputation among the people when this news of his second victory spreads. He trusts his people, and they are willing to die for him."

Baron Woed took a deep breath, looked around the room and then continued. "That leaves us with two choices. First, we convict Baron Stoutheart by his own testimony and execute him for his admitted crimes, plunging the country into civil war as the people destroy everyone on this council for killing their hero. Second, we make him king, despite his crimes, and plunge the country into war with the other Crystal Kingdoms as they respond to the news. Who am I to argue with fate? I prefer the option where I stay alive longer. Perhaps the baron's ingenuity will work on a larger scale as well."

Gavin was stunned. He hadn't recognized this group as the highest court in the land, able to both judge and execute him. He was on a knife's edge.

If they didn't execute him, how could they want him to lead the whole country? He was less qualified to lead Riland than he was to run the barony. He had stepped up to lead the barony, and then the battle because he had to. But the whole country? He shook his head. "The people deserve better than me. Can't I step down and leave it all in better hands?"

Baron Woed leaned forward. "I'm afraid you misunderstand the situation. I doubt anyone here *wants* the mess you've made, or the dangers of leading Riland into war. That, and the will of the subjects in the city, will save your life today."

Baroness Lightmore stood and addressed Gavin. "You, sir, are a poor judge of your own character if you believe the people deserve better. You have my support because I see you as our best option, not because I wish to hide behind you like a craven dog. Your heart is in the right place, and your love of the people is clear to me." She retrieved an epee in a narrow scabbard from her adviser, strapped it about her waist with a practiced flourish and stood beside Baron Woed. She drew the fencing weapon and placed its wicked, unguarded point on the floor as she looped a small bag's tie over the grip.

Baron Woed nodded to the baroness. "I'll stand with you for a common goal, despite our differing opinions." He drew his saber, held it point down against the floor, and hooked his own small bag of crystals through the guard, then tossed a challenging glare about the room. "Are you men and women going to join me, or shall we talk each other to death first? You must see by now we have no real choice."

The remaining baronesses rose in a wave of unified support, followed by the barons who rose with varying alacrity. Within a minute all stood before Gavin offering swords and crystals in open rebellion against the traditions of the Crystal Kings.

If the gathered barons felt they had no choice, the feeling came to roost most strongly in Gavin's heart. Despite his wishes, he saw no better way to protect the people and to keep them from fighting and spreading death and chaos.

Gavin rose and faced each, in turn, starting with Baroness Lightmore. He took each sword and bag and returned them with a firm clasp of hands.

As he reached the last, he said, "You will need your crystals and your swords. It is I who must give crystals to you, especially if we are to restore order and defend ourselves from further invasion. We will stand together against aggression."

Baron Perandi raised a hand for Gavin's attention, and then said, "Baron Stoutheart? This is not even close to how it is normally done, but it appears we will have to be flexible about such things as we move forward." Several cheers rose, confirming the statement.

Rider Faven called the noisy group to order with a loud blast on his whistle. Once the chatter died out, he said, "We have addressed the most critical items, and have little time to waste. You have your assignments. We will reconvene after the coronation and treaty are complete. This meeting is adjourned."

Gavin returned to his table to stand between Draken and Faven, the shock of the rapid change of events seeping into him. He stared at the desk as his mind raced to figure out the next step.

Draken said, "The bets cancel. I don't owe you anything, Faven."

Gavin looked up, brow furrowed. "Bets? What bets?"

"I bet Master Draken," Faven pointed with a thumb, "that you would gain a majority on the first vote."

Draken replied, "And I bet him that before you were done talking, you would destroy the whole process."

Gavin shook his head in dismay. "Can I outlaw gambling?"

As with all bureaucracy, plans did not flow as smoothly as Gavin had both hoped and feared. He wanted everything resolved with the upcoming coronation and treaty, yet felt panicked at the responsibilities being placed upon him.

Even with all the changes, some things were the same. One of his jobs was to be seen by the people, but it was now within a more secure environment. The courtyard of the palace was open to all who didn't mind being disarmed before entry. One crew hung banners between pillars on an elevated walkway that bisected the courtyard. Another set up chairs all around the perimeter. They were in a rush to prepare for the open-air coronation to be held late the next morning. Within the castle, tailors worked in shifts to prepare clothing suitable for a coronation.

Gavin understood the rush. He didn't like it, but Riland needed someone to sign a treaty with the Graven Kingdom.

Another complication arose with the rules about who would sit where. Castle staff assured him everything was under control, but the rules mystified him. All Gavin knew was that King Ithan was to be an honored – yet well-guarded – guest, seated in one of the most prominent positions.

Another area had been set aside for the families of Adrian's men who had been held prisoner. Gavin hadn't been there for the reunions, but he had hand-delivered candles to the families who lost husbands, fathers, and brothers in the war.

The visiting, freshly-minted barons and baronesses were to be seated prominently as well. It was not lost on Gavin that a gathering of nearly every baron in the kingdom could be turned into a target again, so security was tight.

Captain Zachary nodded to Gavin across the courtyard, and Jase shadowed Gavin everywhere. It was like the guards never slept, watching over him every moment. Although Zachary still wore a sling from the fight with the prisoners, he and Captain Haverson traded off shifts supervising the palace guard. The merged forces of palace guards and the barony guards were a formidable force.

Saleena and Willem searched the edges of the palace wall across the courtyard as if they hunted for something. Willem pointed and took Saleena by the hand to hurry over and inspect some intricate carvings on the castle wall.

Even in the short time he'd known Willem, the boy had filled out physically from his improved diet and seemed taller and more self-assured. Now that Willem no longer had to hide and cower, or appear insignificant to avoid trouble, his visage changed for the better every time Gavin saw him.

Gavin still felt the pain of unexpected change and loss at seeing Saleena with Willem, yet he knew they were a wonderful team when it came to training, even though they were far too young in the eyes of his growing contingency of counselors and advisers. They made a great couple, too. Gavin strode over to them where they stood near the wall.

As Gavin approached, he heard Willem say, "It's not perfect, but they should be able to hide in the carvings and decorations with no problem. I could even take them along one of the little passages up to the downspout gargoyles."

Gavin was right behind them when he said, "What passages?"

Saleena jumped, and then glared. "Taking sneak lessons from Adrian?" She held on tight to Willem's hand while they looked over the exterior of the building.

Willem gave up trying to free his hand from hers. "Sir, I need a place to station the cats during the ceremony. They should be out of sight, but with easy access. These walls have channels and passages the cats can climb through."

"That would put them away from the action. Have you checked to see if you can place them under the seating? There may be time to fashion custom seating that's mostly enclosed to hide them. Come to think of it, under King Ithan's chair may be the perfect spot." Gavin grinned at the thought.

He paused, thinking back on when he received the report of the prisoner attack. This was the first time he'd seen the pair since their arrival because of all the demands on his schedule. "You know, the two of you did great work defending the people from that prisoner breakout. I had no idea you'd trained so many people. It's been hard for me to step back and let people do what they're good at without feeling like I'm dumping all the work on them."

Saleena spoke after a couple of false starts. "We didn't train more people. Da and I agreed that he should try more than one crystal. I know you said not to, but we figured out the pattern to it, and knew it was risky to have so few guards over so many prisoners."

Gavin frowned. "He could have died. Was that his first attempt?"

"No. We started a day or so after you left and found Adrian. We were going to tell you."

Gavin ran his fingers through his hair. "So, that's why he looked ill. This is no good. I can't have you bypassing me and hiding what you do. If you disagree with me, fight for what you believe, but please don't hide it. I can't have the top two trainers in the kingdom running around behind my back."

Saleena said, "Despite our saving everyone, you're telling me that I have to get you to agree with me first? That's hardly fair."

Willem said, "Wait. Top two?"

Gavin ignored Willem. "You want to talk about fair, Saleena? They've set me up to become king, so they don't have to take the blame for the coming war. I get to be the target of the remaining Crystal Kings. How is that fair?"

Fair was nice, but he needed trust more. "Who else besides you two could train our people to defend against the invasions we've already been promised by King Ithan? We don't have time for anyone else to become the experts you already are. You may not know military tactics well, but you have the control side down better than anyone. If you can train people to control a group of animals without killing them, we'll need that advantage. I also expect the two of you to spend time working for the good of the kingdom as advisers. Even more, I need you both as friends. I have to surround myself with people I can trust to protect me from the ones who I can't trust."

Gavin placed a hand on each of their shoulders. "Please. I want the two of you to be friends I can count on, friends I can always trust, and friends who will tell me when I make a mistake. We need to be honest with each other, especially when you disagree with me. I don't know everything and don't always know what's best. You proved that."

Willem grinned. "Thank you, sir. You've given me much more than I could ever expect."

Gavin returned the grin. "And you've become critical to the defense of the kingdom. No pressure."

At the nearby archway into the castle, the voice of Master Quincy carried out to them. "Baron Stoutheart took my advice to heart and distributed the grain among the people, while I accepted the personal burden to bring whatever remained. I made that sacrifice for the people."

Willem's smile faded and turned to a well-contained rage. Between clenched teeth, Willem said, "That leech did no such thing."

"Remember, Willem. Friends trust friends. This is one I can handle. At our next council meeting, I will call attention to the details of our evacuation. Would you mind me calling upon you to fill in necessary details?"

Willem gave a reluctant nod.

Gavin peeked around the corner in time to see Master Quincy walk into the castle with Baron Perandi. If Gavin guessed right, Master Quincy would have a hard time convincing that particular baron of anything at all.

"Do I have to wear all this?" Gavin was dressed in more finery than he knew existed. He waited for his cue to make his way to the courtyard outside the palace. Music and singing filtered into the waiting area inside the chapel. Upholstered chairs covered in detailed embroidery sat near an exquisitely polished table. Where they had found the delicately scented flowers this late in the fall was a mystery. The finery of the room bothered Gavin as much as his ceremonial robes did.

Draken grinned at his discomfort. "The people insist. How can you inspire their admiration in punctured, dirty armor and muddy boots?"

Gavin fidgeted. "I'm hungry. Can't this wait?"

Draken rolled his eyes. "The courtyard is full, and the program is underway. If it's any consolation, Lindy has taken over the kitchen and organized a banquet for several hundred of your most devoted friends and enemies. She's cooking for you as well, so you'll be fed before the day's out. But first, the coronation."

It had been a minor coup to arrange for Brother Cleo to perform the coronation ceremony. There was no telling what sort of politics had come into play among the religious hierarchy, and Gavin had no desire to learn how they had come to an agreement. He had even less desire to interfere in the process. All he knew was that it had been decided quickly and without fanfare or any sign of discord.

Tover had come in earlier and shared a detailed report with Gavin concerning the second battle. Gavin could have done without the descriptions of men trampled and torn apart by the large war animals under Tover's control.

Adrian said, "My spies reported back on the footmen I led away from the main army."

Gavin turned to stare. Adrian hadn't been in the room a few moments earlier, and the door to the courtyard remained closed.

Adrian continued as if he had been part of the conversation the whole time. "The enemy scouts figured out that the rest of their army was under guard, so they beat a hasty retreat. They're ill-equipped and will suffer on their trip home, particularly since that path has been cleared of people, crops, and game. With your approval, I'll have a group monitor them all the way to the border. The Graven commander and enemy forces we release with the treaty can join them."

Gavin nodded. "Do it. Watch them from a distance unless they stray, and protect the locals as needed. Make sure they know you're watching, but not how many are with you."

"You didn't expect me to be straight with them, did you, sir?"

Tover brightened. "Another bit of good news is that the badger passed the crystal from King Ithan's bear, and it's in fine shape. Now that it's been cleaned, that is. It wasn't broken after all." He dangled the crystal on a chain.

Gavin shrugged to settle the odd formal clothing, and then said, "Good. I've got the master crystal here, so I'll wear it for the coronation and the treaty ceremony. That should be a nice piece of symbolism that won't be lost on King Ithan."

Tover became much more somber, clearly with more on his mind. "Also, about Saleena. I know the two of you were always close friends. She'd do most anything for you, good sir. I don't want her to get the wrong impression from you."

Gavin said, "Right. We discussed our plans yesterday."

Tover said, "But sir, you have obligations. You can't just make plans, then break her heart like that."

Gavin stopped and backtracked in the conversation, mystified. He adjusted the stiff collar. "Like what? She and Willem agreed to be my chief crystal trainers."

Tover's mouth opened, then closed as his eyebrows raised. "Oh. Right then, good sir. Never you mind then."

Draken turned to Tover. "Did you think that –"

Tover put his hands out defensively. "Oh, no. It was nothing. Forget it. Children don't tell their own fathers nothing any more. I'll have to redo the whole talk now for Willem."

Before Gavin could figure out what Tover was talking about, Draken grinned and said, "Besides, His Majesty here has been taken care of by our treaty team."

Gavin stepped away and glanced between the two men. "Wait. Did you think that Saleena and I ...? What about the treaty team?" Everything came at him at once and overloaded his ability to think. His shirt was scratchy, too.

Draken pointed to a long document on the polished table. "King Ithan nearly peed himself when we told him the Cats of the Apocalypse are part of the formal guard for the treaty signing. I think he and most of his men have never actually seen the cats, aside from the wounds they left on his men. Rumors from King Ithan's men are that we trained something akin to invisible mountain lions. Some of the men will be in bandages for weeks.

He's only heard that horrific triple yowl of theirs, like some hideous three-headed monster.

"You'll want to read that treaty before you sign it. Your treaty committee decided the only way to seal the peace and keep Ithan from invading again is for you to marry his daughter. She's about your age, so all the better. I hear she's clever, too. Well, the committee had some input from me on that point, but they wrote it into the treaty on their own. Once the princess is delivered here, and the proper covenants are made, her father will be free to return home. It's not much different from the baronial agreements where children are married off for land, trade, or power. This is merely on a bigger scale."

Gavin sat back down. "It's like a nightmare. Not only do people act in my name without my permission, but they've also taken over every part of my life without even a by-your-leave. I thought this would take longer. I won't be able to so much as pretend to decide anything for myself by the end of the day."

Draken said, "What did you think you were getting yourself into, sir? Good leaders give themselves to their people, and you've done that. Most of the people out there will give themselves in service, however you call on them, because they trust you. You've also gained their love along the way. This is what you are meant to do."

A distant chime sounded to signal Gavin's entrance into the courtyard, and Gavin jumped to his feet and tugged the collar away from his neck.

Draken bowed as he waved toward the door. "Your people need you now, sir."

Gavin clamped a hand on Draken's shoulder and nodded. He smiled nervously as he marched out through the double doors into the courtyard to meet and claim his people as their new king, and for his people to claim him. The clouds in the sky still floated like dreams, teasing him and out of reach, but new dreams filled his heart, all within his grasp. The crowd roared as he strode into view.

CHAPTER

TWENTY-FIVE

The quiet of night filled the castle as the pooka padded down narrow secret paths wearing the black cat known as Doom Bringer. The animal's name could prove accurate, but only time would tell as events of the long game played out. But now it was time to fulfill a promise made long ago and prepare for his next move.

The animal was surprisingly easy to control, even with the interference of the crystal worn at its neck. He arched his back and stretched, exposing his claws. They were the claws of a predator, and the animal's keen reflexes told of their regular use. The animal had been trained far beyond its natural inclinations. Most beasts the pooka had encountered over the past centuries were driven by masters who used brute force and rigid control. Mankind had lived and died by force for so long, it was easy to lose hope. Few had the patience for the finesse shown by this cat's master.

No, this was more than skill in training. Deep within, the cat not only cared for its master, but it was also fiercely dedicated to him and proud to serve. This mutual empathy was one of the prized goals of the pookas. If the humans learned to feel for and understand others, even animals, they would be stronger.

The pooka squeezed out of the hidden passage and into a hall lined with closed doors, simple in design. The floor was clean and well-worn by centuries of passing feet. Near the end of the hall, the light of a small lantern escaped around the edges of a door with a gap at the bottom. A man inside breathed, but not with the sounds of slumber.

The task ahead was unpleasant but necessary. The pooka steeled himself and slipped along the edge of the hallway, peering under the door to see if this was the human he was after.

An involuntary purr escaped his throat, driven by the cat at the sight of the man seated on a stool reading from a book. The pooka allowed the sound to continue and looked deeper through the cat's feelings to search for this man. Brother Cleo. Yes, this was the one. He slipped under the door.

The man set his book aside on a rough wooden shelf. "Hello, Doom Bringer. What brings you here?" He scratched the top of the cat's head, increasing the rumbling in the animal's throat.

The pooka rallied his control, and with extreme effort formed words, awkward with the animal's tongue. "I bring him to speak with you."

The man's eyes widened. "I see. I am honored by your visit. My master's master spoke of you when I was a boy. He raised me to follow the path." The man stood, and bowed with a hand over his heart before he placed his hands together, fingers pointed outward.

This man was barely middle-aged for his kind, but he had been taught the proper responses with an accuracy beyond most human abilities. It was a relief to have finally found him. Better than that, he was a fine resource for the Trial.

The Priests of Order had long been the contacts among humans for the pookas. The techniques and plans to cut crystals were first shown to the priests, who had passed the information to the Crystal Kings in an age gone by. The priests considered the relationship a good match to their divine obligations as they cared for mankind's spiritual needs. They protected the people, and the pookas provided a tool for their work.

With guidance and occasional help from the pookas, wars were fewer and more controlled in scope as the long-range plans progressed. Each pass through a Trial of Warfare, where the Accords were broken, brought them closer to a lasting peace. It was counter-intuitive, but the progress was clear as the humans slowly gained more and more crystals over the generations. As they controlled and worked through their animal servants, an under-lying empathy grew along with the number of crystals created. The people grew marginally in wisdom with each Trial in a mixture of self-driven change and external influences. It was time to see if they needed a push.

The cat's scratchy voice said, "We cross a tipping point in our plan. Will the plan lead to a stable state this time, or will men kill each other in vast numbers and start over as with past Trials?"

The man sat on his stool and rubbed his chin. "There is no question men will kill each other as they ever do. The Accords prevent many deaths between Trials, yet the people still shrink in numbers due to their continual violence."

"Our eyes and ears are limited here. Will the Graven Kingdom be joined with Riland? It is their best hope to survive."

The man frowned. "How could you have possibly set up the alliance between the kingdoms? The odds of success were horribly small."

"The merger was the goal. A position of power has more chance of success. If it fails this generation, we will wait for the next. The winner was irrelevant."

"No, it's more relevant than ever. This time, your champion and catalyst is King Gavin. He will defend his people out of love, and he will do anything to save them. He's young and sometimes feels unworthy to lead, but he is a good man and an independent thinker. The people see that. He is to wed the Graven King's daughter in the spring to seal a treaty. He didn't even consider the possibility of executing King Ithan."

Such empathy was a good sign, but it was clear the man before him worked at some hidden goal with his speech. The pooka waited patiently. He must decide to support this new king or put his efforts with another.

After a few moments of silence, Brother Cleo spoke again. "Something unusual has driven us to set aside the Accords this time. This Trial will be different."

"What change? Our plans must account for change." Unexpected events could set back or destroy generations of work and influences.

The man pulled a cord from his neck and held out a rough lump of stone. Its pattern drew the pooka in as he padded closer to look.

The crystal's shape and symbols were crude and sparse, yet the stone resonated like the flawless faceted crystal at the cat's neck. Its simplicity sang despite its alien coarseness. The tune was new and foreign to the pooka. He memorized its design as it twisted on a cord before his borrowed eyes.

He followed the stone's wispy link and noticed the bird dozing in a cage above the man's desk.

The cat's voice strained to form words again. "This changes everything.

It may be the last Trial no matter what we plan. Guard your king well, or this chance may be lost. Convince him the Accords are all forfeit. Use what he has discovered. I must go now."

The pooka pulled his thoughts back to his body in a damp cavern far beneath the castle. If the humans could produce crystals a hundred times faster through their clever discovery, they would accelerate their own timeline with little intervention. For good or ill, crystals would be commonplace within a generation. Perhaps sooner. The final goal was centuries closer than expected if everything could be aligned in time.

The pookas' capstone project must accelerate to match. To show the humans their own nature could be the key to an era of progress for humanity to propel them out of their endless wars. Done wrong, it could doom them. He slid through the rough cracks and seams to warn the others. The six pookas had steered the Crystal Kingdoms via their friendship with the Priests of Order for centuries. Now everything pivoted on months.

THE END

ACKNOWLEDGMENTS

I must thank my earliest of readers on this story who saw it as a rough stone in need of polishing in an online critique forum. Ethan Motter, Velentino Bailon and Jim Mulcey gave me some great early feedback. At the next stage, some good friends who are also writers looked at it. Among that group are Jay Barnson and Jana Brown.

Jay and I regularly share information on short story markets, and we compete to see which of us will get into anthologies or magazines. We will share a table of contents for the first time this year. He encouraged me to submit the first short story I had published in this century. Part of my writing incentive comes from Writers of the Future winner Julie Frost who puts most short story writers to shame with the sheer number of stories she has out looking for a home at a given time.

Chuck Workman helped me with story elements as my content editor. Interestingly enough, Jana was assigned as my line editor, and she didn't even make me cry with her edits. She's also the reason the book has a map. Holli Anderson proofed the story and gave me some important feedback. The Immortal Works team has been great to work with.

I quite possibly would not have written this book if not for the strong local writing community and members of the League of Utah Writers who cheer me on. There may be something in the water here that produces great writers. Three examples of this wonderful community are Paul Genesse who always has something positive to say about anyone, Bob Defendi who believes everyone deserves to hear their name shouted with joy, and practices said shouting often, and Dave (DJ) Butler who gives back to the community by hosting a variety of events featuring the arts and sciences.

All of those groups pale compared to what I owe to my dear wife Kelly for her patience and encouragement.

ABOUT THE AUTHOR

John M Olsen reads and writes fantasy, science-fiction, steampunk, and horror as the mood strikes, and his short fiction is part of several anthologies. He devoured his father's library in his teen years and has since inherited that formidable collection and merged it with his own growing library hoping to pass a love of learning on to the next generation.

He loves to create things, whether writing novels or short stories or working in his secret lair equipped with dangerous power tools. In either case, he applies engineering principles and processes to the task at hand, often in unpredictable ways.

He lives near the Oquirrh Mountains in Utah with his lovely wife and a variable number of mostly grown children and a constantly changing subset of extended family.

Strap on some goggles and see his ramblings on his blog:

johnmolsen.blogspot.com

CPSIA information can be obtained
at www.ICGtesting.com
Printed in the USA
FFHW021347170219
50551196-55886FF

9 780999 020524